OLD BONES NEW BONES

A DCI BOYD THRILLER

ALEX SCARROW

GrrBooks

OLD BONES, NEW BONES

Published by GrrBooks

To my first fan and constant fan. Thanks, Dad, for all your help and support. x

1

The first grains of dirt dappled the young man's cheeks and mouth, as if he'd been caught in the act of eating a chocolate brownie. The second handful of dirt looked somewhat less comforting as dark granules stuck to the drying gel of his open eyes.

That unblinking gaze; the slowly milking irises were accusing. The body tucked into the shallow grave with the toy soldier clutched in one hand was too much for him to look at any longer. He finished burying the body, determined not to watch as it disappeared bit by bit beneath the earth. When it was done, he stamped the ground down, pushed some leaves and twigs across and turned away.

The last thing he did before he pulled away in his van was tie some flowers to the signpost to mark the layby. He'd come back. He'd promised.

2

Dave Webb had been aching for a piss since turning off the M25 and this was the first layby he'd come across where he wouldn't be peeing in full view of the steady north-bound early-morning traffic. He pulled in to find a van had already parked up there.

Not to worry – provided it wasn't a female driver, he was good to go. In fact, he'd reached the point of no return.

He was going whatever.

He jumped down from his truck in a hurry, raced across the overgrown picnic area and charged into the scraggy patch of woodland beyond. It was a close-run thing.

He emerged a minute later to see the other vehicle was still in the layby. It was either someone with a bladder ten times bigger than his or...

Nah, he wasn't going there.

As he waded through the knee-high grass, he spotted the other driver coming out from the woodland ahead of him. Not striding out zipping his flies or adjusting his belt but taking slow-as-treacle backward steps away from the bushes and into the picnic area.

'You all right, mate?' Webb called out.

There was no response. The man looked as though he was in shock.

'Mate? You okay?'

This time the other guy reacted. Jumped out of his skin, in fact. He turned to look at Webb, eyes out on stalks.

'You okay?' Webb asked again. 'What's up, mate? Seen a body?' he quipped.

The man hesitated, then nodded. 'Uh-huh.'

'What?'

'A... body.' He pointed at a dark space beneath some bushes.

'You're shitting me?' Webb strode forward, lifted up a low-hanging bough of a tree and shoved aside some stinging nettles.

'Fuck me.' He felt his legs shaking as he took in the unearthed human bones in front of him. He backed up, turning round to face the other driver, his eyes wide. 'We need to call the police, mate.'

'What?' The man stared at him blankly, his eyes perfect Os in his chubby face.

'Call it in?' Webb repeated as he fumbled in his jeans for his phone. He pulled it out and then tutted. 'Shit. Shitty signal. You got a phone on you?'

The other man shook his head. 'No. It's in the van.'

'Well, let's get it and call –'

'I gotta go,' the man said, turning away from Webb and stumbling through the tall grass back towards his vehicle.

'Mate!' Webb shouted. 'I think we're supposed to call the police and stay!'

'*You fuckin'* stay!' the man replied. 'I've got... deliveries...'

Webb watched him pull the van door open. 'Hey!! Mate!'

The man flipped him a finger, turned the engine on and ground the gears. Webb jumped back as the van lurched forward along the layby, hovering impatiently at the exit for a succession of trucks to pass before he had a safe enough gap to pull out.

Wanker. Dave grabbed a quick snapshot on his phone of the van's rear number plate as he watched it recede southwards towards Hastings.

3

DCI Boyd watched Ozzie chase the sea away. The daft spaniel was convinced his ferocious barking was the one thing that was keeping that dangerous big frothy wet stuff from sliding all the way up the beach and devouring Hastings.

He shook his head as Ozzie once again turned his back on the sea and sauntered up the beach with a cocky 'job done' swagger in his step, only to be doused from behind by another merciless wave.

Boyd let his gaze rise up the gentle incline of the shingle beach to the old town.

He had to admit this town was growing on him. It had been three months since the move, and their old place in London was starting to feel like someone else's past.

He'd been to Hastings before, as a young boy on holiday. He had vacation memories of the place to compare with how it looked now.

The seaside town was going through a personality change. In a way, much like Boyd, it was moving – through necessity –

from one life into another. Hastings was trying to leave behind its slightly grubby, cheap-as-chips weekend-B&B-break reputation to become something more modern and hip. A budget Brighton, an easy-going Eastbourne.

His pocket buzzed. He fished out his iPhone, then realised it was his police-issue phone that was ringing.

Work. Not Emma.

He changed phones and saw DS Minter's name on the screen. Boyd recalled that Minter was on nights this week. It would be nearing the end of his shift right about now. He'd be getting ready to close down his computer and gather his jacket. Next, the crazy bastard would go and do an hour in the White Rock gym, then – *and only then* – head home to get his beauty sleep.

'Minter,' said Boyd, 'not that it isn't great to hear your lovely Welsh singing voice, but can't this wait? I'll be in – in half an hour.'

'Morning, boss – there's nothing lovelier than a Welsh accent to wake up to in the morning! Thing is, there's been a buried body discovered in a layby and I thought I'd give you a heads-up that it'll be waiting for you as soon as you clock on.'

'What are we talking, old or new?' asked Boyd. Minter had his full attention now.

'Old bones, boss. Up on the A21.'

The A21 was the main road that stretched from London to the south coast. It was an hour from one end to the other, provided you weren't caught behind a container truck or the interminable Sunday driver.

'How far up?' Boyd scanned the beach for Ozzie, holding up his lead to signal that it was time to go.

'Fifteen miles or so out of Hastings. Up near Lamberhurst where it goes dual carriage for a bit,' replied Minter.

'Okay. Thanks. Anything else come in overnight?'

'Apart from the usual pissheads? Nothing,' said Minter.

'All right. I'll take a look on the way in, so no need to wait for me,' said Boyd, hanging up and noting that Minter was probably desperate to finish his shift and work on his pecs. He shook his head. *Weirdo.*

4

Boyd hurried home with Ozzie. His daughter, Emma, was still fast asleep in her bedroom so he left Ozzie in the lounge where he could perch on the back of the sofa and gaze out of the tall bay window at the comings and goings outside. At this time of the morning there'd be kids walking down Ashburnham Road to school, dog-walkers, maybe even an entitled cat or two pacing slowly past his front garden. Doggie TV at its finest.

Boyd climbed into his Renault, letting it run some warm air to clear the condensation on his windscreen. The tail end of April was still delivering the occasional frosty night. He sped things along by wiping away the moisture directly in front of him with the sleeve of his jacket and then set off with a wave to his curious, head-tilting dog in the window.

The A21 was the usual arse-magnet of a road at this time of the morning, clogged going north with those insane enough to work in south London but live down here. On the other side of the dividing barrier, the road was frustratingly empty.

He had his iPhone plugged into the car and was letting it play random tracks in its storage. This produced a not-displeasing, eclectic mix that ranged from Ludovico Enaudi to Dizzee Rascal.

Just a few miles after the A-road had become double lanes and he could pick up a bit more speed, he spotted the blue flashing lights of a patrol car and a CSI van parked in the layby on the southward side. He took the next exit and overpass, and doubled back, finally pulling into the layby five minutes later.

He got out and watched the creeping northbound traffic that he'd just escaped. Without fail, every driver was rubber-necking as they inched past. It was the forensics technicians in their bunny suits that were drawing curious eyes – everyone presumably hoping to catch sight of a leg or an arm dangling from a covered gurney.

Glimpsing those inquisitive faces, he had an unwelcome flashback from a little over two years ago. Faces just like these glancing at the wreckage of two trucks and one sandwiched car, and a tall dark-haired man beside it – on his knees, sobbing, as blue lights flickered halos around him.

This morning's blue flicker was coming from a patrol car parked at the entrance to the layby, posted there to stop anyone southbound from pulling in to make use of it.

Boyd flashed his warrant card at the traffic cop, then approached a stern-looking woman in a dark trouser suit who had a clipboard under one arm and a steaming Thermos flask cap in the other.

'Morning, Leslie,' Boyd said to Leslie Poole, the crime scene manager.

'Morning, sir.' She handed him her clipboard. 'Could yourself sign in, please? I've just poured me tea.'

He scribbled his name, the date and time below a short list of names. He could see Sully's name above his and glanced over at the CSI van parked in front of a truck. He handed the clipboard back to her.

'Where's the bloke who found it?' he asked.

She nodded over towards the layby's overgrown picnic area.

He could see a young female PC talking with a male civilian – the lorry driver he guessed, and an older sergeant, who was nodding as they spoke. The sergeant spotted Boyd, left the PC to it and wandered over. Boyd recognised his face but couldn't for the life of him remember his name.

'Just come on shift, sir?' the sergeant asked.

Boyd nodded. 'I've come straight from home actually.'

'It's a very old body, sir.' He pointed towards a row of bushes and stunted trees at the back of the picnic area. 'I didn't think we needed to tape up an evidence perimeter over there.'

'Okay. Makes sense for now,' Boyd said. He nodded at the sergeant, then headed towards the scene.

Even though it was fully daylight now, the sky was overcast and heavy with a thick lid of cloud to seal in what was shaping up to be another grey and damp April day. It was eight o'clock in the morning, but the headlights on the far side of the carriageway made it look as though evening was closing in. He caught the strobing flashes of the photographer taking shots of the body and site, and noticed Kevin Sully suiting up beside his van as he waited for the photographer to finish.

'Morning,' said Boyd.

'Ah, I thought I was going to bump into Minter this morning,' replied the forensics co-ordinator.

'He's on nights. Just clocked off,' Boyd said.

'Well, so am I,' Sully retorted. 'But, behold, I'm still here. Don't tell me – he had a pressing appointment at the beautician's? Cheekbones needed sanding? Pecs needed polishing?'

'We're currently on a department overtime ban,' replied Boyd. 'Otherwise I'm sure he'd have jumped at some time and a half.' He nodded at the civilian standing with the PC. 'That's our finder, is it?'

'I presume so. Why don't you go and ask? Don't be shy now,' said Sully, straightening up and picking up his bag.

Boyd raised a tired brow at him, then made his way over. 'DCI Boyd,' he announced as he reached them.

The PC nodded and responded, 'Morning, sir.' She had the fresh face of someone who'd just come on shift rather than the are-we-done-yet look of someone itching to get home.

'Who've we got here?' he asked.

'This is Dave Webb,' she said. 'He called it in.'

Webb looked ten years younger than Boyd, but Boyd was pleased to note that the man was sporting a more generous paunch than his – the curse of the long-distance driver. He realised he was staring and swiftly raised his eyes. He really did need to stop comparing bellies. That or actually do something about his.

'Morning,' he said to the slightly pissed-off-looking Webb. 'I'm sure you want to get under way as quickly as possible, so...' He looked at the PC. 'You've got his contact details?'

'Yes, sir.'

'Good.' He turned to the lorry driver. 'I'm DCI Boyd. I just have a few questions, then we'll let you go on your way.'

'Cheers,' said Webb. 'I've been waiting here for well over an hour, mate.'

'Sorry, Dave. But it *is* appreciated, and it won't take much longer. So... you were the one who found the body, were you?'

'No. There was another bloke in a van who did. I'm guessing he stopped to take a piss too.' He glanced at the PC. 'Sorry, love.'

'I've heard far worse, mate,' she replied.

'Why isn't he here?' asked Boyd, looking around.

'Fucker shot off, didn't he? Said he was running late.' Webb shrugged. 'Left me to call you lot, and he knew I had no bloody signal too.'

'We'll need his statement,' said Boyd. 'Can you give me any details about him? Did he give you his name and number?'

Webb shook his head.

'A description? Vehicle model, make...?' Boyd pressed.

'I can do better than that, mate,' said Webb, grinning and pulling out his phone. 'Got his reg.'

Boyd squinted at the photo. 'Mind if I...?' he said, holding out his hand. The lorry driver handed over the phone and Boyd spread his fingers to scale up the picture.

'Well played, Dave' he said, nodding. 'It's legible.' Boyd returned the man's phone. 'Can you text that photo to this number?' he asked, giving him one of his cards.

'Then can I go?' Webb asked. 'I'm gonna get in trouble, mate.'

'Yup. Then you can go.' Boyd nodded. 'But we'll need you to drop into the station in the next few days to give us a formal statement.'

'What? I'm heading to Kent tomorrow,' said Webb. 'Then France.'

'That's okay. There's no big rush,' Boyd said. 'Just sometime in the next week is fine, when you're back. And thanks again.'

Webb huffed irritably. 'Right.'

'Call me when you're coming in,' Boyd said, indicating the card in Webb's hand. 'I'll have you in and out as quickly as possible.'

He watched as Webb turned and hurried back to his truck, then waded through the tall grass of the picnic area. It looked like the crime scene photographer had finished documenting the site; Sully was heading in Boyd's direction with his bag of kit slung over one shoulder.

They met beside the picnic table. The trees surrounding the site, stripped naked by the winter, were just beginning to bud. The bushes and brambles beneath looked like bundles of ochre razor wire. The only green came from the small clusters of eager nettles looking to steal a lead heading into spring.

'How was our trucker?' asked Sully.

'A bit shaken,' said Boyd, 'but keen to get on his way.'

'Ah, well, maybe *he* did it,' Sully whispered conspiratorially. 'Case solved.'

'If only life were that simple,' Boyd said with a sigh.

Sully raised a hand at the photographer as he passed by. 'See you at Malley's, Wednesday?'

'Yarp. Will do,' the photographer called back over his shoulder.

'What's Malley's?' asked Boyd.

'It's a games bar,' Sully replied.

'What? Like a sports bar?'

Sully turned to look at him in mock horror. '*Board* games, Boyd, please!''

'You mean like Cluedo?' Boyd grinned.

Sully sighed and shook his head. 'Right. Because we don't do enough of that all day long. You need to drag yourself out of the seventies, Boyd. Board games have moved on.'

'Hungry Hippos?' said Boyd, still grinning.

Sully dead-eyed him. 'Oh, good grief... You look as if you've spent a bit too long playing that one. No. *Chess* is a board game, Boyd.'

'That's what you play, is it?'

'No,' Sully said slightly defensively. 'I play Dungeons and Dragons.'

Boyd tried to suppress a smile with little success.

'Oh, smirk away – it's chess-like, strategic. It's complicated stuff,' Sully huffed.

'Right, so not just grown men playing around with little action figures and weirdly shaped dice then?'

Sully rolled his eyes.

'Whatever keeps you off the drugs and booze, eh?' Boyd offered as an olive branch. He nodded at the area in the bushes that the photographer had been circling. 'Shall we?'

5

The bones were located just beyond what would have once been the tamed grass around the two picnic tables with fixed benches.

Through the bare branches, Boyd could see that the woodland went back about thirty feet to a barbed wire fence with a farmer's field beyond, littered with crows hunting the fresh-turned soil for goodies. Their collective cawing was a continuous white noise, almost loud enough to rival the steady grumble of northbound traffic and the occasional whoosh of a lorry heading south.

The picnic site had a forlorn feel to it. A mean-spirited little recess with knee-high grass that had rightly earned its place as a pee break for truckers and squawling kids, and little more. Anyone who'd pulled over here for a flask of tea and sandwiches – if anyone ever had – would have had little sunlight, little view and little desire to linger.

Sully stepped into the undergrowth, pushed aside a low scratchy branch and squatted down to get a closer view of the unearthed bones.

Boyd remained standing where he was on the edge of the open picnic area.

'*Dem aulde bones*,' pronounced Sully with an accent that Boyd had no chance of identifying. Not a pirate this time. Instead something, he presumed, that was meant to sound like a grizzly old Celtic soothsayer.

Sully reached out with his gloved hands and lightly probed the loose soil, plant roots and the bones that had half-surfaced. Scratching around, he reminded Boyd of Gollum hunched over in his underground dwelling, surrounded by fish heads and hunting for his *precious*.

Boyd gave him another minute or so before clearing his throat. 'Well, what do the spirits tell you?'

Sully sighed, clicked his tongue thoughtfully, then looked up. 'Dead, a while I would say,' he said.

'Great,' replied Boyd. 'Thanks for that. You got a rough idea of how long it's been down there?'

'At least ten years,' said Sully. 'That's going on the root incursions. The bones, of course, could be older.'

Boyd took another step closer and hunkered down. The body didn't look complete. Something, presumably foxes, or a dog, had dug it up and had been having a fine old time with the bones. They were scattered in the dip in the ground, some a few feet away beneath the brambles, mistakable for old branches or twigs at first glance.

The rib cage, the skull and the pelvis were the instantly recognisable pieces, and those had been kept together in the ditch, united and tangled up in the remaining dark threads of clothing.

'Give me a ball park, Sully. This century? Last?'

Sully had a pen in his hand that he was using to prod, poke and lift pieces of the body. He pointed at the bottom of the skeletal remains. One and a half legs were still in the ditch. The complete leg was bent at the knee and shrouded with a dark wet and threadbare material. But the remaining foot was quite clearly wearing a Nike trainer.

'I want to say... certainly *not* Tudor,' Sully offered.

Boyd nodded. 'Okay. Tell you what. I'll leave you to snuffle around in there and wait for the sensible answers in your report.'

Sully smiled. 'Good idea.'

Boyd stood up and turned round to look back at the overgrown area and the congested road beyond. He really couldn't imagine anyone in the history of this little piece of transport landscaping had ever stood on this spot and said, *'Darling, here's a perfect spot for lunch. Let's crack open the champagne and make a start on those vol-au-vents.'*

He could, however, imagine countless occasions when some irritable and tired father had shouted out, *'You should have bloody well gone when we stopped back at the service station!'*

Boyd sat down on one of the benches. The warped and flaking wood creaked beneath him.

His gaze settled on a signpost. It was the standard white 'P' on a blue background and beneath it a rather optimistic depiction of a stickman and his child sitting at a table. Beneath that, tied to the grey metal post, Boyd spotted a bunch of almost fossilized flowers.

If it was possible, it made this slice of *terra oblitus* seem even more godforsaken and melancholic. Roadside shrines – Boyd hated them; they broadcast a sense of aching loss like forgotten radio beacons. A signal beamed out to no one in particular that someone had once died here. That someone was missed and still remembered, at least, as long as the flowers were refreshed. There were always two sad stories behind flowers like these – that of the person who'd died, and that of the person who'd placed them there.

He made his way over to the PC and duty sergeant. 'I'm heading back to Hastings,' he said. 'Tape off this layby and let the highways people know this one's going to be out of use for a while.'

'Right, you are, sir,' said the sergeant.

Boyd cupped his mouth. 'Sully!'

Sully glanced back over his shoulder. 'What?'

'I'm off!'

Sully shrugged and resumed scratching and scraping at the dirt, shouting over his shoulder, 'And I need to know that *because*?'

But Boyd was already in his car.

6

Boyd pushed the double doors in from the stairwell and was greeted with the familiar noises of the CID's main floor: someone yawning too loudly, the ping of the microwave in the kitchenette, the trill of a desk phone.

There were usually eighteen detectives here on a day shift and four on nights, though that day/night ratio ebbed and modulated depending on any ongoing investigations. Since the Nix case back in February, there'd been nothing major that had required specific use of the Incident Room and DCI Flack had moved his core team back into it to continue work on his ongoing county lines operation.

Boyd made his way through the open-plan labyrinth of cluttered desks, plastic potted plants and trip-hazard waste bins to his desk and set down the paper cup of tepid McCoffee he'd picked up on the way back into Hastings.

'What time do you call this, guv?' DC Okeke was tapping in details from a handwritten statement, her eyes remained on the screen as she typed irritatingly quickly.

'About quarter past *mind yours*,' he said good-naturedly,

shaking off his jacket onto the back of his chair. 'How was your weekend?'

'*Mind yours*, yourself!' she replied, then: 'Not great.'

'Why? What happened?' Boyd asked, settling himself into his chair.

'Jay got into a fight with someone at the club.' Okeke rolled her eyes.

Her other half was a furniture restorer by day and a bouncer by night. Carpentry was his love, but it was looking large and scary outside a nightclub that paid the bills and – Boyd suspected – gave him a bit of a buzz too.

'I said he should hand his notice in. We don't really need the money,' she continued.

'He got into a fight?' Boyd frowned. Jay had an intimidating amount of muscle on him and had proved he could look after himself at the Sea Breeze Campsite a couple of months ago – but he didn't strike Boyd as the type to brawl unnecessarily.

'Well, actually he was jumped,' she admitted, 'by some scrotes that he'd turned away earlier in the evening.'

'Jesus, Okeke. Is he okay?'

'Battered and bruised. Nothing broken, thank God. But... they jumped him coming home. It could've been knives, I told him. Jay's a big guy, but a scrawny little squirt with a penknife could do enough damage to finish him off. I don't want him to do it any more. I said I'd pay the bills if he wanted to try and build up the carpentry side. Invest in some advertising or something.'

'But his male pride...? *You're fighting crime on the streets, I can manage a couple of idiots at a nightclub...?*' Boyd said.

Okeke nodded. 'Right. Exactly that. At least we're trained, kitted out for it and have backup.' She finished what she was doing on the computer. 'Anyway. I presume you're late because of the A21 layby thing?'

'Indeed I am,' Boyd answered. 'I've just got to wrap a few things up and I'll fill you in.'

At the top of his 'to do this morning' list was a report he needed to finish off on an assault in Bexhill. A neighbour-versus-neighbour grudge that had been running for decades and had ended with one attacking the other with a blunt Saxon sword. Luckily for the attacker he wasn't facing a murder charge; a trip to A&E had resulted in stitches for his neighbour and a charge of aggravated assault for himself. Boyd glanced at his watch. He should only need to give this another hour or so before he could pass it along to the CPS. But… those bones in the layby. Switching mental gears back to completing yesterday's paperwork really didn't appeal to him. But, short of pulling up an incredibly long list of outstanding misper cases, there wasn't really anything productive he could do on the A21 layby bones until Sully had reported back and the forensic pathologist had had a chance to review the body. Boyd sighed and turned to face his computer.

BOYD CLICKED 'CLOSE AND SAVE' on his aggravated assault and emailed it onwards to their CPS liaison. His stomach gave a loud rumble. He checked the time. It was ten to one.

Bang on.

Emma had been hectoring him for the last few weeks about the lunchtime fish and chips he'd got into the habit of grabbing down on the pier. Boyd had tried making the case that the walk downhill to the seaside and, more importantly, the walk back *uphill* afterwards, more or less burned off most of the calories.

Emma had destroyed that argument by showing him on her phone how few calories an hour's worth of stiff walking burned off and then how many calories were in an average portion of cod and chips.

So here he was. Proud owner of a brand-new Tupperware container full of some weird-looking lentil-and-black-bean something-or-other that needed to be microwaved.

Boyd was waiting by the machine, watching it slowly rotate and irradiate his meal, when DSI Sutherland cruelly wandered into the kitchenette with a Cornish pasty.

'Morning, Boyd,' he said cheerfully.

'Afternoon, sir. Swap mine for yours?'

Sutherland raised a defensive hand in front of his pasty. 'Not on your life!' Then he ducked down, screwing up his Penfold eyes behind his glasses as he peered into the microwave's mesh-covered window. 'What the hell have you got going on in there?'

'The diet I've been sentenced to for the rest of my bloody life,' Boyd said with a sigh. 'Or at least until I get back down to fourteen stone anyway.'

Sutherland looked him up and down. 'You don't look bad for ten years or so behind a desk,' he offered.

'That's very kind of you, sir, but it's what I'll look like in ten more years that worries Emma,' said Boyd.

'Emma?' Sutherland looked puzzled for a moment. Then: 'Oh… that's your *daughter*, isn't it?'

'Daughter. Tormentor. Abuser. Food Nazi.'

Sutherland smiled. 'Well, once you get past fifty you can sack that off. No one's going to be asking me to model budgie smugglers any time soon.'

Boyd worked hard for a moment to prevent that image of Sutherland from forming. Too late.

'She's worried about my heart,' said Boyd. 'Being tall as well as overweight supposedly puts additional stress on the circulation system. Apparently I'm a high risk.'

Sutherland, of course, didn't have the height to worry about.

The microwave pinged and Boyd pulled out his plate of lumpy black-dotted beige.

Sutherland peered at it and pulled a face. 'Oh, that reminds me... you went to check out the body this morning?' he said chirpily.

Boyd looked down at his bowl of mush and could see why the DSI had been reminded to ask. 'Uh, yes, sir – I did.'

'And? Was it decomp old, or *bones* old?' he asked, sliding his pasty onto a plate, then into Chef Mike. He tapped a few buttons and the machine started whirring again.

'Just bones, sir.'

'That'll be on BBC Southeast tonight, I've no doubt. We'll have the Time Team lot with their JCBs and jackhammers on that, I bet,' Sutherland said. 'Anything interesting?'

'I'm waiting on Sully to get back to me. I suspect he's still out there playing archaeologist.'

'Do we know if it's male or female?' Sutherland asked.

The clothes had just been dark shreds; there'd been no tell-tale clumps of scalp and hair on the skull – sometimes enough of that lingered to give you a suggestion. But not this one. The trainer, though. He remembered: a Nike one. Hose and scrub it down it'd probably be almost as good as new.

'Sully says male, but the pathologist will give us a clear yes/no on that,' Boyd replied.

7

Emma was heading out of the front door just as Boyd was heading in.

'Hey, Ems... where you off to?' he asked.

'I'm meeting Daniel?' she said, intoned as a question, as if he should already know that. 'I told you this morning I was going out with him tonight?'

'Oh, right,' Boyd said. 'Sorry, love. I forgot.'

He was still trying to get used to the idea that she had a boyfriend. It was a very recent development. She'd met him when they'd both tried out the pub grub at Ye Olde Pump House down the hill on George Street. It was a welcome development, truth be told. His daughter really hadn't had a social life to speak of since Julia and Noah died. Maybe a handful of friends from her old secondary school who'd kept in touch and periodically sent her a text. But not often. They were all off at their universities and colleges of choice, now that post-Covid normality had been restored, and busy enjoying themselves.

And here, like a gift from the heavens, was Daniel. The floppy-haired young man from behind the bar. He looked just like every other guy his age: drainpipe arms and legs, an Adam's apple that bobbed like a cork, and hair that was so extravagantly side-parted from above one ear that it looked like a seventies comb-over. He was all hair, rattling metal bangles and eyeliner. The pale young gothic whippet was making his daughter happy. Even though, in Boyd's opinion, he looked like a cross between Edward Scissorhands and Beaker from the Muppets. Boyd could have hugged him from sheer gratitude.

Of course, that could change in the blink of an eye, if Danny Boy decided to mess Emma around.

'I've made dinner and put it in the oven,' she said. 'All you've got to do is put the oven on.'

'Thanks, Ems.'

She squeezed his arm, stood on tiptoe and planted a light kiss on his cheek. 'Don't wait up, Dad.'

And with that she was gone, all but skipping down Ashburnham Road and already on her phone.

He let himself in, closed the door behind him and then directed his attention to Ozzie, who was spinning circles in the hall and enquiring noisily about dinner time.

'All right, all right,' said Boyd, trying to manoeuvre past without tripping over him.

He fed Ozzie in the dining room, the bowl's scraping sounds echoing off the high ceiling as the dog attempted to lick it forensically clean. Then Boyd grabbed a lead and some poo bags and they headed back out, downhill to the old town and onto the shingle beach beyond.

His thoughts turned back to Emma as he strode downhill. After losing her mother and younger brother, she'd been forced into looking after him, obsessing over him like he was some hopelessly fragile potted plant.

So, after moving down here, settling in and all the worrying about whether it had been the right thing for her… it was good to have Daniel come along. At their age you never knew how long these things would last, but it was getting her out and she was smiling.

She was living again.

It was cause for celebration, and perhaps a little selfish commiseration.

She'll be off, Bill. Off and away. Julia's voice in his head. *But that's what we want for our girl, right?*

'Right,' he muttered.

And then it's your turn, Bill. I'm not having you turn into some lonely old sod.

Boyd looked down at Ozzie. 'I've got Ozzie.' The dog looked up at him on hearing his name. 'We're going to be just fine, aren't we, old boy?' Boyd and his rescue dog of uncertain age rattling around together in that large, echoing Victorian seaside home.

I meant a woman, Bill. Not a dog.

He laughed. She'd always managed to make him do that with great ease.

'Right,' he muttered again.

It took Ozzie half an hour to find the right spot on the shingle to do his business, and Boyd was beginning to get cranky with him. It was cold and windy and fully dark by the time they were heading back up the hill.

He was just getting his door keys out of his pocket when the front door jerked open.

'Hey!'

A male voice. Boyd dropped his keys on the ground.

'Sorry, dude. Didn't mean to startle you.' It was Daniel.

Boyd bent down to pick up the keys. 'I thought you guys were going out tonight?' he said.

'It got cancelled,' said Daniel. 'So we brought back a Chinese. You okay with Chinese?'

Boyd grinned. That sounded a lot better than the healthy

horror that was waiting in the oven for him. 'Yes, I do,' he said, cheering up fast.

'Cool. Emma's serving up.'

Ozzie nuzzled his way forward to get to the young man, who dropped down and cupped Ozzie's head in both hands. 'You a gorgeous boy? Yes, you are. Yes, you are!'

Ozzie wiggled his way into the house and Daniel stepped back to let Boyd in. He led him down the hallway to the dining room at the back.

'We're in here,' he said unnecessarily.

Boyd entered into the dining room. 'Christ, what's this?' he said, looking around.

'What do you think?' called Emma from the kitchen. She'd put a row of various shaped candles on the mantelpiece and a dark red cloth across the table.

'I love the look of your house, Mr Boyd,' said Daniel. 'So cool and gothic. It's got a sort of Addams Family feel to it.'

Boyd heard glasses clinking in the kitchen.

'It wasn't a design choice,' he said. 'We just haven't got around to decorating all the rooms yet. We've only been here a few months.'

'Three actually,' said Emma.

'Oh, right. But this room,' said Daniel, 'is lush. Burgundy leather on the walls, dark wood. Love it, love it, love it.'

'I don't think it's leather,' said Boyd. 'Just some satin-finish paint on textured –'

'But let's keep it like this,' interrupted Emma, coming in with a bottle of wine and three glasses.

'I thought you wanted to lighten everything up?' Boyd said, bemused. 'Pine parquet flooring? Magnolia walls?'

Emma looked at him as though he was talking about someone else. 'What? No! This is so characterful, so rich. Come on... *everybody* does magnolia and pine.'

'Right,' said Boyd. Quite literally, two days ago, she'd been banging on about how dark, moody and oppressive some of the rooms were.

'I mean... your rooms are big enough to get away with it,' said Daniel. 'This is like Marilyn Manson does *Downton Abbey*.'

Emma nipped out of the dining room and came back with half a dozen takeaway cartons. 'It looks even better by candle-light, don't you think, Dad?'

Boyd rewarded her with a heavy-lidded smile. 'Yes. You'd have to be crazy to want to splash boring magnolia over it all.'

She shot him a warning glance. 'Right.' Then she smiled. 'Hope you don't mind that I asked Dan back?'

'Not at all. Good to have a chance to –'

'Interview him?' she cut in, a wry smile on her face.

'*Meet* him,' said Boyd, taking his jacket off and hanging it over the back of his chair. 'Don't worry, I won't do a Jack Byrnes on you.'

'Jack..?'

'*Meet the Parents*?' said Boyd. 'De Niro's character?'

Daniel shook his head. 'Sorry, not seen that one, Mr Boyd.'

'*Boyd*'s fine,' he said. 'That's what everyone calls me.'

'Dad hates his first name. Bill.'

Daniel looked puzzled. 'Why?'

'The *bill*?' said Emma, setting her plate down at the head of the table. 'Nickname for the police?'

'Oh, right, yeah.' Daniel nodded and laughed.

'And because people gravitate towards *Billy*,' said Boyd. 'Billy Boyd sounds ridiculous.'

'But it's William, properly, right? On your birth certificate?' Daniel asked.

'Yup,' said Boyd. 'But three seconds after starting at work I'd have been called Willy, and then it would have been an endless procession of knob gags.'

'Even Mum used to call him Boyd.'

'Only when she got really peed off with me, Ems.'

'Oh, right. Yeah,' said Daniel. He suddenly looked awkward. 'Mr Boyd, let me offer you my comis–'

Emma shook her head at him sharply. Daniel's mouth snapped shut.

'Wine?' offered Emma. They both nodded and she poured a glass of red for all three of them.

She got up. 'I'm just going to put some music on.' She headed off down the hall to the lounge.

Boyd could see the lad was squirming in his seat.

I should tackle this now. Get it out of the way.

'Daniel, I'm guessing Emma's already told you. We're *half* a family.'

He nodded.

'It was a car accident. It was sudden. It... came out of the blue, as these things usually do. My wife and son were killed instantly.'

'I'm so sorry...' mumbled Daniel.

'These things happen unfortunately. It was a few years ago. I won't say we're fully mended people now, because the truth is that never really happens. But it does mean we can mention them now and again without suddenly bursting into tears.'

Daniel smiled. 'Right.'

A female vocal drifted into the room. It was soothing. A band Emma loved. Boyd wanted to say Florence something, but he wasn't sure. She came back down the hall. 'This okay with everyone?'

Daniel nodded, hugely relieved by the look on his face, to have a change of subject. 'London Grammar. Love their stuff.'

Emma began to open the takeaway cartons.

Boyd turned back to their guest. 'So, Daniel, let's start with an easy one: what's the plan? What's the Big Life Plan?'

Daniel grinned. 'In five years... I'm in LA polishing my Mercury Award beside my infinity swimming pool, snorting coke off the back of my gold-plated –' He raised both his hands with a jangle of bracelets. 'I'm joking about the coke!'

Boyd smiled. 'Musician?'

'Bassist.'

'No kidding. That's what I used to play!' said Boyd. 'Badly,' he added.

'Oh, yeah, that's right,' said Emma. 'That's how you first met Mum, wasn't it? At a gig or something?'

'A crappy gig,' said Boyd. 'I think there were less than a dozen people in the audience.'

'During the week,' said Emma, 'Daniel's band play down at the Dolphin Inn. That's the pub right by Rock-a-Nore.'

'I know,' Boyd replied. 'Been there. Remember?'

'Oh, yeah.'

'What's the band's name?' asked Boyd.

'His band's called Mad Priests,' she answered for him.

'I like it.' Boyd nodded. 'Cool name.'

'Come on – let's tuck in before it all gets cold,' said Emma.

THEY POLISHED off two and a half bottles of red between them, and after several hours comparing Spotify playlists, listening to some of Daniel's band's music (rough round the edges but promising, Boyd thought) and arguing good-naturedly about politics, they went up to bed.

As Boyd said goodnight to them both and watched them stagger up the stairs, he realised tonight was a milestone night; it was the first time his daughter had had a guy over to stay. It had finally happened – without her awkwardly asking or him clumsily fluffing a yes answer. After all, she was a woman of twenty-two now and, thinking about it, asking would have been weird.

'Night, Dad,' Emma called out.

'Night, Boyd,' Daniel echoed.

Smiling to himself, he turned and settled down with Ozzie on the couch in the lounge. It looked like there was less than half a bottle to finish off. He poured himself a generous glass.

'What do you think?' he asked quietly.

I like him, replied Julia.

He did too.

Shall we keep him?

He chuckled at that. Daniel reminded him a little of himself at that age. He'd played bass in a band, had been all willowy and floppy-mopped – though he'd never gone as far as bloody eyeliner. He was sure his younger self had been less articulate about things, less aware of the world.

Boyd approved of his daughter's choice. Daniel seemed like a great lad.

He went to bed feeling good, feeling... like he was properly off duty. That was it. Off duty. Off the clock from both work and parental angst.

He lay on his back for a while and watched bare branches and dappled light from the street lamps perform shadow theatre across the bedroom ceiling.

8

The Ellessey Forensic Services building had once been a remote village church. Its flint and clay walls featured tall, narrow stained-glass windows, and what had once been the surrounding graveyard was now a gravel parking area and a well-kept corporate garden.

It was situated just outside the town of Battle, but isolated enough in Boyd's opinion to be considered in the arse end of nowhere.

Okeke found a parking spot near the main entrance and Boyd climbed out of the passenger side. If he'd been a bit smarter last night, he'd have poured that last half a bottle of Malbec away.

'Thanks for getting me out of the cubicle farm, guv,' said Okeke. 'I feel like I've been chained to my desk for weeks.'

'I got you out so you could drive. I'm not even sure I'm entirely legal yet.' Boyd winced.

'Heavy night?' she asked.

'Emma brought her boyfriend home,' he said. 'We "partied" – as the youngsters like to say.'

'Ahh.' She smiled. 'And is he a nice lad?'

'Yeah,' Boyd replied. 'He'll do me.' He slammed the car door shut behind him and groaned at the noise. 'Look, I'm not exactly match fit this morning...'

'You want me to take the lead?' she asked.

'Yeah, I'm not great with cadavers on the slab.' He had a flashback to the previous night's barbeque ribs in hoisin sauce. 'It's probably better if I stand back a bit today.'

He pushed the glass door open for Okeke and she smirked at him as she stepped past him into the reception foyer.

The receptionist, a young man in a casual checked and collared shirt, looked up from his tablet. 'Good morning, can I help you?' he enquired.

Boyd rested his elbows on the marble counter. 'It's DCI Boyd and DC Okeke to see Dr Palmer.'

'One moment,' the young man said, raising a slender finger as he started tapping the screen in front of him.

Okeke was busy admiring a large potted cheese plant, up-lit by a spotlight and casting a jungle-like pattern of shadows across the ancient vaulted church ceiling. 'I want a cheese plant this size,' she said. 'It would swamp my lounge, though.'

Boyd imagined the same plant in the corner of his oversized lounge. He could probably fit half a dozen of them in and still not feel encroached upon.

He turned back to the receptionist, who was still caressing his touchscreen. 'Anything on the horizon yet?' he asked.

The receptionist looked up from his screen. 'Sorry?'

'There's a lot of –' Boyd wiggled his index finger around – 'going on. Is it *that* complicated to check an appointment calendar?'

There was a flash of irritation on the young man's face. 'I'm letting Dr Palmer know you're here,' he said. 'Take a seat and I'll have someone come and get you.'

'It's probably plastic, you know,' said Boyd, joining Okeke next to the cheese plant.

He'd just plonked his bum down on the seat when a young woman Emma's age appeared through sliding glass doors, bearing a couple of visitor's tags on lanyards.

'Boyd? O-kee-kee.'

'Like... *Oh, car key*,' Okeke said with a smile.

'Oops, sorry about that,' replied the young woman. She handed them the lanyards and led them through some smoked-glass doors into the rest of the small Norman church. It had been gutted of everything except an old stone font. The floor was a smooth, richly stained and varnished oak that made their footsteps loud and echoey. In the middle of the floor were a couple of pieces of Hirst-like forensically themed 'art' in glass cases.

'Those are both Von Hagens,' the young woman said, following Boyd's gaze. He paused briefly to look at one of them, a male figure, completely stripped of his skin, showing muscles, tendons, staring eyeballs and bared teeth. He was posed sitting at desk with a chess set on it, considering his next move.

'How about one of these in your lounge?' Boyd said to Okeke.

The young woman seemed mildly irked. 'It's an actual original,' she said. 'Not a mould.'

Boyd nodded. 'Right.'

'Beautiful, isn't it?' She pointed at the theatrically lit exhibit. 'You know, that was an actual person once upon a time,' she said. 'The process is called plastination. You give the body a very long bath in acetone; it draws out all the water and preserves the soft tissue. Then it has another long soak in liquidized silicon. Everything that once was soft tissue is gradually replaced with plastic.'

'What about the bones?' Boyd asked.

'Oh, those are original.'

He looked at the flayed face of the chess player. 'And this bloke was fine with all that, was he?'

She smiled. 'He was, of course, dead first.'

She led them through another set of doors that took them out of the old church into what was clearly a low-ceilinged modern extension.

'I think we're in studio three,' she said, leading them down a coolly lit hallway and stopping outside a door. She tapped four numbers into a keypad and the door clicked softly. She pushed it inwards. 'Dr Palmer, your visitors.'

Boyd stepped in first, Okeke behind him.

The room didn't have the cold, bright and clinical ambience he was expecting. No white tiles on the floor and walls; rather, both were an expensive-looking dark granite, which made the room feel more dungeon than operating theatre.

The room's lighting was a calming, womb-like amber. In the centre stood an examination gurney beneath a crucifix arrangement of bright ceiling spotlights.

There were two people beside it, in green scrubs and gloves.

The one on the left raised a hand. 'Morning. I'm Dr Palmer. DCI Boyd, is it?'

He nodded. 'And this is DC Okeke.'

'Pleased to meet you both.' Palmer turned to the man next to her. 'I hope you don't mind – I've roped in a colleague of mine, Dr Esquerra. His expertise is in archaeological forensics.'

Boyd offered them both a quick nod. 'Archaeological? How old are we talking?'

'It's not an ancient Saxon, I'm afraid,' said Palmer.

'Well, it was wearing a Nike trainer when we found it, so no surprises there,' said Boyd.

Palmer laughed politely. 'The degraded condition of the soft tissues suggests it's been in the ground for maybe fifteen to thirty years.'

'Is it male or female?' Okeke asked.

'Male,' said Palmer. 'Adult but young. Almost certainly between seventeen and twenty.'

'It's a big ask, I know, but do you have a cause of death?' asked Boyd.

Palmer nodded. 'We actually have a very good idea. With a cadaver this old, that's unusual. We can usually tell you about the injuries sustained and make a best guess about which one of them might have led to death. But this one looks straightforward.' Palmer beckoned them both to come closer. 'Let me show you.'

Okeke stepped forward into the glare of the ceiling lights. Boyd remained where he was.

'DCI Boyd?' she prompted.

'I'm good back here, thanks,' he said.

Palmer gave him an understanding and slightly patronising nod.

'I'm feeling a bit under the weather,' he explained. 'I wouldn't want to sneeze over your body.'

'Fair enough,' she said, whipping the cover off the examination table to reveal the body. An odour wafted out to greet Boyd: a mixture of pond water and chemical toilet.

On the table lay a cluster of bones wrapped in the ink-black shreds of material that he'd briefly glimpsed in the muddy ditch. They were now laid out on the examination table in a recognisable simulacrum of the human form.

'Just so you understand how we're dividing the task,' Dr Palmer explained. 'I'm looking at the remaining soft materials, Dr Esquerra is looking at the bones. Do you want to explain the aging first?' she asked her colleague.

Esquerra nodded. 'Of course.'

He leant over to point at one of the legs. When the bone starts growing, there is no flaring here; the bone is more or less a straight shaft. This shaft is called the diaphysis. A separate wider growth of bone begins to develop here; this wider bit is the epiphysis. During adolescence, these two bones begin to fuse until they become completely one, and we then have the recognisable flared end of the tibia.'

He tapped the end of the bone with a gloved finger. 'This process begins at the age of fourteen or fifteen, and the fusing is complete by nineteen or twenty.

'On this one the fusing is complete, but only recently. If you want an age, as Dr Palmer said, I would give seventeen to twenty.'

Okeke bent over and peered more closely.

'Right,' said Boyd, more than happy to take his word for it. 'So, Dr Palmer, you mentioned the cause of death was straightforward?'

'The *likely* cause of death,' Palmer added. She pointed to the cadaver's rib cage and an unmissable – even from where Boyd was standing – puckered mouth of leathered skin that had curled back on itself to reveal the scarred rib bone beneath. 'A single forceful stab wound to the chest. Aimed at the heart, almost certainly.'

Dr Palmer gestured at the rest of the body. 'There are no ligature indicators on what's left of the skin around the throat. No impact marks on the skull. As for the torso, there are signs that animals have been having a go at that, add to that, twenty or more years' worth of degradation, there's little inside that's intact enough to diagnose any other peri- or post-mortem injuries, I'm afraid.'

'Can you be any more precise on how long it's been in the ground?' asked Okeke.

Dr Esquerra looked irritated. 'No. Like I said, between fifteen and thirty years.'

'That's pretty loose,' said Boyd.

'Forensic taphonomy is not great at producing a precise year,' Esquerra explained.

'Did our forensics people send you enough information on where the body was located?' asked Boyd.

Palmer nodded. 'We got a very detailed report from Kevin Sully. A layby off the A21.' She looked at him. 'I know it. On trips back from London I've stopped there myself a couple of times.'

Boyd couldn't imagine it was for the same reason as the trucker.

'To answer calls, emails,' she added quickly. 'Certainly not to picnic. From the pictures of the soil, it looks very wet. Not great drainage. The layby's in a bit of a dip, if I recall correctly?'

Boyd had to cast his mind back to driving over there yesterday. Yes, the road did descend and rise slightly. He nodded.

Palmer shrugged, then indicated the twisted brown skeleton on the table. 'Twenty years, give or take five either side, is as precise as I can get with what we have. Carlos?'

'Yes, I would agree with that,' he said.

Boyd clapped his hands together. 'Well, that's a bit better.'

'Well, I'm afraid we're not going to get a lot more from these bones.' Palmer gestured at a collection of sealed evidence bags on a table nearby. 'You're more likely to have luck with those items.'

'What's over there?' Okeke asked, wandering over.

'Clothes,' Palmer replied. 'Very degraded. A Nike trainer. And a wooden figurine.'

'A figurine?' Boyd moved to join Okeke at the table.

'Yes,' Palmer confirmed. 'It looks carved. There are some flecks of paint on it still. It looks a little like a chess piece...'

9

Boyd placed the evidence bags carefully on the back seat and then plugged in his seat belt as Okeke started up the car. The noise spooked about a dozen rabbits that had been masquerading as mole hills on the beautifully tended lawn outside the church façade of the EFS building. They scarpered en masse for the trees.

'How're you feeling, guv?' Okeke asked as she pulled away.

'Rough, but functional,' he muttered. Getting outside, and away from the smell of formaldehyde without running out early, was a merciful win. With hindsight, he probably could have stepped forward with Okeke and been fine.

'So, dead fifteen to twenty-five years ago,' said Okeke. 'We're talking what... mid to late nineties?'

'Jesus, that's going back a bit,' Boyd said. He tried to think of some cultural markers. 'Back in the time of Shrek and the Spice Girls.'

'Yes. That's the end of the nineties,' said Okeke. She shrugged a little guiltily. 'And *yes*, I was a little Spice Girls fan.'

He shook his head. Where had the time gone?

'You getting all nostalgic?' asked Okeke, smiling.

He grinned sheepishly. 'I *was* actually. I was trying to recall what it was like back then. It was all *Cool Britannia* and millennium bugs. Emma was only a thought; Jules and me were living in a flat in Hammersmith. What about you?'

'Ah, I was twelve, thirteen. Totally loving Scary Spice's attitude.'

He laughed.

'Do you remember Furbies?' she asked. 'I remember the fight my parents had to get me one for Christmas.'

'Christ, yes. The stuff of nightmares. Whoever thought a chirping hairy dwarf bird with staring homicidal eyes would be a great idea?' He snorted. 'There were punch-ups over those. And now they populate landfill sites across the world.'

'You're kidding,' said Okeke. 'They populate eBay as collector's items more like.'

She turned out of the grounds of the Ellessey Forensic Services and onto a country lane.

'So,' Boyd recapped. 'We've got a male, nineteen to twenty-one, buried twenty-odd years ago. What else do we know?'

'Well, there's the wood figurine?' said Okeke. 'Is that going to help us do you think?'

He shrugged. 'Perhaps. It could be symbolic. It has to be important, right? For the killer to make sure it was buried with him.'

'Some kind of ritualistic thing?' she asked.

'What, like some kind of voodoo doll?' Boyd shook his head.

'I was going to say a Christ-on-a-cross, perhaps?'

He nodded. 'Could be. Or it could be something belonging to the boy? Something that was important to him?'

'Do you think the killer would care?' she asked.

'Maybe. Some sort of guilt reflex. Could even be remorse.'

They were quiet for a while, both of them running

scenarios through in their heads. Okeke finally turned to look at him. 'Okay, so someone knocked the boy down on the A21?'

'And then, having run him over, they stabbed him to death?' Boyd raised a brow.

'Stranger things have happened. Could have been a Mercy killing. The boy was in agony and dying. He ended it quickly.'

'Eyes on the road, please, Okeke,' he warned.

She returned her full attention to the road as they approached a blind corner.

'And the figurine?' he asked.

'I'll try,' she said, shrugging.

They lapsed back into silence, both lost in their thoughts.

IT WAS AFTER LUNCH, another microwaved Tupperware container full of some healthy lentil-based gloop that Emma had prepped for him, when Sutherland, responding to an earlier email, invited Boyd to his office for a chat.

Boyd knocked on the office door and Sutherland eagerly waved him in.

'Take a seat,' he said.

Boyd pulled a chair out in front of Sutherland's cluttered desk and sat down. 'So, let's start with a cause of death.'

'A single stab wound to the chest. But it's an old body, almost completely skeletal. Whatever happened, happened two decades ago. There's a clear knife mark on two of the ribs.'

Sutherland steepled his hands together, elbows on the desk. 'How sure was the EFS pathologist about the age of the body?'

'There were two of them, sir. She'd brought in a bone expert. Are you asking about the age of the victim, or how long it's been buried?' Boyd asked.

'Give me both,' Sutherland said.

'Well,' Boyd said slowly, 'they were more certain about the age – but a little looser on how long it's been under the ground. The boy was nineteen to twenty-one. He was white. He was wearing what looked like jeans and a hooded sweatshirt and a pair of Nike trainers. Nice ones by the look of the one we found. And the pathologist found a wooden figurine in his hand.'

'Sully didn't spot it?'

Boyd shook his head. 'She said they had to dig the remains of it out of his hand. I guess over twenty years, the whole thing, flesh and wood, became fused together.'

'It was a wooden figurine, you say?' Sutherland stoked his chin, thoughtfully.

'Yes, they said it looked like a chess piece.' Boyd said. 'It's hard to tell to be honest. There's not much left of it.'

Sutherland was nodding his head, staring into the distance.

'That seems to have triggered a thought?' prompted Boyd.

'I... *damn it*... yes. It rings a bell.' Sutherland's eyes narrowed behind his spectacles and his forehead rumpled into fleshy ripples of concentration. 'I vaguely recall a case of an unidentified body; it was another force, not ours – a boy in a grave, clutching a wooden figure.'

Boyd leant forward, willing Sutherland to dig the memory out of his head.

'Damned bollocking ball sacks,' Sutherland uttered eventually. 'It was a long time ago. I think I was in uniform back then.'

'Okay,' said Boyd. 'Well, that's helpful. It's something I can trawl for on LEDS.'

LEDS – the Law Enforcement Data System – was the Big New Shiny version of HOLMES that Sussex Police, as well as several other forces looking to appear forward-focused and snuffling for brownie points, had offered to trial.

Boyd hated the bloody interface, which had clearly been designed to favour the younger police personnel brought up on tablets and smartphones. He'd only used it so far on his work PC, with the old bastard's interface option of mouse/keyboard.

Sutherland pressed his lips together, unhappy at the thought of upscaling a historic murder inquiry into something larger and more expensive.

'Keep me posted,' he said finally.

10

Boyd sat down at his desk, cracked his knuckles and prepared to spend the afternoon wrestling with LEDS.

The problem that came with software that prided itself on sophistication was the complicated options hidden behind meaningless icons and nested dropdown menus. However, he figured, if he could navigate a Sky Plus settings menu – which was no mean feat these days – he surely had a fighting chance of sniffing out some of the more basic search functions.

By about three in the afternoon, and after a long fight, he'd negotiated an agreement with the system that had it quivering unhappily on the very limit of his keyword enquiry budget.

The keywords themselves were bundled along with a tick list of filters that included all the usual things: demographics, like age, race, gender, location, nationality; and the typical MO indicators of manner of death, post-mortem tampering and body disposal method.

Boyd gave the search a broad canvas: 1995 to the present, which LEDS raised a metaphorical brow at. With a caution from the system that he was being a somewhat greedy bastard with computer bandwidth, he clicked on the 'search' button and went to grab himself a coffee up in the canteen on the top floor.

THE CANTEEN WAS PLEASANTLY QUIET – it was one of the few lull moments between shift ends and shift starts. He saw Warren waiting to be served at the counter and walked over to join him.

'What're you getting?' Boyd asked.

Warren glanced round at him. 'All right, sir. Well... I realised I had need of a bacon sandwich.'

Boyd looked at his watch. 'At this time? Your mum won't be pleased with you – not if you can't eat her dinner.'

Warren opened and closed his mouth a couple of times, unsure how to respond.

'Sorry, Warren, I'm yanking your chain. Ignore me,' Boyd said, grinning.

'Oh, right. Thanks for that, sir.'

'Look, I'll shout your sandwich for you – it's the least I can do,' Boyd said, feeling a little guilty. 'So, I'm glad I bumped into you here. I've got a job for you before you clock off today.' He dug out his phone and pulled up the photograph that Dave Webb had sent him. He zoomed in on the registration number. 'Reckon you can run that through ANPR and get me the name of the owner?'

Warren nodded, pulled a pen out of his jacket and scribbled the number on the back of his hand.

'Is it important, sir?' he asked.

'Sort of. Could be. He's the berk who found the body in the layby this morning, and then buggered off, leaving it to someone else to call it in. I want him in to question him,' Boyd said.

'If I get the details... you want me to invite him in for you?' Warren offered.

'Yeah, if you can get him to come in tomorrow, that would be awesome. Then I can give him the bollocking he deserves.'

'Maybe he had another body in his van?' said Warren.

'Let's not jump...' It took Boyd a moment or two to realise Warren had said that with a glint in his eye.

'Just jerking your chain, sir,' he said, smirking.

~

'Got a moment?' asked Boyd.

Sutherland waved him in and clicked his mouse to close something down on the screen. Boyd was almost certain he'd had a game of solitaire up.

'What is it?'

'I got two hits. One, an unidentified teenaged male body found in North Wales. He was also buried in a layby. The words "carved figure" turned up in the SOC report. It was found along with the body, but not held in the hand.'

'When was that?'

'2001.'

'And how old was the victim?'

'Around sixteen.'

'All right. And the other hit?'

Boyd had actually, vaguely, recalled the name when he'd seen it on the screen. 'A Leon Martin. He was the suspected killer in the case above, but the evidence was all circumstantial, though the timing was spot on.'

Sutherland seemed to sit to attention at the mention of Leon Martin. 'Argghh. I know that name. I know that!' he exclaimed.

Boyd continued: 'I pulled up a potted case synopsis. The

Sun dubbed him the Ken Doll Killer. I've put in a case-file release request to the Cheshire Constabulary.'

Sutherland let out a wheeze of relief. 'That's it! I remember. He got that nickname when the police inspected his house. They discovered he posed the bodies in his house, like dolls, then he'd taken photos of them.'

Boyd remembered the case too. It had been back in 2001 when he'd been a lowly PC. 'What was all the posing and photographing all about?'

Sutherland grimaced. 'Who knows why these weirdos do what they do? Gratification? Attention? He wasn't in the headlines for long, though – because of the whole 9/11 thing.'

'They found his vehicle parked conveniently by a cliff in the north of Wales if I remember rightly,' Sutherland continued. 'There were a few of his belongings inside. He supposedly threw himself into the Irish Sea.'

'But you're not convinced by that?' Boyd said.

Sutherland shrugged. 'If I recall, the consensus in the media was that it looked *too staged*.'

Boyd nodded. He hadn't been as news focused back then. He'd been a young man, training on the job and recently married to Julia, and a new dad on top of that. His nose had been stuck in various Blackstone manuals, trying hard to make the police thing work, because, well, he had responsibilities.

Sutherland shuffled the papers on his desk. 'The Cheshire Constabulary weren't that convinced by the staged exit either. It was all too convenient.' He looked at Boyd. 'Why did the enquiry flag up the Ken Doll Killer?'

'It was a hit on the term "carved figure". I've only got two excerpt sentences from the case file. One is a listing of contents in a room, the other is a reference to one of the killer's photographs of his victims. But his victims also match the profiles of our case and the other one, don't they?'

Sutherland nodded. 'Young lads.'

'Right.'

'Right, well... I suppose you'd better get on and acquaint yourself with that case file, Boyd.'

11

'Hello? Guv?'

Boyd looked up from the case file and saw Okeke standing over his desk. She had her coat over one arm.

'You look like you're a million miles away there.'

'Yeah. Just having a look through this file,' he said absently, eyes firmly fixed on the multiple printed sheets in front of him.

'A few of us are heading down to the pub for a pint,' Okeke said, noting that Boyd was still looking a bit spaced out. 'The pub on the pier,' she added. 'You want to come along?'

Boyd checked his watch. It was gone half five. The rest of the afternoon had just slipped away from him.

'One pint won't hurt, I suppose,' he said, shuffling the papers back inside their folder.

Ten minutes later, she'd managed to round up those who were coming and herd them out of the building, down the hill to the White Rock Theatre and across Verulam Place onto Hastings Pier.

They were eight in total, spread out in chatting, smoking, vaping pairs, with Boyd and Okeke bringing up the rear as they made their way across the decking towards the Bier Garden pub, situated halfway down the pier.

'How's the case-file reading going?' she asked.

'You're too young to remember the Ken Doll Killer, aren't you? It was back in 2001. You'd have been how old?' He glanced across at her.

She shook her head. '2001? So I'd have been fourteen, fifteen? Busy reading *Harry Potter*.'

He laughed. 'Right.'

'And that's definitely our man, is it?'

Boyd nodded. 'I think so. It's looking that way.'

'So what's with the name? The Ken Doll Killer?' she asked.

'The police found photographs of his victims, collected in albums at his farmhouse. He'd posed their dead bodies to look as though they were still alive, playing games, watching TV, that sort of thing.' Boyd grimaced. 'Can't say I've seen anything like it before.'

Okeke pulled a face. 'Does this weirdo have a name?'

'Leon David Martin,' said Boyd.

'And is he interviewable?'

'Nope. He's dead.' Boyd looked at her. 'He threw himself off a cliff in North Wales. His body was never recovered. The police at the time were suspicious that it might have been staged. But that was over twenty years ago. If he were alive, he's not turned up or tripped up or left behind any flagged markers on the system in all this time – which for a serial killer is unusual. It's unlikely that he just stopped, so, things being equal, he probably *did* throw himself in.'

Okeke puffed her lips out. 'That's a rather theatrical departure.'

'Isn't that what narcissists crave? The fame? The attention? Only his swan dive was quickly overshadowed by the Twin Towers in New York being knocked down.' Boyd shrugged.

'So, I'm presuming our layby body fits somehow with this Leon Martin's victims?' Okeke said.

'It looks like it,' Boyd replied. 'That carved figure he was holding. There were others a little like it in the posed pictures and logged among the contents of Martin's farmhouse.'

'Does the timeline fit?' she asked.

'It doesn't *not* fit.' He shrugged again. 'If Sully and Dr Palmer could have been a little more precise on exactly how long the body's been buried there, we might have been able to say for sure.'

'Arghh!' She made a face on his behalf. 'Bloody science, eh?' She paused thoughtfully. 'What about the *trainer*?'

'What *about* the trainer?'

'I heard the body was wearing a Nike trainer, right?'

'So?' Boyd said.

'Well, you might get lucky there.' She spread her hands. 'Nike tend to change their design every year. Well, they do now. Maybe they didn't back then, but it might be worth asking to see if a trainer expert can date it?'

Boyd gave her a bemused look. 'And is there such a person?'

She screwed her face up. 'Of course! It's like a field of study these days. I bet you could do a degree in Nike history now. If you wanted to...'

Boyd wagged a finger at her. 'You're a bloody genius, Okeke. If you're right, that is.'

'I am,' she agreed. 'Just remember to mention that the next time Her Madge descends from the heavens to kick arses and bestow blessings.'

Boyd nodded, but mention of Chief Superintendent Margaret Hatcher set his mind trundling off in a different direction.

Since the fire at the Sea Breeze Campsite and the closing down of the Nix case, he and Hatcher had only had one meeting during which they'd had what seemed to be a very nuanced conversation about one thing, when in fact it had been a conversation about something else entirely.

I know you think I steered the investigation away from looking at Nix's financial affairs, Boyd. I know you suspect I'm somehow tied in. Well... mind how you go there, sunshine. I'm keeping a close eye on you... seemed to be the subtext.

Well, that went both ways. She could be sure about that.

Boyd really had no idea whether she was corrupt or not. He didn't think she'd had any direct dealings with Nix himself – he wasn't so sure about the Russians Nix had been mixed up with, though. He wondered if he'd ever get answers now. Nix and his Russian girlfriend were all dead, their bodies missing at sea. And the Russians seemed to have disappeared. End of story.

Nothing to see here.

Apart from that little 'parting gift' that was delivered to his front door.

'So how was this Martin bloke picked up?' Okeke asked, saving him from his thoughts.

'I've only skimmed the file – but it looks as though his last potential victim managed to escape him, somehow. He was found wandering along the side of the A55 in Cheshire, not far from the Welsh border. He was spotted and reported by a number of passers-by, walking barefoot along the hard shoulder, looking distressed and disorientated.'

'Blimey,' she said. 'That's rough.'

Boyd nodded. 'He was a young lad, Kristy Clarke. He was able to give the police enough information to identify the place he'd been kept captive. The police swarmed Martin's farmhouse, in case there were other victims on the site.'

'And were there?' she asked.

'There were the photos and signs of others, before Kristy, but no one else was there, no bodies. The cops found his vehicle – a van – parked near a cliff off the north coast of Wales. His clothes, his wallet...'

'And they thought he'd gone over,' Okeke said.

'Yeah, well that's what it looked like.' Boyd nodded. 'We should probably join the others,' he added as he pushed the glass doors of the pub inwards.

'I'm buying,' she said, following him inside. 'What do you want?'

'I'll have a glass of diet Coke,' Boyd said. 'Thanks, Okeke.'

'Seriously?' She looked at him and sighed. 'Guv. It's Friday. You're going for an after-work pint with your all-male – except me – CID workmates. Shall we try that again?'

'Ah, good point,' he said, nodding. 'Better make it a pint of Caffrey's – and when Emma tells me off, it was peer pressure and you'd better back me up.'

12

Boyd returned home just after ten, having left his car parked back at the police station. He'd have to sodding well walk to work tomorrow morning. One pint of Caffrey's had become two that became three.

He had an unread text from Emma. She was out with Daniel again, who had a gig. The text said: *Don't wait up*.

He reheated the meal that Emma had made the previous night and let Ozzie out into the overgrown back garden to do his business.

Boyd regarded the scruffy gone-to-wild garden. *That* was another job on his to-do list. The previous owners hadn't touched it in years by the look of it.

After dinner, he sat on the couch, Ozzie's head on his lap, his eyes on the TV – and his mind inevitably circled back to Leon Martin, the Ken Doll Killer. Disappeared, presumed dead, for twenty-one years.

The case file, put together by the SIO Mike Gratton back in 2001, had been absent of any conjecture or speculation as to *why* Martin had done what he'd done. DCI Gratton's pragmatic footprint had been stamped across it with the omission of any guesswork or unsubstantiated theorizing. There'd been no attempt at profiling Martin – why would they? They *had* him. From what Boyd had read so far, it was a very dry account.

Boyd wondered about the environment that had produced the Ken Doll Killer. The family details were slim. Leon David Martin was born in 1976, was the only child of John and Arlene Martin. They were originally from North Wales. John had been in the army and was badly wounded in the Falklands war. He'd come home in 1983 with disfiguring burns and a bad case of undiagnosed PTSD. The family relocated to the farm in Cheshire when Leon was eleven, where John Martin turned his hand to poultry farming.

Leon had been pulled out of his secondary school after the first year to be home-schooled by his mother. There had been no reason given, but Boyd noticed that Gratton had made some notes in his case file to follow up on any records of social service home visits. When he was eighteen, Leon's mother died of cancer and six months later John Martin hanged himself in a barn. With no other next of kin, Leon inherited the farm and had apparently lived there until September 2001 when Kristy Clarke had escaped and Leon Martin had supposedly threw himself into the Irish Sea.

The photographs Leon Martin had taken of the boys – young men, really – fitted with the 'trophy keeping' that was common to serial killers. They were all of corpses but posed as if they were still alive and living with him. There were pictures of his victims on the sofa, propped up as if they were watching TV, a beer can wedged in one hand, a TV dinner placed on their lap. There were photos with a man, presumed by Gratton to be Martin, in shot too – 'selfies' taken long before that word even existed. Martin had coloured over his own face with a felt-tip pen – presumably to disguise his identity. Although... a psychologist might have read into that something more nuanced – a guilt response? Disassociation with the crime?

The images in the case file were only a sample. The rest – and there were hundreds of them – were logged as being in evidence storage at Cheshire Constabulary's headquarters.

In one of the images Boyd had spotted what looked like the carved figurines mentioned in the report. They were lined up on a TV dinner tray on a boy's lap, his head drooped down as if studying them intently. The figures looked to Boyd as though they could be toy soldiers of some sort – uniformly standing to attention.

There were also a few 'out-take' photographs in the case file. Those that hadn't made the pages of Martin's macabre albums, which the police had found in a filing cabinet in the basement: images in which skin discolouration was too pronounced to ignore, where sub-dermal pooling had produced dark unsightly bruises that were too large to hide behind a cushion or any other prop.

Boyd stretched, shoved Ozzie from his lap and stood up. He was knackered, and Martin could wait until tomorrow. He took a glass of water upstairs to bed, trying to remember, as Ozzie shot past him, just when the 'no dogs in the bedroom' rule had fallen by the wayside. He undressed down to his jocks and pulled the quilt over him as Ozzie curled up on what would have been Julia's side and presented his back to Boyd, snuggling backwards until they were virtually spooning.

'Jesus, Ozzie... shall I get you a hot-water bottle as well?' Boyd grumbled, swinging an arm over Ozzie's chest and falling asleep to the steady rustle of his dog's breathing. As he drifted off, he wondered whether the boy from the A21 layby had been in one of those photographs and whether the little nub of rotten wood excavated from the tattered remnants of leathered flesh of the fist had been one of those figurines sitting on the TV tray.

13

'Mullen's waiting for you,' said DS Minter, 'and he's majorly pissed off we made him come all this way to give a statement.'

'Well, he shouldn't have buggered off when he was supposed to stay put,' muttered Boyd. 'All right, which room's he in?'

'Interview room three. Have fun, boss.' Minter carried on down the corridor, jacket slung over one shoulder.

'What's his full name again?' called out Boyd.

'David Mullen,' Minter called back.

Boyd grabbed two cups of coffee and a KitKat from the vending machine and took them with him into the small interview room.

'Here you go, David,' he said, placing them on the table. 'Thanks for coming in.'

Dave Mullen, shaved head and goatee beard, looked at the peace offering with contempt. 'It's Dave,' he said, 'and why've I been kept so fucking long? I do have a job to do, you know!'

'Well, Dave,' said Boyd, looking him in the eye, 'you know

as the first person to find that body, you were obliged to call it in, then wait there until the police arrived?'

'I had deliveries.' Mullen replied sullenly.

'I'm afraid that's not really a good enough answer,' Boyd said. He took a deep breath. Interviewing arseholes like Mullen drove him round the bloody bend.

'Well, it'll have to be good enough,' Mullen shot back. 'I've got deadlines in my line of work.' He looked at his watch. 'Just like I've got today. I've been sitting here for half a bloody hour already.'

Boyd didn't correct him. It had been ten minutes, that was all. He pulled out his work phone and laid it on the table. 'Mind if I record the interview?' he asked.

'Isn't there supposed to be a proper machine that makes a beep sound?'

'The beep machine that records interviews lives in another room,' said Boyd. 'Phone okay instead?'

Mullen shrugged his consent.

'We'll do this as quickly as we can and you can be on your merry way,' Boyd said. 'Now then...' He sipped his coffee. It was still too hot to actually drink. 'Tell me how you found the body.'

Mullen sighed. 'I stopped at the layby, went for a piss, and I found it.'

'Okay. So, winding back a step or two, why this particular layby?'

'I know it. I pass it several times a week.'

'Doing your delivery job, I take it?'

Mullen nodded.

'Delivering what?'

'All different things. Depends. I'm freelance. Like Amazon deliveries,' Mullen said.

Boyd nodded. 'Okay, so is this a regular run?'

'Yeah. And the A21 has bugger all in the way of service

stations and pit stops. So that layby's the last one where you can take a *private* piss before you get stuck in traffic heading south.'

'So you pulled over. Parked up...'

Mullen nodded. 'Got out, went to the overgrown area at the back, and I was just unzipping when I saw those bones.'

'Okay. So did you instantly recognise them as *human* bones?'

'No. Not instantly. Took me a moment to realise what I was looking at. I thought they were dead branches at first.' Mullen reached for his coffee.

'What was it that convinced you they were human remains, Dave?'

'The skull. Obviously.' He took a quick sip, then set the cup down. 'You don't mistake one of them, do you? Jesus.'

Boyd nodded in agreement. 'So what did you do next?'

'I sort of just backed up, didn't I? It put the fucking shits up me.'

'And that's when Mr Webb joined you?'

'Who's that?' Mullen looked confused, which, Boyd thought, was an improvement on the hostile looks he'd been giving so far.

'The other truck driver,' said Boyd. 'David Webb.'

'Right, yeah.' Mullen nodded. 'I suppose I called out something, and he came over to see if I was all right and that's when I showed him the skull.'

'And who was it decided to call it in to the police?'

Mullen took another sip of his coffee. 'I can't remember. Maybe him. Maybe me.'

'It was him.' Boyd leant forward. 'He told me you weren't that keen about doing it. Said you "shot off".'

'Well, I left because he said he'd call. I thought it was all sorted. So I went. Like I said, I've got deadlines. There's barely time to stop for a piss. Normally I've got a bottle on me.'

'A bottle?'

'To piss in. Saves time.'

Boyd grimaced at the image.

'So, what's this about then?' said Mullen. 'Is this a murder, or something?'

'That's a distinct possibility, Dave,' Boyd said. 'I'm almost certain it wasn't suicide.'

Mullen pulled a face. It took Boyd a moment to realise he was smiling. 'Ha. Funny, mate. Was the body a young or old one?'

'Young,' replied Boyd. 'We don't know a precise age. We're waiting on the forensics.'

'Right. *Old* body, though, yeah? Been buried a while, right?'

'It was a pile of bones, so yeah.'

Mullen's face seemed to slacken slightly. Boyd, watching him closely, continued. 'You ever heard of the First Finder Principle?'

Mullen shook his head.

'It's when the guilty party is the one who "finds" the body. It's a way of getting yourself ruled out early. Sometimes the guilty party will make sure they get their hands dirty at the scene of the crime, so that later they can claim that's when DNA contamination occurred.'

Mullen flushed red. 'What're you saying? That –'

'I'm not accusing you of anything, Dave,' Boyd interrupted. 'I'm just asking if you're familiar with the concept. That's all.'

'Why? I mean... no. I haven't heard of that. Why you asking me that?'

Boyd smiled. He realised he was starting to enjoy himself. Of course this nob-head hadn't heard of the First Finder Principle. He'd just made the term up.

'God! Wait! You think –'

'I just thought I'd float the idea, Dave,' Boyd said in a calming voice.

'Hey, I just found it, mate! That's all! I didn't *have* to point it out to the other bloke, did I? I could've just left it for someone else to find.' Mullen was starting to sound panicked, which, Boyd thought, was very satisfying.

Mullen pressed his fists down on the table and started to get up.

'Relax.' Boyd raised a hand. 'It's okay, Dave. I don't really think you did it.'

'Well, then why fucking say that shit?!' Mullen spat.

Boyd shrugged. 'Just testing the water.'

He let Mullen sit silently for a few more seconds, then finally flashed him a quick and courteous smile. 'Okay then,' said Boyd.

'That's it?'

'I just need you to sign this...' He slid a form across the table.

'What's this?' Mullen asked, suspicious.

'Your permission for us to transcribe the interview. And that you're aware the interview was recorded.' Boyd pointed to where he needed to sign. 'Sign there, date there... and name in blocks there.'

Mullen did his bit, then pushed the form back across the table.

'And for your troubles, Dave... here's a free KitKat, courtesy of Sussex Police.'

Boyd walked him out of CID and pointed him towards the stairwell that headed down to reception. He handed Mullen a business card with his number on it.

'Call me if you can think of anything else that might be helpful, okay?'

'Yeah, right,' replied Mullen, tossing the card over his shoulder.

Boyd watched Mullen descend the stairs before turning back through the double doors and into the muted hubbub of the CID floor.

He'd just sat down when his work phone buzzed on the desk beside him. It was an unknown number.

'DCI Boyd,' he answered.

'It's Dave.'

Boyd wondered whether the miserable bugger had left something in the interview room.

'Dave Webb? The truck driver? You said I had to come in and give a statement?'

Boyd nodded. Jesus, were all delivery drivers called Dave these days? 'Yes. When's suitable?'

'I'm on my way up to London to pick up a load. This afternoon I can do.'

'What time?' Boyd asked.

'Dunno. Four, maybe?' Webb sounded irritable too. Maybe that was another delivery driver thing.

'That's fine. I'm on duty until five thirty. Just mention my name to the desk sergeant when you come in.'

Webb hung up without a goodbye.

FOUR O'CLOCK CAME AND WENT. Webb finally arrived at five fifteen. There was no bloody coffee and free KitKat for him.

Boyd placed his phone on the table in the interview room. 'Do you mind if I record?'

'Dunno. Do I need to lawyer up?'

'I don't know. Are you living in the United States?'

'Huh?'

Boyd shook his head. 'You're not a suspect, Dave. You're just giving me a statement for last Friday morning's incident, that's all. I'm recording it because I'm the muggins who's going to have to type it up later on.' He sighed inwardly. *Here we go again*, he thought as he pressed the screen on his phone to start the recording.

14

DSI Sutherland was perched on Boyd's desk, waiting for him to arrive for work. His arse cheeks had spread inside his beige office trousers like bread dough and completely engulfed the corner of the desk. It must have been uncomfortable for Sutherland wedged up there, Boyd thought, as he stepped around Sutherland's extended legs. He planted his coffee cup down beside his keyboard a little more loudly and territorially than was necessary. Sutherland, taking the hint, stood up.

'Can I get you a seat, sir?' Boyd asked innocently.

Sutherland didn't look his usual chirpy, round emoji-faced self this morning.

'Are you all right, sir?'

Sutherland pulled a local newspaper out from behind his back as though he was presenting Boyd with a bouquet of flowers. 'It's in the *Argus*! Already, for God's sake!'

Boyd took the local paper from him and read the headline.

Missing Victim Of Ken Doll Killer?

It was on the front page, no less. There was a picture of the layby, complete with police cars and CSI van parked up.

'At least they put a question mark in the headline,' said Boyd. 'It's not a statement of fact. They're just ask–'

'This is serious, Boyd,' Sutherland snapped. 'This should've been a spare-time case. But now, with a headline like this? We're going to have eyeballs on it. I'm going to have to put dedicated officers on it.' He sighed. 'I simply don't have the budget capacity to spend on a bloody cold-case operation because the local paper's got itself all worked up.'

Boyd nodded. 'Right.'

'It's a bloody nuisance! There's enough *actual* policing to get done without this kind of nonsense.'

'Sir, it's just *speculation* that it's Leon Martin,' said Boyd, 'And he's long dead, so there's not much more we can do other than try to identify the body. Even the press will be aware that after all this time it won't be easy.'

That seemed to calm Sutherland down a little. 'How quickly do you think you'll be able to ID the victim, Boyd?' he asked hopefully.

'Well, we've got an angle on his trainer, that might give us the year he went missing. If we can review all the photos Martin took, we might be able to match up the trainer in one of those.'

'Good, good. I want this done before the *Argus* starts attracting the attention of bigger national rags. Let's not have another bloody freak show of a press conference on our hands.'

Boyd nodded. He'd rather not have to go through one of those again.

'By the way, good shout on recalling the wooden figure,' said Boyd. 'If he *is* one of Martin's victims, we'll get some brownie points for remembering that.'

Sutherland seemed to perk up a little. He adjusted his glasses and blinked repeatedly behind the thick lenses. 'All right, Boyd. Grab a couple of junior officers to help get us an ID. Quick as you can, though, eh?'

Boyd nodded. 'Will do.'

BOYD LOOKED at DC Okeke and DC Warren, neither of whom seemed particularly thrilled to have been pulled away from their desks to the kitchenette.

'Avengers *Assemble*!' said Warren as he waited for the kettle to indicate it was actually doing something.

Okeke eye-rolled. 'It's way too early in the morning for that.'

The freshly filled kettle finally began to gurgle softly. Boyd placed the contents of Gratton's case file on the small round table between them. 'So, we've got some old bones that need to be matched up to an old case. Warren?'

'Yes, sir?'

'You've heard about the layby body case – we touched on it briefly in the canteen yesterday?'

'Yes, sir, the Dave Mullen guy. And it was on the local news this morning.'

'Right. Well, that pile of bones may be linked to this.' Boyd indicated the paperwork in front of them. 'The Ken Doll Killer case.'

Warren frowned. 'What's a Kendal Killer?'

'Ken *Doll* killer, Warren,' Okeke said, laughing.

Warren still looked perplexed.

'You've heard of Barbie dolls?' she asked.

He nodded.

'Well, Barbie had a boyfriend doll,' she continued, 'called Ken.'

'Oh,' said Warren, his eyes lighting up, 'you mean like the one in *Toy Story*!'

Okeke nodded.

'Okay, now we've cleared that up,' said Boyd, 'Leon Martin – the serial killer – posed his dead male victims just like dolls, hence the snappy name.'

'Right.' Warren nodded. 'I get it.'

'Aaand we got there in the end.' Okeke patted his back in a big sisterly way. 'Well done, little man.'

He shrugged her hand off irritably. 'I'm not five, Okeke.'

'"The one in *Toy Story*?"' she said in a high voice, smirking.

'Piss off,' Warren muttered, shaking his head and grinning.

'So...' Boyd rapped his knuckles on the table to get their attention. 'Unofficially, kids, we are now a probing team to see if these cases are, as I suspect, linked.'

'And officially?' asked Okeke.

'You're still on general duties.' He tapped the cover of the file. 'I want you both to read this cover to cover, but I'm going to get you started with the gist of it.

'In September 2001, a young man called Kristy Clarke is found walking along the A54 near Kelsall, wet, barefooted, traumatised, suffering borderline hypothermia, and he claims he's been abducted by a... well, as it turns out, a serial killer. He managed to escape and give the police the whereabouts of the killer's farm.'

'Farm?' Warren rolled his eyes. 'There's always a farm or a basement involved.'

Boyd looked at him. 'Serial killing is not exactly a hobby you can fit into a front room,' he said.

'True that,' agreed Warren.

'How did he escape?' asked Okeke.

'The killer Leon Martin decided that he wanted to go out in a blaze of glory and take Kristy with him. By "blaze of glory", I mean drive his van off the edge of a Welsh cliff into the Irish Sea.'

'Okay.' Warren nodded. 'Impressive.'

'Not for Kristy,' said Boyd. 'He was seventeen at the time. A boy still, really. A rough sleeper. Martin had picked him up and offered him a bed for the night. That, we presume, was his hunting MO.'

'Jesus,' said Okeke.

'So what he did with his victims was kill them, then – while the body was still relatively fresh and photogenic – pose them in his basement as though they were just hanging out together.'

'Basement,' said Warren, looking at Okeke. 'Told you.'

Boyd ignored him and carried on. 'He had it set up like a man cave, sofa, beer fridge, dart board, old pinball machine... and he took photos until, well, his victims didn't work any more as "live" models.'

'And then he buried them?' said Okeke.

'The police assumed so. Around the same time, there was a case of an unidentified teenaged male body found in North Wales, *also* buried in a layby *and* with a "carved figure" mentioned in the SOC report. There was no hard evidence to link it to Martin, but it all seems a bit too coincidental to me. Of course, the cops couldn't interview Martin, because he'd supposedly vanished over the edge of a cliff. He left his van and his possessions nearby.' Boyd shrugged. 'If he jumped, chances are his body would never be recovered.'

'And did he?' Warren asked.

'That remains to be seen,' said Boyd. 'Now, Kristy Clarke, despite being young and very traumatised, was also very helpful. He gave the police a pretty good picture of Leon Martin's state of mind. And by all accounts... Clarke had the presence of mind to engage with Martin during his ordeal, to form a bond that made it difficult for Martin to kill him.'

'Isn't that odd, for a serial killer?' asked Okeke. 'I mean, they're supposed to be unable to form attachments.'

Boyd shrugged. 'Apparently that's not always the case. Anyway... according to the file, Kristy thought something had spooked Martin, maybe a sort of *Crimewatch* appeal on local

TV. Tied in with the body discovered in that layby in North Wales. There's only circumstantial evidence to link that body to Martin, but *that*, together with his inability to kill Kristy, most likely sent him into a downward spiral – which ended with him bundling Kristy into the back of his van with the intention of driving them both off a cliff in Wales.'

The kettle was beginning to gurgle noisily.

'So that's the potted version, anyway. Read the file carefully yourselves, though.'

Warren was absently stroking his half-arsed attempt at a goatee. 'I don't see the connection, though, sir. Why's our layby body been linked to this?'

'The timeline matches. The victim profile matches, but, most importantly, the body in the layby was found to be clutching a small carved wooden figure.'

Warren looked up from the table with sudden interest.

'Yeah. It's a little creepy actually. Both the 2001 body and our layby bones were found to be clutching a carved figurine. These figures also appear in the photographs taken at the farm-house. They look like some sort of toy soldier to me.'

'What kind?' asked Warren. 'Like a Second World War one? Napoleonic?'

Boyd dug a page out from the pile of paperwork and held it up.

'To be honest, it looks like one of those beefeaters that guard Buckingham Palace,' said Okeke, squinting at the copied photograph on the page.

Boyd nodded. 'Or it could be a Chelsea Pensioner. Or a Coldstream guard, maybe? In any case, our primary job is just to ID the body,' Boyd said. 'And hopefully bring some closure to a family that's been waiting for far too long. If we can confirm this is one of Martin's victims along the way, then that's great.'

'But we're not going to be taken off general duties to focus on this?' Okeke said, raising her eyebrows.

'Nope. It's just extra in-tray fun 'n' games for you both,' said Boyd. 'I thought the pair of you were starting to look a little bored at work.'

'Great,' she said with a sigh. 'Thanks for that, guv.'

'If we can put a name to the body, it's all brownie points for us,' Boyd reminded them. 'I've pulled up a list of unresolved mispers to get you started – our bones are likely in there somewhere. Okeke, we've talked about the Nike trainer. You said you can nail down the year they were produced?'

'I said I could try, yeah.'

'Good. Then that could give us a more precise timing. Warren, you're on the outstanding mispers going back twenty... twenty-five years.'

Warren's face dropped. 'There'll be thousands!'

'*Tens* of thousands,' said Boyd, wandering across to the gurgling kettle to flip it off before it had a seizure. 'I did try to bring the numbers down a bit, but unfortunately for you I got interrupted by a phone call –'

Warren grinned. 'Thanks, sir. I'm sure it was nothing to do with LEDS being too computery for you...'

Boyd laughed. 'Cheeky bastard. Well luckily for you we should have enough information to narrow it down to a mere few thousand or so. Okeke's trainer should help bring that down even further.'

'And if he isn't one of Leon Martin's –' started Okeke.

'Then it's our historic murder investigation,' Boyd replied, 'and we're starting from scratch. I'm going to reach out, though, to the force that investigated the previous body and Martin himself. Speak to the SIO if he's still around.'

Okeke cocked her head. 'Which means you're pretty sure Martin's the culprit?'

Boyd poured water from the kettle into his mug. 'Given the previous body was buried in a layby and was also buried with a carved figure, there's a more than a strong possibility.'

'How many victims were there?' she asked.

'They identified, I think, seven clearly different victims from Martin's photo collection, one of whom could have been the one found in 2001, but there could easily be more.'

Okeke and Warren exchanged glances. This case had suddenly got a lot more interesting.

15

After he'd finished his microwaved lentil-and-something-stringy lunch, Boyd took a short walk outside to clear his head. He spotted Okeke and Warren having a lunchtime cigarette, sheltering from the spitting rain beneath the portico entrance to the vehicle park. Warren looked like a naughty schoolboy caught smoking behind the bike sheds, and Okeke, a sixth-former who'd lured him into the dirty habit.

'See you both inside,' he called out, tapping his watch.

Bloody smokers. He used to be one. But now that he wasn't he understood the irritation that non-smokers felt towards their co-workers with all their extra, unlogged fag breaks and dodgy timekeeping.

Back at his desk, Boyd spread out the case file and dialled Cheshire Constabulary's division headquarters, asking to be put through to their CID room.

'CID, DS Paul Owen speaking.'

'All right?' he replied. 'This is DCI Boyd down in Sussex CID. Do you still have a Michael Gratton working there?'

'Gratton?' There was a pause. 'No, I don't think so, mate. Hang on...'

Boyd heard a voice in the background. The phone rustled as DS Owen covered the mouthpiece and the almost identical soundscape of the CID floor up north was temporarily muted. A moment later, the noise returned.

'You mean DCI Mike Gratton?' Owen asked.

'Yeah,' Boyd replied.

'He retired about seven years ago,' said Owen. 'Can anyone else help?'

'It's about one of his cold cases from twenty years back. I really need to speak to him personally. Is there a way I can get in touch with him?'

'Hang on a sec...' The line rustled as the phone's mouthpiece was muffled once again. Boyd could hear an exchange of voices, then Owen came back on. 'I'm going to transfer you to our super. Hold on a minute.'

The line clicked, rang a couple of times and was answered by another male voice.

'DSI George Harper speaking. Who am I talking to?'

'DCI Boyd, Sussex CID,' repeated Boyd. 'I was trying to get hold of Mike Gratton, the SIO on the Leon Martin case from 2001.'

'Oh, blimey... that's going back a bit.' Harper sighed. 'The Ken Doll Killer, right?'

'The very one,' said Boyd.

'Mike retired a few years ago.' There was a pause. Then: 'He's not that well, to be honest with you.'

'Oh? I'm sorry to hear that,' said Boyd. 'Would it be possible to talk to him still, or is he too ill for that?'

'Well, can I give him *your* number and, if he feels well enough to call you, he can contact you?'

'Sure,' Boyd said, and read out his mobile number.

'Okay, I'll pass that along, DCI Boyd,' Harper said, and hung up

SOMETIME MID-AFTERNOON, DC Warren came over to stand in front of Boyd's desk. 'Sir?'

'Yes?'

'I've pulled a list of outstanding missing persons and filtered it down a bit, but I'm still looking at thousands of them. That seems like a lot of mums to be cold-calling.'

'It's called *detecting*, Warren,' Boyd said. 'If our job title was based on a different verb like – I don't know – *fannying*, you might have a point.'

Warren rolled his eyes.

'Come on, Warren,' Boyd said, trying to keep the exasperation from his voice – really, some of these younger DCs seemed to be in danger of losing the ability to actually think for themselves. 'There'll be cases and categories you can rule out. Have you limited the search window to cases reported between 1995 and 2005?'

Warren nodded. 'Can I rule out any regions, sir?'

'No, let's keep it national for now; we know Leon Martin had a van. You could prioritise the ones who were repeat runaways, difficult ones who *didn't* want to be found and returned home.'

Boyd's mobile started buzzing on the desk.

'Okay, off you go then, Warren. Make me proud.' He picked up his phone. 'DCI Boyd.'

The voice on the end of the line sounded thin and weak. 'This is... Michael Gratton...' His words were broken by the sound of something mechanical clicking and wheezing.

'Ah, right. Thanks for calling me back, sir.'

'No problem. Mike... call me Mike. I'm retired.'

'Okay, Mike. Well in that case, I'm just Boyd. So, you were the SIO for the Leon Martin case, is that correct?' he said.

'Aye.'

'And was that from beginning to end?' Boyd asked.

'For my sins... ' Gratton's voice sounded breathless; his answers were quick and short as if every word was an oxygen choice.

'I spoke to – I guess he was your replacement – DSI Harper? He said you're not a well man.'

Boyd heard a wheezy laugh that sounded like the fluttering wings of a bird trapped in a paper bag. 'You could say that.'

'Is talking right now going to be too difficult for you, Mike?'

'Yes...' Gratton replied, 'but... talking *any* time is difficult. So...'

'Right. I'll get to the point. I don't know if the news has reached you, but we discovered an old body buried beside an A-road layby outside Hastings. I know it's a fair way from Cheshire, but there are markers that might link to Leon Martin and we think it's old enough to be one of his victims,' Boyd said.

There was a long pause. Boyd could hear beeping in the background. Gratton sounded as though he was surrounded by medical machinery. He could hear Gratton's breathing over the phone, a steady Darth Vader-like rasping.

'We found a small, carved wooden figurine in the boy's hands,' Boyd continued. 'It looks like a soldier. A guard of some sort.'

'A Coldstream guard,' whispered Gratton.

'Right,' said Boyd. 'The ones with the tall bearskin hats.'

'His father carved them. Leon's father. He used to be one.'

'His father? John Martin?' Boyd felt a sudden kick of adrenaline. 'Then, shit... it really does seem like we might have found one of his victims.'

'Looks that way,' Gratton said, a note of excitement creeping into his tired voice. 'Apart from that other one… we never found any of the other bodies.'

'You sound certain it was linked.'

'The carved figure looked like one of those in his house.' Gratton took a breath. 'Victim profile and timeline matched. Just not enough forensics to nail it.'

'We have a forensic lead in the form of one of his trainers,' Boyd went on, 'which may give us a specific year, if they're limited edition. Possibly even a region where they were purchased.'

'That's good news, Boyd. Wait… they can do that?'

'I know, I know. Modern technology, eh! It never ceases to confound and amaze me.'

Gratton wheezed out a laugh. 'It would be… nice to finally give one of those poor lads… a name.'

'Yeah,' said Boyd soberly. 'That's what we were hoping too.'

'Might even provoke the bastard,' said Gratton, so quietly that Boyd wasn't entirely sure he'd heard him correctly.

'Provoke? Sorry, who?' he asked.

'Leon Martin,' Gratton replied.

It was Boyd's turn to sit there, silent, breathing down the phone.

Gratton spoke again. 'I never thought… he threw himself in.'

'You don't say that in your case file,' Boyd stated.

'Aye, well, I don't present opinions… Leave that to barristers.'

'You think he staged it?'

'That's what my gut says, aye.'

'Based on what?' Boyd asked.

'Some of the things Kristy Clarke said.'

There was another long pause. Boyd listened to the sound of the mechanical wheezing for a few moments. It sounded like a ventilator.

'Might be easier... discussing this in person...' Gratton said finally, pulling in another long, rasping breath. 'Always nice to get... a visitor, you know?'

'You in a hospital?' Boyd asked.

'In one of those you don't walk out of... A hospice.'

The last time Boyd had been in a place like that he'd been a teenager saying goodbye to his grandfather. The place had been designed carefully to gladden failing hearts: warm colours, large windows with views of a forest, freshly cut flowers, and Vivaldi piped gently through the wall speakers. The irony was, the harder they tried to fill the place with cheer, the sadder it all felt.

'Right. So whereabouts are you?' Boyd asked.

'Saint Barnaby's Hospice in Boston... google it for the... address.'

'I will do. Is there a good time for me to drop by?'

Gratton did his fluttering laugh again. An unsettling sound that Boyd was convinced would end with a solid electronic tone and the sound of electric paddles being charged up.

'Anytime. I'm not going anywhere, Boyd,'

16

Boyd drove up to Boston the following morning. His satnav had promised him a very doable three-and-a-half-hour drive, but it had no idea about the extra time needed to allow for the slow northbound A21 traffic at that time of the morning.

For the first forty minutes he found himself sitting in exactly the same shuffling jam he'd observed from the layby last week.

He arrived at St Barnaby's Hospice just before midday. The building looked like a converted Victorian warehouse and sat flush with, and looming over, the River Witham. Across the river he could see St Botolph's Church with its tall gothic tower that was known locally as the Boston Stump. It looked like a piece of Hogwarts had been torn out of the wilds of Scotland and parachuted in on an unsuspecting market town in Lincolnshire.

There was actually a police station in the turning just before the hospice, so Boyd parked his car in one of their staff slots and went to the front desk to make sure the desk sergeant was aware he wasn't a cheeky civilian trying to blag some free town-centre parking.

He walked up the road, turned into the entrance marked St Barnaby's, and showed his warrant card at the hospice reception.

'I'm here to see Michael Gratton,' he said.

The receptionist did a double take as she noticed the police ID he was holding up. 'I'm pretty sure Mr Gratton isn't the man you're after, detective,' she said without smiling.

Boyd couldn't work out if she was joking or not, so settled for, 'Well, obviously I'm not here to arrest him,' while maintaining a straight face.

She looked back down at whatever she'd been doing on the computer screen. 'Is he expecting you?' she asked.

'Sort of, yes, he is,' Boyd replied.

The receptionist picked up her phone, spoke quietly into it, listened for a moment and then nodded and hung up. 'He's in room nine,' she said, tipping her head to the right.

Boyd made his way along a hallway, passing several partially open doors, through which he glimpsed similar-looking small rooms filled with flowers, cards and beeping equipment. The hushed ambience took him right back to that one visit to see his grandad.

The door to room nine was half open. Boyd rapped his knuckles on the door. 'Is it okay to come in?' he called through the gap.

A nurse came out of the room and answered on Gratton's behalf. 'He's awake,' she said, then she disappeared into the next room. Boyd stepped in slowly, feeling that anything faster might be seen as inappropriate for a place like this.

Mike Gratton, the retired detective superintendent, lay on a bed surrounded by monitoring equipment and wearing an oxygen mask over his nose and mouth. The wheezing and clicking Boyd had heard over the phone wasn't some mechanical ventilator as he'd suspected but Gratton's own laboured effort to keep breathing.

Gratton looked like an old – well, *very* old – man but Boyd had looked him up and knew that he was only sixty-six.

'DCI Boyd?' Gratton wheezed.

Boyd nodded. 'I wasn't sure whether to bring grapes or a six-pack of Carling,' he said.

The oxygen mask shifted subtly. From the wrinkles around Gratton's eyes, Boyd guessed he was smiling. 'A bottle of Jack... would've been bloody... well appreciated.'

Boyd sat down beside his bed and looked around at the equipment. 'This doesn't look particularly promising.'

'Aye. I like to think of it as... my evil lair.'

Boyd laughed. 'Which button does the death ray?'

Gratton grinned beneath his fogged mask. 'Don't tempt me.'

There were half a dozen touchscreens and monitors making it look, Boyd thought, very Mission Control. 'Can any of these fancy screens pick up Sky Sports?'

'Be handy,' Gratton replied.

Boyd got the impression that the retired DCI was the kind of person who called a spade a spade, and not the type to tiptoe around a sodding great big elephant in the room.

'How long have you got?' he asked.

'A few weeks... if I'm lucky. The cancer... it's bloody well everywhere,' Gratton said.

Boyd had never mastered the art of offering sympathetic platitudes. He'd be the first to admit he was utterly tone deaf when it came to judging the right amount of inflection to put into his voice and the right words to say.

'I'm sorry to hear that, mate,' he said.

'Aye, well, it's self-induced... Had a twenty-a-day habit... most of my life.'

'Me too. Until I quit,' Boyd said, realising that he'd better get to the point; Gratton was looking tired after just those few sentences. He lifted the flap of the shoulder bag he'd brought with him.

Gratton's eyes darted, almost hungrily, to the bag. 'Is that... Leon Martin's case file?'

'Yes,' Boyd said, pulling it out and setting it on his lap.

'You're sure that... your body's one of Martin's?' Gratton asked, barely audible.

Boyd nodded. 'Pretty sure.' He pulled a couple of glossy pictures out of the folder: the rotten stump of the carved wooden figure sitting beside a metric ruler, and a copy of the picture that showed the soldiers on parade on the TV dinner tray. Despite the damage due to twenty-one years of corrosion, the solitary soldier, pretty obviously, came from the same platoon.

'Like I said on the phone, our body fits the timeline and the victim pool that Martin was trawling. And there's the carved figure.' Boyd leant forward, holding the photos closer to Gratton's face. He lowered his voice. 'You said on the phone that you had reason to believe that Martin didn't go ahead and kill himself.'

Gratton nodded. 'Staged it.'

'What makes you so sure about that?' Boyd asked, returning the photos to the file.

'Kristy Clarke. You read the interview... transcripts?'

Boyd nodded. There were a lot of pages, Gratton had taken his time with Kristy all those years ago.

'He suspected...' Gratton stopped and took several deep breaths to catch up on the oxygen he needed. 'He suspected Martin had *allowed* him to... escape. So he could tell us everything.'

'Now that bit *wasn't* in the report,' Boyd said. 'Did he say that to you?'

Gratton nodded. 'When the recording machine was off.'

'Why? Why didn't he say it again on tape?'

'Worried it might implicate him... as an accomplice, or if Martin was alive he might come after him.'

Boyd took a moment to piece that thinking together. In the transcripts it was very clear that Kristy was in a fragile state of mind, terrified that Martin would somehow find a way to get to him, Freddy Krueger-like.

'So Kristy thought that Martin had primed him with the idea that he was off to Wales to drive them both over the cliff... then deliberately slipped up, giving Kristy the chance to escape?'

Gratton nodded.

It made some sense. It was clever, Boyd thought – making your last victim an unwitting part of the escape plan. But young Kristy, terrified and traumatised though he was, seemed to have seen through it.

'Any idea what made Martin decide to flee?' asked Boyd. 'I know that a body had been found, but was there anything to point towards him at that stage?'

Gratton shrugged. 'Not at that point... it was all over the news and it scared him.' He took a sip of oxygen. 'Made him think police were closing in.'

'In the interviews, Kristy mentioned that Martin's behaviour was already becoming erratic. Kristy said he was scared Martin would top himself, leaving him shackled in the farmhouse?'

Gratton nodded. 'That body being found was... the last straw.'

'So you think, to avoid having to kill Kristy and worried that the police were on to him, Martin left his van parked near the cliff and made it look like he threw himself over?'

'I had my suspicion... at the time,' Gratton said. 'But you know what it's like. It all tied up; Martin was gone; we had no more bodies, even though we tried digging up a number of likely places around the farm. Nothing. No leads... Case closed.'

'And then?' Boyd asked.

Gratton hunched his shoulders. 'Made a new life... under another name... who knows?'

'That's not an easy thing to do.' Boyd wasn't convinced. It was almost impossible to live off the grid for more than a few months.

Gratton pulled the mask away from his mouth so that his words weren't muffled. 'We never recovered a body... from the sea.' He lowered the mask over his nose and mouth again.

'Right,' said Boyd. Every word Mike spoke was an effort. He could see that. But really – not recovering a body meant little. The sea was lively there, battering away at Wales' north-west tip. The current was strong; Martin's body could just as easily have washed up on the Irish coast and become a John Doe for the Garda to puzzle over.

'Look, Mike, our interest on this case is primarily about ID-ing *our* body and working out whether he definitely is one of Leon Martin's. For the record, I think he is. The carved figure is pretty much the clincher for me.' Boyd was beginning to feel hot in the small room. He took off his jacket. 'What do you think the deal is with those?'

'I've no idea,' Gratton said, taking another blast of oxygen. 'It wasn't explored, those figures... We had to re-allocate resources... 9/11 happened.'

Boyd nodded. There was no need to explain. In the wake of that September day, there had been a lot of pressure on the UK to co-operate with US agencies to round up sympathisers and 'hate preachers' and, of course, pressure to stay mindful that something similar might happen in the UK.

'Leon Martin did a thorough job.... of erasing his identity... from the farm,' said Gratton.

'What do you mean?'

'He'd emptied the place of personal effects, photos of himself, his parents... Little there.' Gratton reached for a glass of water. Boyd leant forward and helped him.

Gratton sipped and nodded his thanks. Boyd set the glass back on a side table and waited for him to continue.

'We found ashes: a bonfire of family photos, records. He left... nothing behind about himself.'

'There was no one for you to interview about him?'

Gratton shook his head. 'No family. No friends. Like a ghost,' said Gratton. He smiled. 'I think he *planned* to... disappear one day.'

One of the beeping machines in the room changed tone to a higher shrill note, drawing a nurse into the room like an angry wasp. Boyd got up from the visitor's chair and stepped back to give her some room.

'You're not getting enough oxygen, Michael,' she tutted. 'Just breathe, deeply, slowly.... That's it.' She looked accusingly at Boyd. 'You really shouldn't be making him talk so much.'

'I'm sorry,' Boyd said reflexively.

'He needs to breathe, not gossip,' she chided, turning back to Gratton. 'That's it. Slow. Deep. Good. Good.'

Boyd watched and waited.

The nurse flicked a switch to reset the beeping alarm and lingered beside the bed. 'Good,' she said again, more softly this time. 'You get some rest, Michael. No more talking. All right.'

'Hold on – we're not quite finished yet,' Boyd said.

Her head whipped round. 'Oh, I think you are. He needs his rest!' She had the steely eyes of Nurse Ratched and the no-nonsense expression of Hattie Jacques.

'All right.' Boyd raised his hands submissively. He stepped forward and looked down at Gratton over the nurse's shoulder. His eyes were getting heavy, slowly closing. 'Hey, Gratton?'

His eyes opened.

'Do you happen to know how I can get hold of Kristy Clarke?'

Gratton nodded. He fumbled with his hands at a side table.

'What do you want, mate?' Boyd asked. 'Pencil?'

Another nod.

Boyd reached across and grabbed a pencil off of the Sudoku book that Gratton had been working through and pulled a notepad out of his own pocket. 'Here you go,' he said, handing them both over.

Gratton scribbled something down. Then let go of the pencil and the pad, and slumped back into his pillow.

Nurse Ratched picked up the pad and thrust it towards Boyd. 'There – you got what you wanted, Now I think it's best you leave.'

She had a look on her face that suggested if she had to say that again it would come with slightly more colourful language.

'Okay. I'm going,' Boyd said, tucking his notebook into the case file. He put the file back into his bag and shouldered it.

'Thanks for your time, *guv*,' said Boyd, turning at the door.

He saw Gratton's eyes crease with a smile. 'A while since... been called that.'

'Never gets old, does it?'

Gratton shook his head.

'I'll, uh... I'll leave you to it,' Boyd said to the nurse. He gave Gratton a quick nod of thanks. 'Take care.'

'If Martin didn't jump...' Gratton began, then had to stop to pull in another breath. 'Catch the bastard... for me... Boyd,' he whispered. 'Let me know...'

The machine began beeping again and the nurse glared in Boyd's direction.

Boyd nodded. 'I'll keep you posted. Promise.'

He backed out of the room into the hallway and headed back towards the reception desk, with the sad feeling that DCI Michael Gratton was going to be long gone before there was any more news about Leon Martin to pass along.

17

Boyd's drive back down to Hastings was interrupted by a desperate hankering for a frothy coffee and something laden with naughty carbs to soak it up. He stopped at the one service station he knew like a second home, South Mimms.

It was mid-afternoon; if ever there was such a thing as a quiet moment in the day, this was it. He managed to park right outside the entrance portico.

He went for a pee first, then bought a large cappuccino and something Italian-sounding, toasted and cheesy. He'd just sat down and had taken his first tentative greasy nibble from the edge of the steaming sandwich when his phone rang.

It was Emma.

'*For fuck's sake*,' he muttered. 'I'm in South Bloody Mimms! And she's still watching what I bloody well eat... Hey, Ems. What's up?' he said, squeezing the half-chewed bread into his cheek and trying not to sound as though his mouth was full.

'Nothing much – we're just walking Ozzie. I thought I'd check in and see how you're doing. How was your meeting?' she asked.

'I'm on the way back now,' he said, finally managing to swallow the bread.

'That was quick,' she said. 'Where are you? Sounds like a service station. Are you eating?'

'Busted!' he said, crossing his fingers behind his back. 'I bought a banana to have with my coffee. I'm going to be back about six. Are you going to be in or out?'

'We're out later on. Dan's got a gig tonight.'

'Ah, right. Good for him,' Boyd said, staring longingly at the sandwich on the table in front of him.

He heard Dan's voice in the background, then: 'He said you should come, Dad.'

Boyd smiled. 'That's... that's kind, but I'm not going to be up for some thumping rock club surrounded by Redbull-fuelled teen–'

'It's not a thumping rock club, Dad. It's in the Nelson pub. Rock-a-Nore. Near the net huts? It's a small gig,' she continued. 'More laid-back. There's no drummer – it's an acoustic set.'

'I... hmmm...' he stalled.

'Come on, Dad. Pleeeease. It *is* Friday.'

Ugh, the power of that extended word in the hands of an expert. 'All right,' he said. 'I'd love to come along.'

He hung up and was about to properly test his cheesy-toastie thing for mouth-burn when he remembered the other reason he'd stopped. He pulled the case file out of his bag, located his notebook and flipped to the last page to look at what Gratton had scribbled down.

Capital Reach, Central London.

It sounded like some financial company. He googled the name and discovered it was a small charity group. Their website showed images of a couple of charity shops and street food carts, which presumably was where they made the money to pay for their work. They appeared to be a sort of pop-up soup kitchen and clothes library operating out of the back of a van.

It looked as though Kristy Clarke worked for them. That would make sense, he thought. Clarke had been a rough sleeper once. He'd once been as vulnerable as the people he was now helping. It seemed to fit well with what he'd picked up from Gratton – Kristy Clarke could empathise, seemed intelligent and capable. Somebody who would want to do some actual good in this world.

Boyd called Okeke.

She answered on the first ring. 'How's it going, guv?'

'I'm on my way back down. Look, can you or Warren do me a favour?'

'Sure,' she said. 'What do you want?'

'Martin's last victim, the one who escaped...'

'Kristy Clarke.'

'Yup. Gratton thinks he works for a homeless charity called Capital Reach. Could you look them up and find out, *subtly*, whether he still does?'

'Subtly?' she asked.

'As in... not...' Boyd cupped his hand around the phone's mic and rasped, 'THIS IS THE POLICE...'

Okeke laughed. 'But why subtle? You got some hunch about him?'

'What? No. I'm trying to do some sensitive policing for a change. He may have family, work colleagues who know nothing about what he went through as a young man. So...carefully, okay.'

'Oh, right,' she said.

'Just find out if he's still there, or if anyone there knows him.'

'Okay, guv. I'm on it,' she said, and disconnected the call.

Boyd put his phone away so that he wouldn't be distracted by his email or nagged by the various clickbait news headlines that his phone seemed to think he was dying to read, and let his mind freewheel for a moment.

Kristy Clarke might not *want* to cooperate. He could well have put the whole Martin case behind him, locked up and sealed in his distant past. He might have a partner or friends who knew nothing about it and maybe he just wanted to keep it that way. It would be perfectly understandable. If that had been Emma, Boyd wouldn't want some clunking, clumsy DCI barrelling into her post-trauma life and dredging up memories of the days she was kept captive by a chatty serial killer.

His eyes settled on a family walking towards the service station exit – Mum, Dad, baby in a papoose, daughter swinging from her father's hand like a tetherball.

How many times had he and Julia stopped here on the way up, and the way down, to visit her parents? Stopped and bought a KFC bucket to share in the car. Stopped for a coffee and a cake. Stopped just for one of those emergency 'I gotta go Right Now' moments?

He tucked those memories back into their box. They were like Polaroids, he thought, sadly. Expose them too much to the sunlight and they fade. He picked up his cheesy toastie and took a hearty bite out of it, confident that it must have cooled down enough by now.

'Fuck!' he swore, spitting it back out and wiping molten cheese from his beard.

18

Boyd watched Daniel and his three colleagues unpacking their guitars and plugging in their bits and pieces.

'This takes me back,' he said, settling in his chair and picking up his pint.

Emma smiled. 'Do you miss all that?'

'What, being in a band? Gigging?'

She nodded.

He thought about it for a moment. 'Not really. It was ninety per cent carrying things around, ten per cent actually playing. I wasn't really at the centre of things, just the bassist.' He laughed. 'And not a very good one.'

'Why did they let you join then?' she asked.

'Beats me,' he said. 'Maybe I looked the part.'

'And what look was that?' She grinned; she'd seen the photos.

'Long hair, mopey face. I also ended up writing most of our song lyrics.'

She looked utterly shocked. '*You?* A lyricist?'

'Hey! What's so incredible about that? I can spin a decent rhyme every now and then.'

She nodded, unconvinced. 'Dan writes their lyrics.'

'Any good?'

She hmmed. 'Too crusadey sometimes.' She sipped her drink. 'So your band, Dad? Did you think it was a *serious* thing?'

'For us, it was, yes. We started to do a few festivals.'

'Cool. But you didn't get a record deal?'

'We got pretty near one.' He sipped his pint. 'We picked up a manager who wanted to get us "deal ready". The first thing he said to them was "ditch the bassist".'

'*What?*'

Boyd smiled wistfully. 'It was the right thing to do. I was rubbish. They got a deal I think a few months later.'

'That's really shitty!' she said.

He shook his head. 'Best thing that ever happened to me, Emma. I got on with the rest of my life –' he paused – 'and now I get to lock up bad guys for a living.'

He'd looked his old bandmates up on Facebook during his two years away from work. He'd found Mark, the lead singer, working endless hours as a DPD van driver, and the guitarist and band visionary, Alex, working as a taxi driver. He'd exchanged a few messages with them and learned how they'd had their record deal and bombed. The record failed to earn out on the advance; the sales were pitiful. Boyd had got the distinct impression they still thought that a second chance at success might be just around the corner even though they were in their forties.

'Those guys never made it, Ems. Most don't. Only the lucky few become rock stars and even then I'm not sure how lucky they are. They usually end up addicts or alcoholics… or dead.'

'Jeez, Dad.' She mimed tying a noose round her neck. 'Way to put a downer on things.'

He laughed and sat up straight. 'Sorry, love. Didn't mean to.'

She shook her head. 'You should definitely share that anecdote more often, Dad. It's fun.'

He pulled a mock angry-Dad face and swatted her arm. 'I'm sorry, daughter. Can I get you another whatever-the-hell-that-is to make up for ruining the fun evening you had planned?'

'Oh, that'll help – thanks. Cider and black. And Dan will have a pint of Stella.'

'They'll know what a... one of those cider things is, will they?' he asked uncertainly.

Emma raised a brow.

'Okay, okay,' he said, getting up and making his way across the room. It was beginning to get busy in the pub and he had to hunt for a gap at the bar. He finally found one and ducked so his head wasn't obscured by the shelf of pint glasses; eye contact was critical if you wanted to have any chance of being served.

'Oh, hello,' said a female voice next to him.

Boyd turned to his left to see a vaguely familiar face smiling at him.

'All right?' he replied, buying himself a few more seconds to try and work out where the hell he'd seen her before.

'Are you here for the beer or the band?' she asked.

'Uh... bit of both,' he replied. 'And some nuts. Er, so... what about you?'

A smile was spreading slowly across her face. Boyd wondered if he had something stuck in his beard, or if Emma had snuck up and was doing bunny ears behind him. He couldn't help a quick glance over his shoulder to check.

'You haven't got a clue who I am, have you?' she said, grinning.

'Of course I do. I...' The lie slipped out before he could stop it.

That only made her laugh. 'Go on, then,' she said. 'Where do you know me from?'

Bollocks.

He tried to marshal his thoughts. It had to be someone at the police station. He'd been there nearly three months now and he'd been introduced to so many faces it was all he could to keep the CID lot in his head, let alone the uniformed ones.

She shook her head. 'I'll let you off the hook. I'm the idiot who keeps picking up your dog's poop,' she said with a mock reproachful glance up at him.

'Oh, God! Yes!' he said. 'I didn't recognise you without your dog.'

She laughed. 'Yes, I'm Mia's mum.'

He smiled back. 'Then I guess I'm Ozzie's dad. And I... am so sorry about the poop thing. I'm getting to grips with being a dog owner, but... it's all a bit of a learning curve. Should've rescued a bloody cat.'

'Or an easier breed,' she said. 'Spaniels are quite high maintenance. But that's why I love them. They're crazy and needy in equal measure.'

'Well, that's definitely true,' he said. 'Look, can I buy you an "I'm sorry" drink, for the poopgate?'

'No, I'm good. I'm just getting ready to go before it gets noisy.' She smiled. 'But thanks. Another time maybe?'

He nodded. 'Sure.'

She pointed a finger. 'See you on the beach sometime.'

'Right. Yes. On the beach,' he repeated.

'Armed with your own poo bags,' she added. 'Yes?'

For some reason he found himself saluting, as if her words were a flag being run up a pole. 'Poo bags. Gotcha.'

She nodded a good evening to him, turned and weaved her way between pub tables to the door. He watched her exit, then walk outside past the window, the blustery cold wind spitting dashes of diagonal rain against the glass, as she tugged at her coat for good measure.

19

Since the weather that had been so nice over the weekend was lingering into Monday, Boyd considered walking to work along the cycle path between the shingle beach and Pelham Place parking. On the one hand, he thought, the exercise would burn off that second helping of pudding he'd gone back to the fridge for last night after Emma had gone to bed. It was a chocolate brownie something-or-other that Daniel had given to Emma from the pub's kitchen. Apparently it would have gone into a bin if Daniel hadn't rescued it, and it would have been criminal to waste it.

However, he reasoned, the weather was forecast to change later on, meaning that not only would he have to walk uphill, at the end of the day it would be raining. Probably.

The decision, he decided, was a no-brainer.

~

Boyd tossed the car keys onto his desk and set his coffee down. 'Good morning,' he called out to the CID floor in general.

Okeke was on her phone and threw him a quick nod.

Minter was just in, back on days, his hair still wet from his post-gym shower.

'Morning, boss,' he offered as he squeezed his annoyingly slim waist between two desks to get to the photocopier. 'Have a nice weekend?'

Apart from walking Ozzie along the beach (four times) and a bit of badly executed DIY, it hadn't been the busiest of weekends. 'Not too bad, Minter. You?'

'Training mostly,' Minter said, glancing down at his body.

'For what? The Olympics? You're already ridiculously fit.'

'I'm training for the Iron Man Challenge, aren't I?' he said.

'Right,' Boyd said, looking down at his own stomach. 'Of course you are.' He could still hide his spare tyre inside his loose office shirt, he reassured himself, and the tie he wore long ('Trump length,' Emma often teased) helped camouflage the paunch when he sat down and leant forward.

'When is it? This challenge?' he asked.

Minter hit a button and the photocopier started spitting sheets of paper out. 'My one's scheduled for next month.' He patted his perfectly flat stomach. 'It'll be tough. It's not just *looking* the part... It's *being* the part.'

'What does that even mean?' Boyd grumbled. 'It sounds like something off the front of a bloody JD Sports shopping bag.'

'You have to have inner strength, boss.' Minter tapped his temple. 'Endurance. Crushing the pain. Smashing the wall. Killing the challenge.'

'Right. Okay. Well, that's good,' Boyd said, turning towards his desk, 'and just in case you're at all worried... you don't sound in any way psychotic.'

DC Warren, sitting a few desks away, finally spotted Boyd, pulled out his headphones and called across. 'Sir? You got a moment?'

Boyd sighed and waved Warren to his desk. Warren hurried

over, looking way too eager for first thing in the morning, a stack of printouts clasped in his hand.

'So, what have you got for me this morning?'

Warren set his pile of papers down on Boyd's desk.

'Forty-three cases, sir. All white males, aged sixteen to twenty-one, who were reported missing between 1995 and 2005 and are *still* open cases.'

Boyd looked at the top page and a photograph of a teenager in a Manchester United football kit. 'You've got it down to forty-three already? That's pretty good whittling, Warren.'

'Thank you, sir.' Warren beamed.

Boyd picked up Warren's results. Their A21 body was probably in there, one of the forty-three faces printed on these pages. Short of tracking down the families of each of these young lads and asking for DNA samples for a familial comparison against their body, it was going to have to be old-school police work: phone calls, questioning and paper shuffling. There was no way Sutherland was going to authorise the cost of forty-three DNA swabs and tests for a historic case that wasn't even originally theirs. He'd have a heart attack if Boyd even suggested it. If they could reduce the number down to, say, half a dozen likely candidates, then maybe the brownie points they'd gain by ID-ing a victim of another force's case would tip the balance for him.

'In the back,' said Warren, 'there's an addendum and a list of birthmarks and tattoos that were completely or partially visible in the staged photos that were recovered. I'll go through those and cross-reference with these cases. We may be able to whittle it down further.'

'Same page, Warren, same page.' Boyd smiled. 'Good thinking.'

Warren turned and headed back to his desk to reveal Okeke, who had been waiting patiently behind him.

'And what can I do for you, Okeke?' asked Boyd.

'There's a couple of things, guv,' she said. 'Firstly, I managed to get hold of a product designer at Nike. I spoke to him yesterday afternoon and sent him pictures of the trainer we recovered from the layby.'

'Please tell me they're some sort of limited-edition ones?' Boyd said hopefully.

'No such luck. But he said if we can send it over, they can analyse the tooling on the sole and the stitching on the upper. From that he said he could give us a production year.'

'Good. Send it where? Don't tell me Los Angeles.'

She shook her head. 'No. Guildford. They have a design studio there apparently.'

'Ah, okay.' Boyd raised his eyebrows. 'Well, guess what you're up to today, then.'

'No problem. Happy to do it,' she said.

'Don't forget to sign it out of evidence.'

'Of course.'

'Right,' he said. 'See you later.'

Okeke remained at his desk. 'I said a *couple* of things, sir.'

'Oh yeah. What's the other thing?'

'Kristy Clarke still works at Capital Reach.' She handed him a piece of paper with an address and a contact number on it.

'That's great news. Who did you speak to? What did you say?'

'I spoke to a colleague of his. I said I was from HMRC... double-checking the validity of his furlough application from 2020.'

'Clever.' He looked at the address. 'This is his home address?'

She nodded.

'Good. Thanks, Okeke.'

As she walked back to her desk, Boyd finally reached for his coffee. It was, predictably, cold.

BOYD SPENT the morning looking into Kristy Clarke. Apart from his interviews with DCI Gratton back in 2001, he'd had no further interaction with the police. At least the traumatic experience didn't appear to have pushed him into some self-destructive spiral.

Boyd already knew from the police files that Clarke had been offered help following his interactions with Martin. He'd been offered therapy, secure accommodation and the opportunity to complete his education. Whether or not these had been taken up was not documented.

His thoughts turned to the homeless charity, Capital Reach, whose name Gratton had written in Boyd's notebook. Their Facebook page had a mission statement – to provide an emergency service for *young* rough sleepers. Food, clothing, support and advice was, informed the write-up, just one call away. The charity raised money through a number of social media platforms, and several charity shops situated in south London. They had a few celebrities, musicians and YouTubers championing their work and had a small fleet of a half a dozen vans, each marked with their logo and their emergency number on the side in a yellow-and-black chequered design that was, he thought, reminiscent of a first response vehicle.

His brand-new nemesis – LEDS – informed him that Kristy had a parking permit violation, a social media platform violation marker for sharing a fake news story, a low credit rating (for not spending *enough*, ironically) and a facial recognition tag indicating he'd been at an Extinction Rebellion rally.

Boyd grudgingly admitted to himself that he was beginning to warm to LEDS. For deeper background police work – data mining – it was a godsend, despite its clunky interface and chirpy help boxes that offered explanations that only its coders had a hope of understanding.

And LEDS was the main reason that Boyd was beginning to think that if Leon Martin had faked his suicide, he had to have died sometime since. There just weren't the gaps any more in which a person could easily hide. Certainly not for twenty-one years. Even data going back ten, fifteen years was all linked up now. Sure, there were exceptions. But Boyd was sure that if Martin had been involved in another murder, or even charged with a much less serious crime, his DNA would have been entered on the National DNA Database.

And there'd be a hit.

But there wasn't.

Boyd's attention circled back to Kristy Clarke. Scrolling through the Facebook comments, he came across a user by the name of KLC. That could be Kristy; KLC was an admin on the account. Boyd tapped the initials into the search box at the top of the screen and scrolled through the posts that came up. He'd posted pictures of London street scenes, and of food and new clothes piled into the back of vans, but there was little else.

Clarke's current address was north of Ashford in Kent.

Not so very far away, then. Boyd decided it could be worth his while to drive over and have a chat with him face to face. He was keen to find out, first hand, how Leon Martin had crossed paths with him. It would be very helpful to hear Clarke's version of how and where Martin had originally picked him up. It might help them to get a better idea of Leon's methods ... and perhaps help them to understand where their boy in the layby had come from. In the absence of a name, there was every chance Boyd was going to end up calling him Nike Boy.

There. You've done it already. Numbnuts.

20

Boyd rang the doorbell of Corner Cottage and waited. It took a few minutes before he heard anything, then finally through the frosted glass of the front door he saw a figure approaching. A chain slid on the far side and the door opened a crack.

The gap revealed a floppy tress of grey-streaked brown hair and a pair of dewy eyes behind a pair of rimless John Lennon spectacles. He was on the phone. He cupped it with his free hand, leaned towards the gap in the door and said, 'Just leave it on the porch, thanks.'

Boyd flashed his warrant card. 'Not Amazon, I'm afraid. Sussex Police CID.'

The man scratched his chin and narrowed his eyes as he tried to focus on the card. 'Sussex Police? Jesus. What's happened?'

'I'm DCI Boyd,' said Boyd. 'It's nothing to worry about. Are you Kristy Clarke?'

'Sorry, Helen,' the man said, speaking into his phone. 'I'll call you back later.' He hung up and pulled the door wide open. 'Yes. I'm Kristy. What's this about?'

'Mind if I come in for a chat?' Boyd checked his watch. It was gone two o'clock. He wanted to be back in Hastings before the roads got clogged up with commuter traffic. 'I won't be long.'

'Sure.' Kristy nodded. 'But please tell me this isn't about Leon Martin... *again*?'

Boyd made a face. 'Unfortunately it is.'

Kristy rolled his eyes and backed into the small hallway with a sigh. 'You better come in, then.'

Kristy led him down a gloomy hallway and into the sitting room. He pointed Boyd in the direction of an old armchair. 'Can I make you a cuppa?' he asked.

'I could murder a coffee,' Boyd said.

'Only tea. Green tea, I'm afraid,' Kristy said.

'Green tea it is, then – thanks. White and one sugar is fine.'

'With *green* tea,' said Kristy with an 'Are you sure?' look on his face.

'Yeah.' Boyd nodded. 'Milk and sugar, thanks.'

'Okay-y-y. Well, take a seat and I'll be back in a minute,' Kristy said, disappearing back out of the room.

Boyd sat down in the armchair. It had a faded floral pattern and wooden arms that had been worn and smoothed by decades of use. He looked around the lounge; it had a very old-fashioned feel to it. It was decorated in what Emma would have called 'Laura Ashley chintz' – flowery wallpaper and display cupboards full of dusty porcelain figurines. There was a dining table in the corner and it was covered in paperwork. Also on it was a laptop and a phone. It looked as though Kristy Clarke worked from home.

'Is this cottage yours?' Boyd called out.

'I rent it,' Kristy called back. 'From the charity I work for. They charge me a nominal amount.'

He came back a moment later with a cup and saucer for Boyd and one for himself. Boyd looked him up and down as he placed the tea on a small wooden table. Kristy was wearing an office shirt, unbuttoned at the top with a loose tie, and baggy jeans. Tidy up top, casual down below. He had a bumbling, almost apologetic, Hugh Grant-like quality to him.

'Given we're on the outskirts of Ashford and there's the train link into London, what I pay to live here is a gift,' he said, taking a seat in an armchair opposite Boyd.

'Do you go in to London often?' Boyd asked.

'Two or three days a week. To touch base with my colleague, Helen. And then I do some outreach work in the evenings. I work for a charity called Capital Reach. But I'm sure you know that already. I work from home the rest of the week.' Kristy paused.'Now then... Tell me – did Mike Gratton send you?'

'You remember DCI Gratton?' said Boyd.

'Of course. He sends me a Christmas card every year.' Kristy smiled. 'He's one of the good guys. 'I'm not a big fan of the police in general, sorry... What was your name again?'

'DCI Boyd.'

'Boyd. Like the X Factor winner?'

'That was Boyle, wasn't it?'

Kristy shook his head at his own idiocy. 'Of course.'

'You say you're not a big fan of the police, Kristy?' Boyd said, hoping to dig a bit deeper.

'Not a huge one. No. The Met are way too heavy-handed with rough sleepers. Some of the thugs they have in uniform... But Mike Gratton... Mike's a good guy.'

Boyd nodded.

'How is he?' Kristy asked.

'I'm afraid he's not doing so well these days.'

'He's retired now, isn't he?' Kristy said, sipping his tea.

'Retired and dying,' Boyd said somewhat bluntly. 'He's in a hospice. He's got cancer.'

Kristy frowned, looking down at his tea. 'Well, I'm very sorry to hear that. He was gentle with me... back when.'

'I've read the transcripts,' said Boyd. 'I think he was very worried about how the experience would affect you.'

'I know – he was very good to me,' replied Kristy. 'I mean... in the beginning it was fine. I wasn't aware of what Leon Martin was capable of until a few days after he brought me to his farm.' He pulled the teabag out of his cup and settled it in the saucer. 'So why are you here, DCI Boyd?'

'Just Boyd is fine.' He tried his tea. It was bloody awful. 'We may have found another one of Martin's victims. We're still trying to ID the body at the moment. I thought I should let you know before the national media get wind of it and thought it might help to hear your story, directly from you. It might shed some light on how he found our boy. Where he snatched him from, that sort of thing.'

'Oh, he didn't *snatch* me,' Kristy said, shaking his head. 'He was... kind. Gentle.' He looked over at Boyd. 'When you've been sleeping on the streets for a while you become invisible to normal people. It's as if you're not even human sometimes. So... you know, when someone actually stops and talks to you, like you matter, it's hard not to be won over.'

'And that's how it was for you?' Boyd asked.

Kristy nodded. 'It was on a freezing cold night. He took me to a café, bought me tea, something to eat, and we talked.'

'This was in Manchester?' said Boyd, making notes.

'Right.'

'And how did he convince you to go back to his place?'

'He offered to give me a bed for a few nights, while the cold snap was on. As I said, it was freezing. It wasn't that difficult a decision for me really.'

'It didn't strike you as... potentially dangerous?' Boyd asked, knowing what the answer would be.

'Sleeping rough is dangerous,' replied Kristy.

Boyd nodded. 'So you went with him, back to his farmhouse. And how was he with you? Describe what he was like.'

'I remember he came across as desperately lonely.' Kristy narrowed his eyes as he cast his mind back. 'It was almost pitiful… how he wanted to please me. To make me feel at home.'

'Were there any, I don't know, warning signs?' Boyd asked.

'That he was psychotic, you mean?' Kristy said.

Boyd nodded.

'Until I stumbled upon the stuff in the basement, not really. I mean, he was a little odd, the way he behaved, awkward, you know? It was as though he was unused to interacting with people, but then that suited me just fine.' Kristy paused, trying to find the right words. 'Looking back, he was on a self-destructive tangent.' Kristy placed his teacup carefully back on its saucer. 'I think he was on a path to taking his life, even then.'

'And what happened when you found the stuff in the basement?' Boyd asked. 'Is that when things changed?'

Kristy nodded. 'He had a sofa down there, a fridge, boombox thing, a TV with a Nintendo. It was like a lad's pad. I was obviously drawn to it. Then I found his photo albums.' Kristy lifted his cup and Boyd could see the slightest tremor in his hand. 'There were,' he continued in a low voice, 'at least seven other boys who came before me. I didn't know that at the time. I didn't know what he was back then.'

'I'm not going to ask you to go into detail there, Kristy. It's all on file.'

Kristy nodded, relieved. He sipped his tea. 'Well, anyway. He came down, found me looking at them –' he shrugged – 'and changed instantly. Like a Jekyll and Hyde thing.'

'He knew the game was up,' Boyd said. 'And that's when you became his captive?'

Kristy nodded. 'Right. And from that moment on he knew he couldn't let me go. He had a shotgun, forced me to go upstairs to a bedroom and that's where he shackled me. To the bed frame. They'd been used before, the handcuffs. They had dried blood on them. In the grooves.'

'You said in your interview with Mike that he attempted to kill you?'

'Several times... He came into the room, with his shotgun, and I thought, *This is it,* you know?' His voice was shaking. 'I... and...'

'Kristy... it's okay,' Boyd said, realising how hard he'd been pushing him. 'I've read the interviews you had with Mike. We don't have to cover those details again.'

Kristy smiled gratefully. 'I haven't thought about it in a while. It's still so clear.'

Boyd nodded. 'I know what you mean,' he said. The images of the crash, of Julia and Noah, were so vivid sometimes; it was as though he was there all over again. He pulled his attention back to the present.

Kristy frowned, his trembling hand repeatedly stroking his scruffy threadbare beard.

'Leon became increasingly erratic over the next couple of days. At one point... he even came into the room, aimed the gun at me, couldn't do it, then aimed it at himself.'

'Jesus,' Boyd said.

'He didn't do it, obviously. If he had, I'd be dead now.'

Boyd reached for his tea and took another less-than-enthusiastic sip.

Kristy smiled. 'Milk and sugar really don't go well with green tea.'

Boyd pulled a face and nodded as he set his cup back down. 'Yeah,' he said. 'I might have to rethink that next time. Kristy, tell me about your escape. How did you get away? Mike seemed to think that you thought maybe he'd *let* you escape... so that you could tell the police that he was planning to kill himself?'

Kristy took another very deep breath. 'Well, he came into the room with the shotgun. I was terrified. I thought he'd suddenly talked himself into shooting me dead, but he grabbed me, got me in the van, and we took off.'

'To Wales?' Boyd asked.

'Right,' said Kristy. 'He said it was all over now. The police were going to find us, and that the best thing was to end it.'

'By which you thought that meant...'

'Kill us both. With his shotgun. Halfway there he explained there was a place he knew from when he was a boy, a cliff. That he was going to take us there.'

'But you escaped before he got there?'

Kristy nodded. 'He pulled into a forest layby on the way over and went for a piss. That's when I managed to escape.'

'How?'

'I wasn't manacled to anything. He just told me not to move, then got out.'

'He just told you to stay?'

'He took the gun with him. But... yes. As soon as he was in the bushes, I opened the door and ran.'

'Okay,' said Boyd. 'You ran... and Leon did what?'

'I don't know. I disappeared into the woods and just kept running. I didn't look back.'

'And you think that was his doing? He was letting you go?'

'At the time I just thought I'd got lucky. Very lucky. But... later on, I began to suspect that he'd planned it. To let me go; let me tell the police about the other boys and that he was going to top himself.'

'You think that was his escape plan?'

Kristy nodded and shrugged. 'Clever. When you think about it. Mike told me about the body they'd found. It had been on the news and they had a partial registration for his van. I think it had spooked him and this was his way out. Whether he's dead or alive – I guess it worked.'

Boyd felt he had enough from Kristy Clarke for now. It was

clear the questions were pulling him back to a place he'd long ago moved on from.

'Look, thanks for your time,' Boyd said, standing up. 'And the weird tea.'

Kristy laughed, relieved the visit was over 'You're the one that made it weird.' He laughed again.

'Fair point,' Boyd said, putting his notebook and pen back into his bag, before swinging it onto his shoulder.

Kristy led him out of the sitting room, down the hall, and opened the front door.

'Boyd,' he said quietly, 'there were seven young men in those photographs and – a possible victim – laid to rest. If your boy is one of the seven, and if you find out his name, would you let me know?'

Boyd nodded. 'Of course. It's the least I can do after dragging it all back up again. Take care, Kristy,' he added, before he walked back down the lane towards his car.

21

Boyd arrived back at the station at just after half past four. A build-up of trucks trailing back up the M2 and the M20 from Dover and Folkestone that had spilled onto the M25 had slowed things down to a frustrating crawl.

He dumped his jacket and bag on the desk, glancing up and catching DSI Sutherland's eye as he did so. Sutherland was heading back to his office, a fresh coffee in his hand. He raised his free hand and pointed to his open door.

'I'm just gonna grab one for myself and I'll be with you,' Boyd called after him, to which Sutherland made an 'okay' sign with his thumb and forefinger.

Boyd, looking around the room, noticed Okeke was away from her desk, presumably still out on her Nike trainer fact-finding mission. He could just see her, standing in some super-cool design studio, surrounded by hipsters with topknots and ironic mustard-coloured cardigans explaining the aesthetic curves of the product images on their expensive Apple monitors. He wouldn't be surprised if there was also a meditation pod in the middle of their workspace, and what he thought of as woo-woo music being pumped around the office floor.

He slapped the kettle on, and spooned coffee granules and two heaped spoons of sugar into his mug. He sighed at the sight of the solitary bottle of red-top milk in the fridge and toyed with the idea of trekking to the canteen on the top floor for a naughty cappuccino.

But Sutherland was waiting.

Settling for a uninspiring black coffee, he headed down the walkway to Sutherland's glass-box office.

Boyd knocked and entered. 'Afternoon,' he said.

'Afternoon,' Sutherland replied, pacing briskly around like a restless fish in an aquarium.

'Everything okay, sir?'

Sutherland nodded. 'Just trying to get my ten thousand steps in.' He raised an arm to show off a FitBit. 'I'm so close – just wanted to get the fireworks in before I'm done at work today.'

'Ah, I see,' said Boyd, no idea what he was on about.

'Take a seat, Boyd. You don't mind if I keep going, do you?'

'No. It's not at all distracting, sir,' said Boyd, sitting down.

'So how's it going with our unidentified body?' Sutherland huffed.

'Still unidentified. DC Warren's working away at narrowing down a list of open misper cases. I'm pretty confident our A21 lad is lurking in there somewhere.'

Sutherland puffed past Boyd, slightly pink in the face. 'I heard from Okeke you went to interview the last of Leon Martin's victims? The One That Got Away.'

'Kristy Clarke? Yeah, I'm just back actually,' Boyd said.

'And?' Sutherland rounded his desk. 'What did you get out of that? Anything useful there?'

'Kristy seems like a very resilient man. He's spent the last twenty years trying to deal with what happened to him. I liked him,' Boyd said.

'That's lovely heartfelt stuff, Boyd, but how does it advance your investigation?'

'I thought letting him know about the latest discovery in person was the right thing to do. The previous SIO, Mike Gratton, and Kristy Clarke himself, both voiced a theory that Leon Martin might have allowed Kristy to live in order to help orchestrate Martin's staged exit.'

'The supposed suicide?'

'Yeah. Neither of them is convinced he jumped.' Boyd rubbed his neck, sore from the drive and from tracking Sutherland on his mini marathon around the office.

'So what're you saying? You think Leon Martin's alive still?' said Sutherland, pacing beyond Boyd's peripheral vision.

'No. I suspect it's unlikely that he's another Lord Lucan. I'd say he's dead somewhere. Or possibly serving prison time under another name. But certainly not at liberty.'

Sutherland stepped into view. 'Can you link our bones to the Ken Doll case?'

'I hope so. If the trainer fits the timeline, then I'm almost certain he's one of Leon Martin's. Warren's misper list will hopefully get us the rest of the way over the line.'

'But so far away?'

'He had a vehicle. Makes sense to put some distance down.'

Sutherland came to a halt behind his desk. He remained standing, pondering something.

'Speaking of distance, how many steps?' Boyd asked.

'What?'

Boyd nodded at the FitBit.

'Oh, err... nine thousand, four hundred and seventeen.'

' And you look great on it, sir.'

Sutherland registered the sarcasm. 'Up yours, Boyd. At least I'm doing something about it.' He shot Boyd's midriff a meaningful glance, before sitting down in his chair and gazing at his steaming coffee. 'But if Leon Martin got away...'

'Then, yes...' Boyd said, 'there could be more recent undiscovered victims – if his compulsion to kill, pose his victims and take photographs persisted. But I don't see how. Back then he had a remote farm, a vehicle, his parents' savings, no criminal record and a lot of privacy. After Clarke, he had none of those things.'

'Hmmm.'

'And whatever compulsion was making him do what he did, that sort of thing doesn't just switch itself off because it's inconvenient, does it? If there were more, we'd have heard.'

~

'Oh, so *that's* why he's swimming around in there like a goldfish,' said Okeke, grinning. 'It's about time he did something; he's as round as a bloody football.'

Boyd laughed as they headed down the stairwell to the ground floor, her voice echoing off the walls. After his interviews with Gratton and then Clarke, it was a refreshing tonic to be back in the office with the others.

'When did the trendy Nike guys say they'd get back to you?' he asked.

'They need twenty-four hours or so to compare the treads on ours with a batch sample,' Okeke said. 'They have those for every production run, you know. They keep one set sealed in an air-conditioned archive.'

'Right. Of course they do.' Boyd shook his head. 'Lucky for us – eh?'

'Not only can they give us the production year, they can give us the production month,' Okeke continued.

'That's impressive.'

'I know, isn't it?' she agreed.

At the bottom of the stairwell, he pushed the double doors open for her.

'So, guv, here's a question for you...' She paused. 'What if they come back with a production year that's *after* Martin's supposed suicide?'

'If that happens, then it becomes our own murder case,' Boyd said. 'Though I think that's very unlikely.'

'But if it did,' she pressed, 'that would mean the investigation would scale up, wouldn't it?'

'I would say it'd have to,' he said distractedly, fumbling in his jacket pocket for his car keys, as they headed past the front desk and the bored-looking desk sergeant on duty.

'Or it could mean Martin's still alive?' pondered Okeke. 'Or someone else doing his work... a copycat.'

'I hate that term. It's so bloody *Prime Suspect*,' Boyd muttered, locating his car keys at last and holding them up triumphantly.

She grinned as stepped out into the cold. 'A copycat. How very exciting.'

'Well, don't get your hopes up too much, Okeke,' he said. 'If we ever do find Martin, chances are he'll be nothing but old bones too.'

22

Boyd let Ozzie have the full length of the extendable lead to investigate the twist of rotting seaweed on the shingle, leaving his version of a CC-all memo on it as he went.

'Come on, Oz' he said with a sigh.

Ozzie had slammed his anchors down. Boyd turned round to see he was taking a dump on it for good measure. This evening Boyd had taken special care to come prepared. He dug into his anorak, pulled out the roll of poo bags and tore one off. He doubled back and squatted down to clean up.

'The things I do for you, mate,' he muttered. 'I bet you wouldn't pick up mine.'

Boyd knotted the bag, stood up and looked, automatically, up and down the beach. He laughed to himself as he realised who he was looking for. Every time he picked up after Ozzie on the beach, his first thought was to see whether he'd been spotted by her, being a responsible dog owner. The woman down at the Nelson. Mia's mum.

Alas, his deed had once again gone unnoticed. Why was it,

he wondered, always the one time you fucked up that you had an audience on hand to pass judgement?

Dusk was throwing a peach glow across the shingle and long lavender shadows where the rotten wooden stumps of long-gone breakwaters emerged. The gaudy lights of Pelham Arcade flickered and danced to his right, and to his left the steady glow of the lamps along the pier looked like a string of pearls heading out to sea.

There was no sign of her. He was surprised at the little tug of disappointment he felt.

23

DC Okeke was a dozen places ahead of him in the canteen queue and Boyd really couldn't be arsed to wait in line with the mob of uniformed officers who'd just come off duty and beaten him by mere seconds to the canteen to grab their cooked breakfasts.

He pulled out of the line, strode forward and tapped her on the shoulder.

'Oh, morning, guv,' she said cheerfully.

'Okeke, would you be a mate and get me a –'

'Cappuccino?' she interrupted.

'Yeah. And... a bacon sandwich.'

She raised her eyebrows. 'I thought Emma was rabbit-fooding you?'

'What happens at the station, stays at the station, okay?' he said, not entirely joking.

She pressed her lips together. 'And if she asks me?'

'You'll lie,' he replied. 'Because that's what mates do for each other.'

She sighed.

Boyd grinned. 'I'll square up with you.'

He went to look for an empty table to sit down to wait for her and saw Sully sitting alone, eating a cheese toastie. He wandered over.

'Mind if I...?'

'Yes, actually,' Sully replied. 'Go buy your own.'

'I meant sit with you, not share your bloody breakfast,' Boyd replied, realising belatedly that Sully hadn't really thought he was after his sandwich. He pulled out a chair and sat down. 'How's tricks?'

'Busy, busy, busy.' Sully said, through a mouthful of cheesy bread.

'I do believe I'm still waiting on your report,' Boyd said not-too-subtly.

'And you will have it, my Boyd, after I've finished completing DCI Flack's SOC report.'

Flack had been given a few more officers, by Sutherland, in the wake of another county-lines-related stabbing in a back garden during a house party in Ore.

'Anyway... your case is cold, Boyd. Cold like my wrinkled old walnut of a heart.' Sully patted his chest.

'I didn't know you wrote verse in your spare time, Sully. That's quite beautiful.'

Sully took another stringy bite out of his toastie.

'Do you have any more thoughts on how long ago the A21 body was buried?' Boyd asked.

Sully took his time chewing as he considered his answer. 'I said ten to fifteen years at the layby, didn't I?' he said. 'Well, I'm revising that upwards.'

'Why? What have you spotted?'

'I've just been looking at the photos more carefully. The root penetration through and around the body... I reckon it's probably more like fifteen to twenty years' worth of growth.'

Boyd narrowed his eyes. 'Hang on. Are you just lining your estimate up with the people at the Ellessey labs?' he asked.

Sully's normally dead-pan face twitched with irritation. 'No. Actually. I came to that figure *before* I heard what they came up with, so, with all due respect, you can Foxtrot Oscar.'

'Here you are, guv.' Okeke set a tray down and shoved Sully's plate to one side to make room. She handed Boyd a hot paper bag and a steaming paper cup. 'You owe me four pounds ninety-five.' She acknowledged Sully. 'Morning.'

'Moo-ing,' he managed with a full mouth.

She sat down next to Boyd. 'I got an email from the Nike people,' she said.

'And?'

'My computer crashed. I came to grab a coffee while it reboots. I haven't had a chance to look at it yet.'

'Oh for... ' Boyd stood up, grabbing his coffee and his bacon sandwich. 'Come on.'

'I just sat down!' she protested.

'We'll eat at your desk.'

Okeke sighed, grabbed her things and followed him towards the door. 'Jesus. It can wait a couple of minutes, can't it? You know it'll be another half an hour before it sorts itself out!'

Sully's irritated voice followed them out of the canteen. 'TRAY?!'

'HERE WE GO,' she said, some thirty minutes later, clicking on her inbox. 'There...'

Boyd glanced at her screen. 'From Alistair Bowen-Coulter at Nike?'

'He prefers to be called Ally,' Okeke said. She opened the email and read it out loud.

'Hey, Sam – great to hang out with you yesterday –'

'Hang out?' said Boyd.

She shook her head. 'That's how they all talk over there,

guv.' She resumed reading the mail. '*I sent the treads to our production facility yesterday and they were pretty quick turning it round. The machine-cut patterning is from a batch produced December 1996, in Taiwan. And that's one hundred per cent accurate – like I said, the guys keep good records.*'

'End of 1996? They're absolutely sure?'

She nodded at the screen. 'That's what it says, guv.'

It meant their body fitted nicely within the timeline of Leon Martin's activities. Boyd had been trying not to get his hopes up. As Okeke had pointed out the other day, if the trainers had been dated after Martin's suicide, then that would have been a whole new investigation.

'Good,' he said. 'That's a bloody relief. What's that last paragraph there?'

'Oh…' She hand-flapped. 'Nothing.'

Boyd leant closer. '*Now, how about that drink? Have I earned it?*'

She tutted. 'The bloke was hitting on me all afternoon. Complete pony-tailed weasel. Total preppie idiot.'

'Not your type, then?' He smiled at her obvious annoyance.

'Jay's my type,' she replied. 'So, obviously, the whole flappy-handed designer type *isn't*.'

'And you were there all afternoon, you say?'

'He insisted on giving me a tour of the design studio first.' She sighed. 'It was everything you'd expect it to be. You won't believe this…'

'What?'

'They have a ball pool and a soft play area in the middle of their floor. I'm serious.'

'They bring their kids in to work?' Boyd asked incredulously.

Okeke rolled her eyes. 'I don't think it was for the kids, guv.'

24

Mark Richmond wasn't particularly keen on walking the dogs this late in the evening. It was seven thirty and the sun was just about clinging onto the horizon, but it was going to be almost dark before he got back home.

His shifts at Pound Bargains were all over the place; they tended to be whatever shifts were left over after everyone else had taken their pick. It made planning anything virtually impossible. Like this evening – it had been scheduled to be a *Call of Duty* Clan night – but, at the last moment, he'd had a call telling him to go in for eight for shelf-stacking. So there was no clan gathering for him tonight, and, to top it off, his mum had reminded him that the dogs both needed to be walked before he went out. Which was a total pisser.

Watson and Max were up ahead of him, doing what dogs did best, rooting around grotty bits of undergrowth and getting dirty. He usually called out to them once every couple of minutes to get them to report back in if he couldn't see them. Mum was constantly reminding him that dognapping was an actual real thing – and, according to her, even happened at knifepoint. She'd drilled into him: *Keep them in sight, Mark. Always keep my boys in sight.*

He swore she loved her two fur babies more than she loved him. For fuck's sake, they got Christmas stockings. They even got canine chocolate Easter Eggs.

'Watson! Max!' he called out into the gathering gloom.

Up ahead he could see the dark form of something moving slowly out and away from the wooded area that ran alongside the A road. It was too dark to see which one of the two dogs it was, or even if it was a dog.

It could be a deer.

It was something on all fours, at any rate.

'Watson?' he called.

The dark shape stopped moving. As he drew closer, it became more defined against the greyed-out, darkening backdrop of the field. He turned the torch function of his phone on and aimed it.

Two eyes glinted back at him. Watson.

'Where's Max, mate?' he asked.

Watson was too busy to go looking for his partner-in-crime. He had found something far more interesting to play around with.

Oh God, please. Not fox shit, he prayed. That stuff stank. Watson was the worst for it. He rolled in it first – really putting his back into it so that the stuff got firmly meshed into his fur, then he ate what was left on the ground. He'd prance around afterwards, a smug look about him, as if he'd just discovered the mother lode. And the smell of shit lingered even after a thorough hosing down with anti-fox poo shampoo.

'Drop it!' snapped Mark.

Watson looked as though he was going to be an arse about it. He picked up whatever it was, ran a dozen yards further away from Mark, then carried on chewing his find.

Little sod.

'Right! Come here! NOW!' Mark used the Angry Voice. The one that made his breaking voice go shrill and high-pitched – and made him sound like a total idiot. But it worked. Watson dutifully padded towards him, head low, tail low, but still defiantly hanging onto his prize.

'Drop it!' growled Mark. 'Now!'

With great reluctance, Watson opened his jaw and dropped what he had on the ground a few feet away. It looked like a pale mouse, maybe. Or perhaps it was more likely a baby rat. They came out hairless, didn't they? Little pink squiggly, squirmy things.

Mark stepped over, squatted down and was about to reach out and prod it to see whether the poor thing was still alive, when, at the last moment, he stopped.

The little baby rat had a fingernail on the end of it.

25

'I'm sorry. That's actually not how it works in real life,' said Boyd.

'Oh, no... here he goes again,' said Emma.

'I'm just saying – you can't use anything the suspect says as evidence until *after* they've been cautioned.' Boyd shook his head at the TV. 'It's utter bollocks, that is.'

'You'll have to forgive him, Dan...' Emma said. 'This is precisely why we don't watch police procedurals. Dad tends to moan all the way through.'

Boyd sighed. 'It's just irritating when they don't bother to try and get it right. That bloke there could have just confessed to the murder, how he did it, when he did it, why he did it... All of that, and not one word of it could be used in court because they –'

'Dad?'

'All right,' he huffed. He sank back into his armchair and resumed rubbing the fur up the wrong way along Ozzie's back. He seemed to like that. 'I'm just saying –'

'Dad.'

'Fine. Fine... You guys carry on watching this completely inaccurate shite.'

'It's fiction, Dad. The clue's right there in the word. It's doesn't have to follow the rules – it's not real!'

Boyd rolled his eyes and noticed that Daniel was looking slightly uncomfortable. 'Relax, this is perfectly normal. I moan at the TV, she moans at me, we agree to disagree. Then I make amends by offering to make a cuppa.'

'Red bush tea, please,' she said quickly.

'Dan?'

'White tea if it's no bother. I can –'

Boyd waved away any forthcoming offers of help and got up off the chair, making an old man 'ooof' as he did so.

The series wasn't grabbing his attention anyway. It had lost his interest the moment FBI agent Kate Trent had rolled up at the crime scene on a Harley, wearing bike leathers, pulling her helmet off and tossing her perfectly styled blonde hair.

Why do they do that? It seemed to him that every US crime show needed to feature a cast that looked as if they'd just finished modelling for a catalogue and were filling in their down time by trying to solve a bloody crime.

Boyd went down the hall, crossed the dining room into the kitchen and slapped the kettle on. He was busying himself with cups and tea when his phone vibrated in his pocket. He pulled it out and saw it was DS Minter. Ironically – a cop with catalogue-model looks and a perfectly sculpted body.

'What's up, Minty? You back on nights again or is this a social call?' he asked.

'I shift-swapped with DS Allen. Last minute. He's got family problems,' Minter explained.

'Ah, okay. So, you got a good reason to be calling me a –'

'We got another layby body, boss,' Minter interrupted.

Boyd looked at his watch. It was just gone nine. 'Where?'

'A27, boss. The road that goes over to Brighton. A young lad was walking his dogs and they sniffed it out and dug it up.'

'Shit.' If dogs had sniffed it... 'Are we talking a recent one, then?'

'Very recent. Maybe only a few days. It's another layby, boss.'

'Shit,' Boyd said again. He was tempted to jump in his car and... *Bugger*, he thought, realising he'd just had a couple of glasses of wine with the kids.

'Who's attending?' he asked.

'Me,' Minter replied. 'I'm heading out of the station now.'

'Forensics? Please say Sully.'

Boyd preferred continuity and Sully was good. His findings came dry, opinion-free and well-ordered.

'You're lucky,' Minter said. 'He was working late and about to clock off. Said he'd take it.'

'Good.' Boyd flipped the kettle off. It was too bloody noisy to hear himself think.

'I'd join you, but I've had something to drink.'

'It's okay, boss. I've got this.'

'Good. I'll be in early so we can handover face to face.'

'Righto,' Minter said, and hung up.

Another layby... and this time a *recent* body. Coincidences existed, of course. It wasn't beyond reason that some other murderer had decided a layby would make a convenient place to dispose of a body.

There was, though, another possible explanation. One that made Boyd feel slightly queasy.

That both Mike Gratton and Kristy Clarke had been right.

26

Boyd arrived in the CID room a good couple of hours before his shift was due to start. It was strangely quiet at that time of the morning. There was just Minter pecking away at his keyboard, and two others at their desks, whiling – or more likely *willing* – away the last half hour of their red-eye shift.

Minter looked up from his keyboard, relief plain on his face at the sight of Boyd. 'Early in too, boss?'

'Chat and a coffee, Minter?' he said, gesturing to the doorway.

He took the detective sergeant up to the canteen, which was quiet before the shift-change surge and the breakfast rush. He got Minter and himself a coffee and the obligatory bacon roll, and they grabbed a table in the corner.

Boyd pushed aside the sweetener sachets he'd picked up – this was fast becoming a new habit he wasn't too keen on – and reached for the sugar sprinkler. 'Okay,' he said. 'Hand me the keys to the kingdom.'

'It's another layby body, boss, on the A27. As I said last night, it was a dog walker who called it in, a Mark Richmond. He was only a young lad and was pretty shaken up, as you'd expect. His dog picked up a finger and pretty much dropped it at his feet, if you can believe that,' Minter said.

'So, it's *very* recent, as you thought,' Boyd said. 'Do we know how long it's been in the ground?'

'Sully's preliminary guess was five days. Obviously he's going to refine that if he can. It's another young male, late teens by the look of him.'

'Do we have an obvious cause of death?'

Minter shook his head. 'His hands were bound, and he had what looked like a single stab wound to the chest. There were smooth ligature marks around the neck, suggesting something like electric cable, Sully thought.' Minter looked at him. 'And, boss, ... there was another carved wooden figure.'

The same stab wound as the A21 bones. And the figure. *Fuck.* If he had any hope left that this wasn't related, it winked out right then. 'Same as...?'

'It's a little soldier., Minter confirmed. 'Like one of the Buckingham Palace guards, with the bearskin hats.'

'Right.' Boyd sighed, looking down at his coffee.

'And one more thing. There were some flowers and a message found not too far from him,' said Minter.

'Flowers?' Boyd's head snapped up.

'Yeah, tied to the layby signpost. Recent ones. Very recent. Let me just check my notes...'

Boyd recalled there'd been flowers at the A21 layby too. He remembered wondering how old they were. Had they been picked up as evidence? Shit. He fucking hoped so.

Minter was flipping through his notebook. 'Ah, yeah. There was a handwritten message with the flowers... Boss?'

Boyd grabbed a pen and scribbled on a napkin. *A21 – flowers*. 'What was the message?'

'A line of a poem or a song maybe.' Minter read it out loud.

He was right. The words were from a song, and a well-known one too. If their killer – and Boyd couldn't quite bring himself to use Martin's name yet – had left those flowers, presumably the words meant something to him.

'Right,' Boyd said. 'I want to keep this out of general circulation until we know if it's significant or not, okay?'

'Righ-o, boss. You worried about press leaks?'

'I always worry about them. Because they always bloody happen.' If it wasn't a small cash bribe from a reporter, it was careless chatter in the canteen or down the pub.

'Those words may not lead us to the killer,' said Boyd, 'but we can use them to rule out the idiots that call in pranking us.'

Minter's perfectly sculpted brows lifted in unison.

'Oh, you just wait,' added Boyd. 'You can bet on it. Or that lyric will be all over Facebook as some bloody meme. Yours and my eyes only for now, is that clear?'

'Sure,' Minter said.

'The flowers and message been bagged and logged, have they?'

'Yeah. You want the evidence bag serial number?' Minter asked, reaching for his notebook again.

'Maybe later. Just...' His mind was back on those *withered* flowers. 'Just a sec...' He pulled his phone out and dialled Okeke. There was no answer. He had Warren's number in his recent-calls list and dialled that instead.

Warren answered after a couple of rings. 'Sir?'

'You on your way in yet?' Boyd asked.

'Um, no, err... not yet. I'm just having me cereal. I'm not due to '

'Right. Well, finish up. Can you go to the A21 layby?'

'The body one?'

'Yes – the body one.'

Boyd heard a spoon clink against a bowl... and the muffled sound of a woman's voice in the background. 'It's the guv, mum.' The phone rustled as a hand went over it, and Boyd listened to a muted exchange.

Another rustle and Warren was back on. 'Sorry, about that sir. What do you want me to do?'

'On the picnic signpost, there are some old flowers. Evidence-bag them if they're still there, will you?'

'Right.'

'Thanks,' Boyd said. 'And, Warren –' he paused for a second –' say hello to your mum.'

He hung up and looked at Minter. 'If the same thing's written on those, then...'

Minter nodded. He looked pleased with himself. 'To be honest, boss, I nearly didn't bother with them. You see them everywhere these days, don't you?'

'Too often.'

'Do you think this is going to escalate to an operation, boss?'

'I think that's a given. Don't worry, though. I'll make sure you're on the team. Look... I'm going to talk to Sutherland as soon as he's in. Go home; get your beauty sleep. I may be calling you back in later today once we're up and running.'

~

BOYD COULD SEE through the glass that Hatcher had already descended from the Heavens and had found her way to Sutherland's office. They were deep in conversation.

He knocked on the door, then pushed it open and walked in.

'Ma'am. Sir.'

'Boyd?' said Hatcher with a look of irritation on her face. 'Can it wait? I'm –'

'There was another body discovered buried at a layby last night,' he said. 'A recent one.'

Hatcher and Sutherland exchanged a glance.

'Actually we were just talking about it,' said Sutherland. '*And* the Ken Doll Killer case.'

'That was twenty years ago,' she said. 'Let's not jump to conclusions too quickly. You know how –'

'They're linked, ma'am,' Boyd said.

She stiffened, annoyed at his interruption. 'And you know that, DCI Boyd, because...'

'Because it's a similar MO: similar victim profile; same disposal method.' He looked at Sutherland and added pointedly, 'And we've got another carved figure.'

'Fucking hell,' Sutherland muttered.

Hatcher looked at Sutherland crossly, then back at Boyd. 'What's this?'

Sutherland explained the link with the A21 bones and the photographs in Gratton's case file.

'Can the wooden figures be matched?' she asked.

'I expect the traces of paint on the older one could be chemically matched with the paint on this one. Maybe the wood can be matched... I don't know. I've never looked into that before, ma'am. I'd have to ask Sully.'

In complete contrast to the male officers, Hatcher was almost beaming. She looked utterly stoked about the possibility of landing a serial killer on her patch. 'We'll need to ramp this up, asap.'

'There's also the flowers,' added Boyd.

'What flowers?' asked Sutherland.

He explained Minter's find last night and the old, withered bunch of flowers at the A21 layby. 'We may get DNA off the recent message. We might even get some DNA off the older one, though it's pretty unlikely.'

'If they've got anything to do with it,' said Sutherland, 'they could be for some old RTA that occurred along that stretch of road.'

'I'll get that checked,' said Boyd. 'I've sent one of mine over to the A21 to evidence-bag them if they're still there.'

Hatcher lowered her head and skewered him with a look over the rim of her glasses. 'You didn't get them at the time?'

'No, ma'am, I didn't.'

'Why not?'

Boyd's mouth hung open, exasperated. 'Because the flowers only became significant last night.' He cleared his throat. 'Ma'am.'

'You said *message*,' said Sutherland. 'What was the message?'

'It's on a tag with the flowers. It's a line from a song. It may not be significant at all.'

'What is it?' asked Hatcher.

Boyd realised he was pushing his luck. 'Ma'am, if it's okay, I'd like to embargo that piece of intelligence from everyone outside my core team.'

Hatcher opened her mouth to say something.

'It's not that I don't trust anyone in this station,' Boyd added quickly, 'but it just takes one casual slip and I've lost the exclusive use of a crucial detail.'

Sutherland nodded. 'That makes sense, Boyd.' He looked at the Chief Superintendent. 'Ma'am, he's got a point.'

'I mean, if you insist... Of course I'll tell you,' offered Boyd. 'But... if it leaks at the moment, I'll know it's definitely one of mine.'

'Fair enough,' she replied eventually. 'We had a reporter from the *Mail* calling for a comment about the Ken Doll Killer case, yesterday. Which means their little ratty whiskers are already twitching for this story.'

'As soon as it gets out about the second body, they're going to be like gulls around a chip van,' said Sutherland ruefully.

'If the Ken Doll Killer's come back from the dead, this will be front-page stuff, Boyd,' Hatcher said, a little too enthusiastically.

Sutherland visibly wilted. 'Marvellous. This is going to get expensive.'

Boyd eyed his seniors – one stressing about budget and the other polishing her CV though neither of them paying the slightest mind to the fact that someone's son had just been found in a shallow grave at the side of a road.

'Remind me. Which force dealt with it last time?' asked Hatcher.

'Cheshire,' said Boyd.

'Well, now it's our case.' She offered Sutherland a smile. 'Iain, relax. We can go Dutch with them on the budget.'

'I hope so,' Sutherland replied, sighing. 'Flack's county lines operation has been sucking me dry for the last six months.'

'I can ring-fence a discretionary budget for this,' Hatcher said. 'I have a small magic money sapling going spare.'

'Ma'am?' said Boyd.

She looked at him. 'Yes?'

'So this is now escalating to operation status?'

'Effective immediately. You'll remain as SIO, Boyd.' That came with a pointed look, and a smile. *This is yours... You're welcome.*

Sutherland looked like the father of the bride settling a wedding bill. 'Anything you need, Boyd?'

'I'll start with DS Minter as my second, if that's okay, sir?'

'All yours.'

'And I'll get back to you ASAP with a team pick-list.'

Sutherland nodded. 'I'll book you an operation name.'

'And you'll need to boot Flack and his team out of the Incident Room again,' Boyd said, standing up.

'I'm not sure we need to do that just yet,' Sutherland said nervously.

'Yes, do it,' said Hatcher. 'I'm going to hold a press conference later today, once I've spoken with Cheshire's Chief Super and we've agreed the case ownership. I want to announce we have a team on it already.'

'Don't waste any time, Boyd.' She looked him in the eye. 'The old bones are on the Cheshire Constabulary; the new ones are going to be on us.'

27

Boyd had just sat down at his desk with a fresh coffee when an email came in. It was from Dr Palmer at Ellessey Forensics saying they had taken receipt of the new body and it was the first job on her slate today.

He found the contact number at the bottom of the email and dialled it.

'Dr Karen Palmer,' she answered.

'This is DCI Boyd. I just got your email,' he said.

'Ah, good. I'm going to make a start on it at about ten. You're more than welcome to pop over and observe if you want?'

It wasn't top of his Bucket List. One of the privileges of his rank was supposed to be that he could remain one-hundred-per-cent office-based and send his gophers out instead. But... some errands were too important.

'All right – sounds good,' he lied. He decided to drag Okeke along. He could fill her in on the way there, and she could translate the forensics mumbo jumbo for him. 'We'll be there.'

He dashed off a quick email to Warren, Minter and O'Neal, telling them to wrap up or pass on any other business, and beckoned Okeke over to join him.

~

THEY WERE in the same lab as last time, studio three. But this time it was just Dr Palmer conducting the autopsy.

'So, this is *very* recent,' were her opening words. She pointed at the body. 'This boy is tall for his age – big boned. Six feet, I'd say.' She ran her gloved hands over his torso. 'And lean, which is helpful as you can feel more easily for signs of bloating.'

She shook her head and gently pressed her gloved fingers along the boy's abdomen. 'I'm not feeling any gassy sponginess, which indicates we're looking at fewer than four or five days.'

She circled the examination table and lifted one side of the body up to show off dark discoloured skin. 'Livor mortis stains. But these look undeveloped.'

'What does that mean?' asked Boyd.

'Rotated position post-mortem,' said Okeke.

'Correct,' said Palmer. 'It means the body was in one position for a few hours and then placed in another. Once blood stops circulating, it drains down to the lowest points, which gives you the bruising effect. This body rested on its back for a while, then was buried with the left side upwards. So, we have two sets of livor mortis stains: along the back, and on the right-hand side... pre- and post-burial.'

She opened a folder and looked at Sully's photographs. 'There, see? He was lying on his right side in the ground, knees tucked up.'

Boyd looked at Okeke. 'Could he have been lying flat out in transit possibly? And not in a car boot, either. I can't think of any cars that have an enclosed boot big enough to lay someone flat out.'

'Not in a car, full stop, looking at the size of him,' Okeke pointed out.

'So you're thinking he put him in the back of a van or a truck?' he replied.

Okeke nodded.

Dr Palmer wasn't listening to them; she carried on with her once-around the body, then returned to the far side of the examination table to study a penetration wound on the right side of the chest and a small bruise beneath it.

'Here we have a deep wound caused by a single-edged wide-bladed knife. A kitchen knife would do that.' She pulled the skin apart slightly, the sides of the wound parted like puckered lips. 'It's a deep wound. It would have taken a lot of force. See the bruise? That would probably have been caused by the knife's handle thumping into the chest.'

Boyd glanced but didn't let his eyes linger. 'A single stab to ensure fatality?'

She nodded. 'The boy was strangled first,' she said, pointing at the ligature marks round his neck. 'But that's not a precise science. You can render someone unconscious that way, but sometimes it's hard to know if they're dead for sure.' She shrugged. 'And strangulation time to cause death varies hugely.'

It almost sounded, Boyd thought, as though she'd tried it out on a few hapless test subjects herself.

Palmer continued. 'I mean, that Saudi journalist Khashoggi... The audio tapes recorded seven and half minutes of strangulation before they concluded that he was dead. The stab wound would probably have been for the killer's peace of mind. To check that the victim wasn't faking it.'

She pointed at the red lines around the boy's neck. 'The ligature marks are completely smooth, not patterned, so not rope, or chain. I'd say electrical cable of some kind.' She leant over and lifted one of the boy's eyelids. 'Petechiae on the conjunctiva, eyelids, cheeks.'

'Evidence of death by asphyxiation,' said Okeke quietly. 'You get pinpoint surface haemorrhages.'

'I know what that is,' Boyd said.

'You said you wanted me to translate,' she muttered.

Palmer's gaze slowly descended from the face, the neck, to the chest, then down the left shoulder and arm. 'What are you looking for?' asked Boyd.

'Defence injuries. I was hoping for skin under the nails, but this lad has hardly any nails. He was a chewer, I think.'

'Any chance at all of skin scrapings?' he asked.

'I've swabbed them, so... if he did manage some fingernail-to-skin contact we might get some transference of DNA.' She straightened up. 'Right, so that's the surface check. I'm going to start opening him up. It's not everyone's favourite part, so...' She looked across at her audience.

An image of Noah on the back seat of their car flashed through Boyd's head.

Palmer shrugged and reached for a scalpel sitting in the kidney dish on the corner of the examination table. 'I'm going to start making incisions; if either of you are not that good with this sort of thing, now is probably a good time to absent yourself.'

'I'm fine,' said Okeke. She looked up at Boyd. 'How about you?'

He let out a breath. 'I'm not great with this bit, if I'm honest,' he muttered.

Dr Palmer looked up at him. 'Seriously, then, I'd rather you stepped out now. It's distracting having a *wobbler* in the room.'

Boyd had another flash of Noah on the back seat, a towel thrown across his head, to hide the God-awful mess beneath. He'd seen enough RTA bodies while in uniform to be desensitised to a post-mortem, to some degree. But right now, even before she had started on the Y-shaped incision, he felt himself sliding.

'I'll be fine,' he said.

Dr Palmer was looking at him. Not at all convinced.

Okeke turned to him. 'Haven't you got some urgent calls to make, guv?'

Boyd glanced at her.

'I can stay here and report back with any info… but didn't you mention needing to get the Incident Room set up and the team sorted, ready for when we get back?'

He could have hugged her. She really was a good egg. 'Yeah, you're right. Okeke, I'll just be outside –'

'Good idea,' interrupted Dr Palmer, waving her hand in the direction of the door.

He left studio three and headed down the hallway, deliberately not looking at the plasticized anatomical sculptures in the vaulted hall, and finally made his way past reception, out of the glass doors and into the fresh air.

He took several deep breaths to chase the nausea away. It took him a couple of minutes to be sure he wasn't going to throw up. It really wasn't the body on the slab that had done it – it was the surprise emotional kick in the guts.

… On the back seat in the booster chair. His son. Noah's head is gone from the bridge of his nose up. Just gone. There's hardly any blood on his pale cheeks. Somebody – mercifully – has draped a towel over the clean bisection. In his chubby little hands he's still holding an action figure.

It's an Avenger – the blue one with the round shield.

Boyd tried to focus on his shoes. On the laces and the scuff marks, on the gravel between the left and right foot. On *anything*. Anything to swipe that image away, back into its little box.

'Shit,' he whispered softly.

28

Half an hour later, the glass doors swung open and he heard footsteps on the gravel as Okeke approached him. 'You all right, guv?'

'Yeah. I'm good, thanks. I just had a bit of a moment back there.'

'We noticed.'

Boyd shook his head, disappointed with himself. 'Is she finished already?'

'She's taken some brain and liver samples to check for toxicology tests. She says the boy might have been drugged before being strangled, but she won't know until she gets the toxicology reports back. So she's wrapping up.'

'Right.'

'She did wonder if you needed a sit-down and a cup of tea or something before we go,'

He already felt like a complete idiot. A cup of tea and a biscuit actually sounded quite good – this was beginning to feel like a carb wobble. A sodding great big pastry with lashings of white icing slathered on top would be even better.

He sighed. 'Probably best we get going. Although, if there's somewhere to pull in and grab a coffee and something –'

'Sugary?' she asked, eyebrows raised.

He nodded. 'I'm thinking this might be a carb wobble.'

She smirked. 'Sure, if that's what we're calling this...'

'It is, Okeke,' he replied testily. 'I've done autopsies before.'

She dropped the bantering tone and gave him the benefit of the doubt. 'I get the carb-shakes too,' she replied. 'The trick is not to go crazy and eat ten Mars Bars. A banana will sort you out. Come on – I'll drive.'

Okeke found a decent-sized petrol station just round the corner and stopped to get them a coffee each, and a pot of sliced fruit for Boyd.

'No pastries?' he asked, feeling more than a little irritated as she handed the fruit over. 'You're as bad as bloody Emma. I don't need two mothers on my case.'

Okeke sighed, reaching into her jacket pocket and pulling out a solitary Snickers bar. 'There you go. But eat your fruit first,' she said, waving a finger at him.

'Jesus....' he said, grinning at the sight of the chocolate bar. 'Yes, Mum.'

As they pulled out of the forecourt, he was already tucking into the fruit pot.

'So this boy was holding the same kind of wooden figure as seen in the Martin case file photos,' began Okeke. 'Same MO and burial method as our Nike boy.'

'That's what I've started calling him,' Boyd muttered. 'The sooner we have a bloody name for him, the better.'

He finished the fruit and poured the juice left in the pot into his mouth and quickly fumbled to unwrap the Snickers bar. 'So... the take-away from the autopsy, Okeke?' His mouth was almost immediately full again.

'This one's a big lad,' she said. 'He may have been drugged first, so the killer could handle him, and then strangled and stabbed. This happened about four or five days ago. Then he was transported – most likely in a van or truck – and buried shortly after.'

She glanced at Boyd, happily chomping through his Snickers bar.

'So, four or five days... guv?' she repeated. 'If it was Martin, wouldn't he have been posing him? Taking more photos?'

'If he's still doing that twenty years later.' He looked at her.

'So it *could* be a copycat, then?' she said, adding smugly. 'I said that earlier.'

Boyd finished his mouthful. 'We found Nike Boy twelve days ago. It was in the news eleven days ago, so maybe he got spooked and got rid early. But it's not a copycat, Okeke – the carved figure, remember?'

'True. So... Leon Martin *is* alive, then,' she said.

'We'll see,' he replied. 'The sooner we get DNA results back on our new victim and the soldier, the sooner we'll know.'

'Keep in mind, guv, Leon Martin would have had a major compulsion to do what he did. That's something he'd have had to keep a lid on for twenty-plus years, if it was him.'

'Maybe he just wasn't caught. Most serial killers manage to go about their lives without alerting a scramble team of psychiatrists.'

She laughed. 'But they're still not wired up, right, are they? Most serial killers need two things. To be *able* to kill, and to have a *need* to kill. He wouldn't have been able to stop for that long would he?

'*To be able to kill, and to have a need to kill.* That's catchy. We should put it on a staff mug,' Boyd said drily. 'There are plenty of people who are able to kill, Okeke. Ex-soldiers for one. The need? Well, what's your choice? Anger? Resentment? Disenfranchisement? Revenge? Boredom?' He looked at her. 'Christ... wasn't that Dennis Nilsen's motive? *Boredom?*'

She shook her head. 'I don't think even he knew why he did what he did.'

Boyd's phone buzzed. He finished off the Snickers bar and ditched the wrapper in the passenger well.

'Boyd.'

'It's Warren, sir.'

'Ah. Did you manage to bag those flowers?'

'Yes, sir.'

'And?'

'They're with CSI right now. Kevin Sully's looking over the plastic wrapping for any possible fingerprints.'

'Was there a message card with it?'

'Yeah, but... I couldn't make out what was written on it. The ink's faded. Looks like it's been taped up there for a while, sir.'

Boyd nodded. 'Okay, we're on our way back.' He hung up.

'Well?' said Okeke.

'Well, we've got another bunch of flowers.'

29

Boyd assembled his team in the small conference room. The corridor outside was filled with the slamming and opening of doors, along with the disgruntled sighs and grumbles of Flack's small team relocating themselves from the Incident Room. Yet again.

'All right,' Boyd said, looking around the room at Minter, Okeke, Warren and O'Neal. Sully was also there, sitting in and ready to share his opinions on the forensics so far. 'We have an operation name – Weatherman.'

Boyd had Gratton's case file in front of him, opened so that the pictures from Leon Martin's macabre photo album were spread out across the conference table for all to see.

'For those of you who've just been roped in, this is the sum of the investigation back in 2001. Our murderer was dubbed the Ken Doll Killer by the red tops because of these photographs. They were found at his farmhouse. He'd been posing his male victims like dolls, so to speak… hence the name, courtesy of the *Sun*. You're all going to read the case file this afternoon, but I'll give you a potted synopsis to start you off.'

Boyd proceeded to give his team the bare bones of Gratton's

work: Leon Martin's background, from childhood to living alone on his parent's farm, and then on to Kristy Clarke's escape back in 2001. He went through Clarke's account of his abduction from the streets and his week-long incarceration, before being driven across to North Wales to die alongside Leon.

He then briefly covered the interviews and aftermath, including the discovery of Leon Martin's van with his clothes discarded on the passenger seat, the inspection of the farmhouse and surrounding outhouses by over a dozen uniformed officers, and only *then* – too late to preserve the integrity of the crime scene – the SOCOs.

Boyd paused to look round the table. For once there was no fidgeting or banter, and all eyes were firmly fixed on him.

Satisfied, he moved on to the body discovered in the A21 layby the week before, and the very recent victim found buried beside the A27, including the linking details about the carved figure and the flowers, and the message tag that had come with them. He closed the briefing with his interviews with delivery drivers Dave Mullen and Dave Webb and, of course, the interview with Kristy Clarke – the 'one that got away'.

'Both drivers were called Dave?' said O'Neal, looking at Warren out of the corner of his eye.

'Yes,' replied Boyd. 'Dave and Dave.'

'I think it's been a legal requirement since Brexit,' said Sully. 'Seriously, you're not allowed into France with a truck unless you're called Dave.'

Minter chuckled. 'My dad's called Dave,' he said. 'See, he could drive a truck quite legally.'

'I'm a Dave,' added Warren. 'Middle name.'

'I'm Dave,' said Sully, 'and so's my wife.'

Boyd rolled his eyes.

'Life of Brian, right?' said Minter.

Sully nodded. 'Well spotted, Dave.'

'It's *David* actually.' Minter grinned. 'Although I'll let you call me Davey if you buy me some chips.'

Okeke sighed loudly. 'Are we done... *boys*?'

Boyd pressed his lips together, suppressing a smile. 'Yes, you're quite right, Okeke. That's enough arsing about.' He settled back in his chair, raised his arms and cupped his hands behind his head. 'Okay, so then, that's where we're at. Let's deal with some of the theories.' He gazed up at the bland tiled ceiling. 'The way I see it, it boils down to the following two scenarios. Firstly... Leon Martin staged his suicide and has managed to evade capture for the last twenty-one years under a new identity. The second scenario is that our recent victim was abducted, killed and buried by either a copycat –' he glanced at Okeke – 'or more likely, an accomplice of Martin's.'

O'Neal raised his hand. 'I've got a question.'

Boyd nodded at him.

'What was the message written on the tag with the flowers?' he asked.

'Well, we need to keep something like this to ourselves. It doesn't get spaffed out to the press, okay? It doesn't leave this room. *Is that understood?*'

There was a chorus of agreement from the team.

'Right.' He read out the line.

'That sounds vaguely familiar,' said O'Neal. 'Is that from a song?'

Boyd looked at him incredulously. 'It's a line from a Beatles song, but I don't know whether it's meant to mean anything. It's one to ponder. Before we drill down into lines of enquiry... does anyone have any more thoughts?'

'Do we have any suspects, sir?' asked O'Neal.

'Not at this point. We do, however, have Kristy Clarke, who is the only person who could positively identify Martin if he is still alive today. He's also the only person who really got to know him. He's our best source of information at the moment.'

'What about either of the men who discovered the A21 body?' asked O'Neal.

'O'Neal again,' acknowledged Boyd. 'Someone's had their Weetabix this morning. Well, we know it's not unheard of for the guilty party to present themselves as having stumbled across the body and not known what they were dealing with... It gives them a valid reason as to why their DNA is present at the scene. So, yes, given the discovery of our most recent victim, I'm going to call them back in and get them swabbed and re-interviewed.'

'Do we have any evidence from 2001 that might suggest Leon had an accomplice, guv?' asked Okeke.

'Nothing that was flagged up,' Boyd said. 'Kristy Clarke was quite clear that Leon was acting entirely alone. In fact, in the interviews with the original SIO, he stated he thought coerced companionship was one of Leon's motives.' Boyd shrugged. 'He wanted a friend.'

'More like a pet lamb to the slaughter,' said Minter. 'Do we trust Kristy Clarke's account, boss?'

'We trust nothing, obviously. But...' Boyd spread his hands. 'The documented forensic evidence supports Clarke's account. His DNA was found at the farm. On Martin's parent's bed, on the shackles and in the back of Leon Martin's van. He was in pretty poor shape when he was discovered, and he had abrasions round his wrists from the shackles.'

'What about this case file?' said Okeke. 'Do we trust that? Didn't you say the forensics were a complete mess.'

'They were. It wasn't the SIO's fault; it's just the boots went in too early. They were turning the farm over, expecting to find other captives, or bodies. For that reason, we have to view the contents of this case file as helpful, but not the Holy Bible. Now we're scaled up to operation level, this is our case. We're the active force, and Cheshire are in a supporting role. So we're starting over. The old case file we can use to ink in any gaps, but, where we can, we're going to source. OK then... I'm going to parcel out some tasks. Minter?'

'Boss?'

'I want you to head up to Cheshire and dig into Leon Martin's childhood. Search through Cheshire's evidence archive; interviews with locals who might not have been interviewed at the time. What I'd really like is a better bloody photo of him. Also any possible clues as to what Martin's life would look like under an alias. If he couldn't tap whatever savings his parents left behind, he'd have to work. What was he qualified to do, other than drive?'

'Gotcha.'

'There's no good photo of him... anywhere?' asked Warren.

'We have one school end-of-term photo, and that's it. He's eleven in that and in the back row. It's no bloody good. The original SOCO free-for-all at Martin's farm recovered no family photos. It seems Leon made a pretty good job of burning almost everything there was about his parents and himself.'

Boyd turned to Okeke. 'You can go with him. We need whatever forensic samples Cheshire Constabulary have in their evidence archives back here so we can examine them again.'

'DNA work is twenty years better now than it was back then,' said Sully. 'And cheaper.'

'Quite,' agreed Boyd. 'Let's get everything we can off them, particularly anything that might still have Leon's DNA and that of his parents. We need to make sure they picked out the right profile from all the swabs they took to identify as his. Then we'll get a job lot of testing done at the EFS. Maybe they'll give us a discount with all the work we're giving them.'

He pictured Sutherland, disappearing meerkat-like down a burrow hole with the department cheque book clutched tightly in his little paws.

'Warren... I want you to continue work on ID-ing our A21 victim. I know you've done pretty well at whittling down the misper candidates. I reckon it's time to start doing some home visits.'

'Yes, sir.'

'Take Leon Martin's photos that show identifying marks and tattoos,' Boyd added. 'And a picture of the trainer too. The trainers were new when the victim died. Parents would remember things like that. If we can get an ID, we may get a clue as to where he was picked up by the killer. But, for God's sake, do it sensitively and take a family liaison officer with you. He's definitely a Martin victim in my book, so let's get his name.'

As Warren collected photos, Boyd turned to O'Neal.

'O'Neal, you're working our new body. We need to ID that as soon as possible. You've got a lot more to play with there. If there's a misper report, then it'll be recent. You've got DNA; our lad might just be on the NDNAD, or his fingerprints on PNC for something – you never know.'

O'Neal nodded. 'Yes, sir.'

There were the official roles to hand out too. 'Minter's my second and action log manager. O'Neal, you're exhibits officer. Okeke, forensics liaison with Sully and EFS.' He paused to look out through the glass wall at DCI Flack carrying out his Nespresso machine and gave him a cheeky wave.

Flack's hands were full, but Boyd suspected he'd have loved to reply with a middle finger.

30

'Sausage and chips, please.'

Boyd decided to take his lunch off the pier and down onto the shingle beach. It was a nice day today and he wanted to get his food as far away as possible from the circling gulls before they picked him out as a clueless tourist and descended on him like the pack of thugs they were. Plus, he wanted some headspace. He was well aware that half his team were scattered along the queue leading into the cafeteria.

He picked the point down the beach where high tide tended to shove the stones up into a steep ridge and plonked himself down. He pressed his coffee cup into the shingle so that it wouldn't tip over and started to pick at his chips, keeping one wary eye on the lookout for any feathered scrotes hovering nearby.

He set the carton of chips down between his feet, sheltered from prying eyes.

Stepping up to Operation Weatherman was going to attract press attention. Again. There were no two ways about it. The A27 body, so far, hadn't triggered much in the way of interest up to this point, simply because nobody had leaked (yet) that it was linked to the A21 bones and thus to the Ken Doll Killer.

But that was sure to happen, and sooner rather than later. Hatcher seemed happy to deal with the press this time round. And she was welcome to them.

The trick was keeping the toy soldier and the flowers out of the story. More importantly, the short message that had been left with the most recent flowers.

As for DNA... was there any chance at all that there'd be something still usable on the flowers O'Neal had been sent to grab from the A21 layby? It was far more likely that there'd be something on the A27 flowers and message tag that Minter had spotted, bagged and logged yesterday.

The question that Boyd kept asking himself was why the killer – for argument's sake, Leon Martin – had left them there. They were potentially a forensic gift and, if there were more bodies out there marked by the same thing, wasn't he in danger of flagging up where all his victims might be buried? It occurred to him that he only had to put out a press release asking everyone to check the next roadside shrine they saw for a card with that little message on it, and presumably within weeks they'd have located all his buried bodies.

And inspire hundreds of idiots to copy it as a prank, or post those words on Facebook as some macabre meme?

Maybe not, then. As with the first flowers, any card found would have had its message washed off long ago. And they couldn't very well promote the idea of taking flowers from what would probably be very real tributes to loved ones.

So, anyway, he dragged his thoughts back to the question: why leave the flowers? Was it an act of contrition? Was Martin saying sorry to his victims? Or was it an act of bravado? Leon Martin sticking two fingers up at them?

'Ah! I thought it was you.'

Boyd jumped at the sound of the voice just behind him and

looked round to see the woman he'd got into the habit of looking out for whenever he was walking Ozzie. The one with the dog. Only, her dog wasn't with her right now.

He started to get up, but the shingle clattered and shifted beneath his feet and he lost his balance. He dropped back down rather inelegantly onto one knee. The shifting stones knocked his paper cup over and his coffee drained away into the shingle.

'Bollocks,' he muttered.

'Oh, God, I'm so sorry,' she said. 'That was my fault sneaking up on you like that!'

He picked the cup up. There was a mouthful left in the bottom, which he swigged for some reason.

'Can I get you another?' she asked.

'No, it's fine,' he said. 'Not the greatest coffee in the world, truth be told.'

She smiled and looked up at the looming bulk of the pier. 'The pier café?'

'Yeah. But the chips on the other hand are –' He turned to gesture at the takeaway carton he'd set on the shingle, only to see a gull was already picking its way through it, tossing out chips that were still too hot.

'Oh, for fuck's sake!' Boyd took a step back towards his lunch and threw out his hands to scare it off. 'Yahhh!'

He was successful, but only after the second, closer, louder *yahhh*. The bird fluttered noisily, shedding feathers and dragging his carton a few feet across the stones before giving up and flapping away.

'They really think they own this town,' she said, her mouth quirking up at the corners.

'I'm beginning to think they actually do,' he said, picking up the scattered remains of his lunch.

'I really do owe you an apology,' she said. 'And some more chips.'

He gathered the greasy paper and cardboard, and left the food; already the sky above them was busy with noisy, hovering, curious gulls.

She pointed up the sloping beach to the White Rock Theatre. 'There's a nice café in there. Would you let me buy you a coffee and something warm?'

THE CAFÉ WAS CALLED the Sea View Lounge. A long, curved front balcony window above the grand and whitewashed Doric columns of the theatre's entrance looked out across the beach, the pier and the Channel.

It had the feel of the rear end of some vast cruise ship – the curved wall of windows, the view of the sea. The chandeliers.

'Very nice,' he said, as she returned with their order.

'They refurbished it during the lockdown. It was beginning to look a little tatty,' she said, setting the tray down on the table. 'Coffee in a porcelain cup, rather than a paper one. And a sausage sandwich.'

'That's very kind of you.'

She sat down. 'No problem. I keep bumping into you and telling you off. It's a peace offering.'

'It's not really needed, but thank you very much,' he said, spooning sugar into his coffee and stirring it.

She smiled. 'I'd hate to be thought of as some stuffy old cow who lectures people on how to walk their dogs.'

She definitely wasn't old, he thought; she looked a similar age to him. 'Well...' He spread his hands. 'Thanks again. I suppose we should introduce ourselves. I'm Boyd.'

'Boyd?' She nodded. 'I guess that's better than knowing you as the BBC-bleeped copper.'

'Really?' he said, surprised. 'I'm still known as that?'

She laughed. 'You earned a little social media fame there.' She offered him her hand. 'I'm Charlotte.'

He shook her hand. 'Where's your dog?'

'Mia? She's at home. I'm at work today.'

'Ah, where do you work?' he asked.

'Here,' she replied, smiling. 'I literally am *at work*. I'm the box office manager.'

He nodded. 'Right. That's ticket sales and booking shows and acts to put on?'

'Just ticket sales. Nothing so glamorous or exciting as booking anyone, I'm afraid. And you, Boyd...' She frowned. 'What is that? Hold on – have you just given me your surname?'

He nodded. 'Ah, yes. It's a bit of a habit, I'm afraid.'

'You do have a first name, I take it?' she asked.

'It's Bill.' He shrugged almost apologetically. 'William. Bill for short. But I never use it. It's a police thing, I suppose.'

'I presume your family don't call you Boyd?'

'My daughter calls me Dad. My dad calls me Son.' He shrugged. 'It's a name that just doesn't get used.' He smiled. 'It's going spare.'

'Presumably your wife....' She rolled her eyes. 'Sorry, I shouldn't say that these days, should I? Your *partner* doesn't call you Boyd, surely?'

'She didn't, no.'

Boyd could see a flush of awkwardness on her face. She busied herself pouring a little milk into her tea and stirring it.

He sipped his coffee and sneaked a look at his watch as he did so. It was just gone twenty to two. Another five minutes and he was going to have to make an exit. He took a bite out of his sausage sandwich.

'You've moved down to Hastings?' she half stated, half asked. 'I'm not getting a trace of a Sussex accent.'

'Is there one?' he asked, mouth full.

'Not really. Not any more. Some of the old boys up at the

fishing end still hang on to a bit. Some of the people who've lived here for generations still say *five pound* instead of *five pounds*.'

'I came down from London at the beginning of the year. What about you? Are you a Hastinian...?' One of his team had used the term. He was damned if he could remember it, though. 'That's right, isn't it?'

'Hastonian,' she corrected. She shook her head. 'I'm from Brighton originally. I'm a West Sussex girl, don't you know?'

The conversation lapsed for a moment, and she reached for her tea. Boyd noticed she sipped from the teacup in that pleasingly old-fashioned way – pinkie sticking out from the handle. It matched the genteel environment of the café, as if Charlotte was a part of it, a historical re-enactor brought in to add some authenticity to the place. Even the way she spoke was charmingly out-of-time, as if she'd stepped from the pages of some cosy Arthur Ransom novel.

'I'll have to try this place instead of the pub on the pier some time. It's like sitting aboard the *Titanic*,' said Boyd.

'Oh, I hope not. That wasn't a great success, was it?' She glanced at her watch. 'Oh crumbs, I'm really sorry, but I'm due back at work in five minutes. I'm going to have to take my tea with me and run.'

Boyd drained his coffee cup and stood up. 'Well, thanks again for this – you didn't need to,' he said as she followed suit and stood up too.

'I did,' she said, 'and it was my pleasure. I've enjoyed your company.'

'Me too,' Boyd found himself saying, a little surprised at himself. 'I guess I'll see you on the beach sometime?'

'Yes,' she said. 'See you on the beach.'

He left the café and was halfway back to the station before he realised he could have asked her for her number.

31

Home visits reminded DC Warren just how difficult it was to be a uniformed officer. He realised he didn't miss it at all. Being a uniform involved way too much general public, way too much shouting, way too much reasoning with stoned or drunken morons, and way too many difficult and sometimes emotionally draining conversations with complete strangers.

The previous home visit had been really tough: a boy had gone missing in the early nineties and left behind a mother who had been sucked dry of any will to live. Thirty years of unresolved grief and grinding hope had turned her into a prematurely old woman. Watching the hope flash on her face as they announced themselves on the doorstep, then slowly ebb away as they talked in her front room, had been like watching a slow death.

Mrs Dunn was the second on his list this morning.

She was a woman in her late fifties, short, slim and fidgety, the kind who seemed to have an endless reserve of nervous energy.

'Mrs Dunn?' said the uniformed sergeant beside him.

'Yes?'

'I'm Police Sergeant Gayle Brown and this is DC Warren. May we come in and have a little chat with you?'

'Is this about my Toby?'

She nodded. 'I'm afraid it is.'

Warren watched Mrs Dunn clench her eyes shut and guessed this was the scenario she'd been preparing herself for, for the last two decades.

'Can we come in, love?' Gayle asked.

Mrs Dunn backed up into the hallway and led them both into her front room.

'Take a seat, Mrs Dunn,' said Sergeant Brown.

'Right, y-yes... okay,' said Mrs Dunn, sitting down.

'You can call me Gayle,' said the sergeant, sitting down next to her. 'I'm a trained family liaison officer and DC Warren is with the CID. We've come to talk about your son who disappeared –'

'A long time ago.' Mrs Dunn finished the sentence for her. Warren guessed that she didn't want to be reminded about the number of years.

'Yes.' Sergeant Brown looked around. 'Now, is there anyone else home who could make us a nice cup of tea?'

Mrs Dunn shook her head.

'That's all right. I'll do that while my colleague has a chat with you. Would you like a cuppa?'

Mrs Dunn nodded quickly, then looked over at Warren. 'Are you here to tell me my Toby's...' Her voice hitched. 'Is it that body that was found on the A21 the other day?'

Warren took a deep breath. *Here we go.*

'It's a possibility, Mrs Dunn.'

Her head dipped down. He could see her narrow shoulders flexing and quivering. She was crying silently into her hands. Sergeant Brown had warned him in the patrol car on the way over that this would probably happen.

Warren watched the silent crying, not sure whether to let her finish before asking his questions, or try to find a moment to jump in.

Brown came back into the lounge, presumably to ask about milk and sugar, when she saw the woman's shuddering shoulders and head in her hands, and Warren looking completely unsure as to how to continue.

She squatted down beside Mrs Dunn and rubbed her back softly. 'That's okay. That's okay.'

'Please say you don't know it's Toby,' Mrs Dunn said, sobbing through her hands.

'We think it could be a possibility,' replied Sergeant Brown. 'But we need to be sure.'

'Should I make the tea?' asked Warren.

Brown looked over her shoulder at him and nodded.

Warren got up and found his way to the kitchen and, after opening a number of cupboards, found all that he needed. Five minutes later, he returned to the lounge to find Mrs Dunn dabbing at her eyes with a balled-up tissue.

'There you go,' said Warren. 'Milk, and I put some sugar in too.'

Mrs Dunn accepted the mug from him with a grateful nod.

Brown had pulled up a chair in front of the sofa for Warren, while she sat beside Mrs Dunn. 'I've explained that you need to ask her some questions. And that you have some photographs you need to show her,' she said to him.

Warren nodded. His mouth felt dry; his throat, tight. He hated how nerves made his voice go a little higher than normal. 'Mrs Dunn,' he began, 'the body we found last week dates from about twenty years ago and the forensic people have estimated the age as between seventeen and twenty.'

She nodded. 'Seventeen. That was how old Toby was when he left us. The police weren't interested. No one was interested. We'd had a few rows over silly things. He was in with a bad crowd. He'd been gone for a few weeks before, so they said he was probably just annoyed and would be in touch when he calmed down. Anyway, he was old enough to do what he wanted.'

'Right,' said Warren. 'I think that was a pretty common view back then. It's not a lot better these days, to be honest.'

Delicately. Do this delicately.

'Well, we have reason to believe the, uh... the body we discovered *could* be your son, because the apparent age and the timeline fits.' He opened the folder and pulled out an A4 print of one of the pictures found in Leon's Martin's album. The image had been cropped to show just the bit he needed her to see.

It was a photograph of a Nike trainer that matched the one unearthed from the A21 layby. It was pictured from the side, a foot perched casually on top of the other knee – a lad's way of sitting cross-legged. Warren turned it round so the image of the trainer was standing up.

'I know this is hard, and a long time ago, but... did Toby have new trainers before he went missing?'

She leant forward and studied the image carefully. 'He had trainers...' she replied. 'That's all he wore on his feet, love.'

'Nikes?'

She pulled a face. 'We never could afford those. I bought his things from Woolworths.' Her expression of grief-tinted hope began to fade.

'All right. Let's just try one more...'

He pulled out another photo . A cropped close-up of a hand. A hand holding a Twix-branded Easter egg mug.

'The mark next to the knuckle of the index finger,' began Warren, 'we believe is a tattoo.'

Her face changed. Her eyes widened. 'It is.'

'You recognise that?'

She nodded. 'Silly boy did that at school. A DIY tattoo with a compass and some pen ink. He got sent home for doing it.' She shook her head and managed a little barked laugh. 'And it got infected. He was such a handful. Is it him? It's him, isn't it?' She dissolved into tears again.

'Okay, Mrs Dunn. Thank you.' Warren gently took the photo from her lap and let Brown comfort her.

Almost done. A nod for the tattoo was a win, but Warren wanted this over with. *What the fuck. This is un-fucking pleasant.* He felt like a fraud, like a kid in grown-up police clothes and, at any moment, the adults around him were all going to tell him to go back to playing GTA on his PlayStation.

Brown nodded at him that he should probably get on with it.

'It doesn't look as though the body we found was your Toby, Mrs Dunn. But, from the tattoo you identified today, I'm so sorry to tell you that we do believe that he is dead. We believe he was killed by Leon Martin.'

The name didn't seem to trigger a reaction from her. Warren knew that his nickname was better known. 'The Ken Doll Killer?' he added.

Her eyes widened ever so slightly. 'Oh... God... the man who....'

Yes, Mrs Dunn. I'm afraid so.'

Her eyes darted down to the blank backs of the printouts he held in his hand. 'No. No. No.... Oh, please...'

Warren shoved them back into his folder. 'Okay, Mrs Dunn. It's okay.'

'I want to see,' she said, her voice steely.

Warren looked at her. She had tears streaming down her face, but her eyes were certain.

'Do you have a picture of his face? I need to see it's him. You owe me that,' she added.

Shit. I can't do this.

Warren leant forward and took her hand. 'I want to assure you, Mrs Dunn, these images are... They're not...'

What the fuck word do I use? Gory? Bloody?

'They're not upsetting. To be honest, they just look like they're sleeping. Are you certain you want to do this?'

She nodded and whispered, 'But they are *dead*?'

'I'm afraid they are.'

She chewed her lips, swallowed several times and took a deep breath. She finally held out one shaking hand. 'Okay.'

Warren pulled a sheet of paper out and turned it over. As he handed it to her, he saw the last traces of hope drain from her face.

She had picked out her son instantly. Her face had gone ashen – he'd heard that expression a billion bloody times before, but today he'd actually seen it for the first time. The blood had visibly drained from her face as she pointed at picture six and then backed away from it as though it was toxic.

'It's him,' she whispered. 'That's him. That's Toby.'

~

THEY LEFT the house forty-five minutes later, after a friend had been called round to sit with Mrs Dunn. By the time they had both politely excused themselves, she had regained her composure enough to thank them for bringing her the closure she'd been waiting so long for.

'I'll be back in touch tomorrow,' said Sergeant Brown, as they stepped out onto the front-door step, 'to see if there's anything I can do for you.'

The door closed behind them and they walked down the path to their patrol car. As they reached the gate, Warren glanced back and caught one last glimpse of Mrs Dunn through the front bay window as she sat down in the lounge with her friend and began the long and lonely process of grieving.

'First time you've had tears like that?' Gayle asked, as she closed the gate behind them.

Warren nodded.

'You handled it well, love,' she said.

He felt emotionally drained. The relief washed over him as he climbed back into the car and plugged in his seat belt.

32

Gaining access to Cheshire Constabulary's evidence archive had required a carefully handled courtesy call from Her Madge to their Chief Super. And a lot of pleases and thank-yous from Minter and Okeke as he ushered them resentfully down into the bowels of the HQ building in Winsford.

'Because we've actually kept this investigation listed as inactive rather than closed,' he said pointedly, 'it's not gone across to the evidence warehouse.' He looked at Minter. 'We've kept it close to hand.'

Minter nodded. 'Good to hear, sir.'

'Word is that you've got a new one?'

Minter nodded again.

'Leon Martin?'

Boyd had given Minter a briefing before they'd set off, which basically amounted to *tell the buggers as little as possible.* If he was concerned about leaks in his own team, he was doubly concerned about leaks from a force that were being asked to surrender control of an unresolved case.

The Chief Super lingered as the evidence officer signed

them in. 'Try and be mindful,' he said, 'we had our hands full with post 9/11 wild goose chases back then. It was every pair of hands on deck. So, it's not like Mike Gratton and his team just casually wrapped things up, you know. It looked as though Martin was dead and we had bigger fish to… fry… catch, whatever the damned expression is.'

'I understand, sir,' said Minter.

'Right. Well, I'll leave you in Karl's very capable hands. Anything else you need…?' He left that hanging in a such way that it could have been followed with either 'give me a shout' or 'you can go fuck yourselves'.

Minter and Okeke nodded and chorused, 'Thank you, sir.'

Karl led them down an aisle of wire-frame cages. He unlocked one and handed them each a pair of forensics gloves. 'I've not received a compliance request form to allow you to take anything away with you,' he said gruffly.

'Yet,' said Okeke. 'That'll come.'

Karl stared down at her defiantly. 'Until I do get one, you can look, but it all stays right here, sweetheart.'

He turned and walked off, presumably back to his desk.

She watched him leave and tutted. 'Sweetheart? What bloody decade did he just emerge from? Twat.'

Minter chuckled. 'Been watching too much *Life On Mars*, eh?'

She shook her head and sighed. 'C'mon, we'd better get started. This is gonna take a while.'

The wire cage was large enough to store a small car. It was packed with cardboard evidence boxes sealed with signed and dated tape. Okeke and Minter were here with a very specific wish list from Boyd: a better photograph of Leon Martin, preferably one taken when he was older than eleven, and any personal items of his, or his parents, that had been bagged and tagged at the farmhouse and not messed around with since.

The box contents were all marked 'Miscellaneous from Martin Property – >> 23/08/01'.

'OK.' Minter checked his watch, then looked with dismay at the piles of boxes in front of them. 'Well, it's four o'clock...'

'It's going to be a late one.' Okeke let out a long sigh.

He swiped his hands together. 'We'll treat this like a Secret Santa, okay? You open one, and I'll open one, and we'll see what we see – how's that?'

Minter picked the nearest, scored the tape with his car keys and peeled it off. He pulled back the cardboard flaps and peered inside while Okeke opened another box beside him.

He found himself looking at a row of box files. The labels on the side of the boxes all read: 'Basement Contents – misc photos.'

He checked inside one of the files and caught a glimpse of the endless images Leon Martin had taken and printed. Some of them appeared to have been snipped from larger images. It looked as though Leon had been removing any bits of the image that weren't picture perfect – the parts of his victim models that were too discoloured with dried subdermal blood to make the albums. Minter checked the other box files – they contained more of the same.

He moved the whole lot to one side. 'The boss will want these bringing back,' he said.

'I'll let you explain that to Mr Happy,' replied Okeke.

'What have you got?'

'Parents' clothes by the look of it.' She pulled out a flowery blouse sealed in a plastic bag. 'Shall we take some of it for familial DNA?'

'Worth a try,' said Minter.

'It all seems to have been laundered though,' Okeke said. 'And they died ten years or so before. I'm sure there'll be richer pickings elsewhere.'

'Toiletries are good for touch DNA samples,' said Minter. 'Hairbrushes, toothbrushes, that kind of stuff.'

She stood up straight and looked at him, her head slightly tilted to one side. 'Really? I never thought of that...'

'What?' he asked, opening up another box and lifting the flaps.

She rolled her eyes. 'Nothing,'

Inside the box he found a pile of junk mail. He checked the box's contents description: 'Misc papers/junk mail, hallway/kitchen.' Minter found himself looking at envelopes with plastic windows addressed to J. Martin, Mrs A. Martin, Mr and Mrs J. Martin, 'The Owner' even, but nothing specifically for Leon.

It was entirely possible that Leon Martin just hadn't come to the attention of the junk-mail beast yet. He wasn't that old. Had never lived on his own at this point, if his parents were of a mind to home-school him, then arguably they'd be the kind to give him little independence. No credit card. No phone,

Mr and Mrs Martin had created a ghost out of their son.

'Oh, for God's sake!'

Okeke pulled out a large forensics bag that contained the contents of a bathroom cabinet. She studied them through the plastic. 'There's medicine bottles, toothbrushes, flannels....'

'All thrown in together?'

'Uh-huh.'

Minter tutted. 'Got a proper little cross-contamination party going on in there. That's really shitty bagging.'

'I *know*,' she said, before she could stop herself.

'If it's one bag, that means it's all been logged under one evidence number.'

She stared wide-eyed at him. 'I *know*!'

'We'll take it anyway,' said Minter. 'EFS should be able to unpack the separate genetic profiles.'

She shot him another look.

'You all right?' asked Minter.

'I would be if you could stop mansplaining basic forensics to me,' she muttered.

'I'm just pointing out where they were sloppy, Okeke.'

'I know they were sloppy. It doesn't need pointing out... Oh, whatever. I'll just keep my forensics degree to myself – don't mind me.'

Minter grinned and winked. 'You make it too easy, Okeke,' he said, before delving into the box once again.

She flicked a V sign at his back. A little childish, she conceded, but satisfying all the same.

Minter had resumed picking through the old envelopes. There was so much of this stuff. They weren't going to get back to Hastings until at least ten, and then they'd have to log everything in before going home – presuming, of course, they won the fight to take it away from Karl in the first place. They were both going to be at the Hastings station until gone midnight.

He sifted through another handful of letters and was about to offer Okeke a coffee to make amends, when he struck gold.

33

Boyd had wanted to have the update meeting before going to give Sutherland a briefing, but the round-faced little bugger had decided to invite himself along and had turned up unannounced. He'd brought a family tin of Quality Street 'for the team', which he claimed he'd picked up on the way into work, but, suspiciously, it was already unsealed. Boyd suspected the tubby little sod had been dipping for the good ones already.

'All right – let's get this started,' Boyd announced.

The long table in the Incident Room now had eight people sat round it and was starting to look crowded.

'Let's discuss progress from the last couple of days.' Boyd looked down at his notes. 'Minter? How did it go up north?'

'Useful.' Minter had a slim cardboard folder in his hands. 'We've now got a decent adult picture of Leon Martin to work with.' He opened the folder and pulled out a blown-up print of a young man.

'This is him aged twenty-five. I found an opened envelope from the DVLA in the junk mail from 2001. And a letter for a replacement plastic licence.' He grinned. 'We got very lucky.

The correspondence indicated he'd lost his paper licence in June and was after a replacement. The plastic photo ID cards had come in by then.'

Minter rounded the table, approached the whiteboard and tacked the photograph on to it. 'His plastic licence had gone, but the reference number was there. I got DVLA to dig out the original application and scan the passport photo he sent.'

He returned to his seat and sat down.

'Good job, Minter.' Boyd studied the young face on the whiteboard. 'So he'd be forty-six now. If he's alive. We need to have that picture aged up.'

Sutherland finished chomping on a chocolate and said, 'We should get one of our digital forensics boys to play around with it.'

'What? You mean throw a beard on it in Photoshop?' Sully queried sarcastically.

Sutherland looked at Sully. 'I meant edit the photo to look a bit older,' he clarified.

Sully rolled his eyes. 'So yes, then.' He shook his head, then aimed his comments Boyd's way. 'You need proper forensic treatment. Bone structure changes with age, as well as soft tissue distribution. I suggest you use EFS; they've got some very good digital media nerds over there.'

'How much is *that* going to cost?' asked Sutherland.

Sully shrugged. 'Not my problem. I'm just passing on my informed opinion.'

Boyd nodded. 'We can put it on the tab, can't we, sir?'

Sutherland folded his arms grumpily. 'Why not? I mean it's only money, right?'

'Okay.' Boyd scribbled that down as an action point for himself. 'Thanks for that. Okeke, any luck on finding us some swab candidates?'

She nodded. 'We found toiletries that dated back to when Mrs Martin was still alive. There was a roll-on deodorant for women. I'm hoping the rollerball may have traces of Arlene Martin on it still. There's an old-fashioned shaving set that I presume John Martin used. So we may get some touch DNA from that. The problem is....'

She produced a photo she'd taken of the evidence bag. 'This is how I found it, all in one bag.'

Boyd's jaw dropped. 'Seriously?'

''Fraid so, guv. They had uniforms, not SOCOs, bagging things up there. So, there's going to be a bit of everyone on everything. Leon Martin, possibly some of his victims if he allowed them to use the bathroom and clean themselves, traces of Mum and Dad.'

'So that can go to EFS too,' said Boyd. 'Let's get a cast list of DNA profiles going, then we can try and verify who's who. Cross-reference them with any samples taken and attributed in the original investigation.'

Sutherland consoled himself by grabbing another chocolate from the tin.

'Warren? Do you want to tell your good news?'

Warren's triumphant grin made him look about twelve. 'Yes, sir. We've got an ID for one of Martin's victims.' He glanced down at his notes. 'Toby Joseph Dunn. Reported missing in 1999 by his mum. They had a difficult relationship. He was a bit of a handful apparently. He was a low-priority misper because he was a repeat runaway. His mum said she thought he might have gone to London, because he was always going on about it being the place to be.'

'How was the home visit?'

'Not easy, sir.'

Boyd nodded. 'Those kind of visits aren't. I hear it was pretty hard work with Dunn's mother?'

Police Sergeant Gayle Brown answered for him. 'She was distraught, sir. Very. Understandably. That was a really tough one.' She nudged Warren's arm like a proud mum bigging up her little boy. 'But this young man handled it very well.' If she could have got away with pinching one of his cheeks, Boyd suspected she probably would have.

'Good job, Warren,' he said.

'Thanks, sir.'

Boyd looked at O'Neal. 'How are you getting on with the A27 body?'

'He's Stephen Wooten, aged sixteen,' O'Neal answered. 'He was involved in a burglary and got a suspended. His family home is in Southend, Essex. He was a misper logged with the Met late last year... Lemmesee...' He leafed through some notes and found what he was looking for. 'Yeah, he made a call home a few months later from a Manchester-based number. So, I reckon he was roughing it up there over the last few months. I don't know *when* he was picked up by the killer – got to be recently, right?'

'And deposited shortly after death,' added Boyd. 'Which suggests to me that our chap decided to get rid of him quickly.'

'Boyd?' Sutherland balled up a handful of sweet wrappers and tossed them into the tin. 'Do you think our killer got spooked again?'

'Like Leon Martin's hasty exit back in 2001, you mean?

Sutherland nodded. 'Yes... if we're going with the supposition that this could be Leon Martin, then we know he's prone to panicking.'

Boyd shrugged. 'Assuming it's Martin, then yes, maybe. He could have caught something on the news and decided to get rid quickly.'

'Or maybe Stephen Wooten was too much for him?' offered Okeke.

'Good point,' said Boyd, nodding. 'Wooten was big for his age. If he's got previous form, then maybe he was no shy wallflower either.' He glanced at Sutherland. 'If we continue with the supposition that our killer's Leon Martin, then he's forty-six now. It's possible Martin landed too big, too difficult, a fish for him to cope with.'

'Suggesting Leon Martin's small?' asked O'Neal.

'Not necessarily. He could be unwell, unfit. He's not young any more,' said Boyd.

'Do we have any contact DNA from Wooten?' asked Sutherland. 'Skin under the nails, that sort of thing?'

'They've taken finger swabs,' said Boyd, glancing at Sully who mouthed, *Not yet*. He made a note to chase up Dr Palmer at EFS for the results. They'd had twenty-four hours now. 'We'll find out.'

'What about those flowers?' asked Sutherland. 'And the handwritten message along with them. You felt like there may be mileage in those last time you briefed me.'

'Yeah... on the *old* flowers, the ones at the A21 layby, we've got nothing. No DNA on the cellophane wrapping or the message tag. But that's been out there in all the elements for God knows how long, so no surprises there. I'm also waiting for EFS to let us know with the A27 flowers. If we get a profile, then the first thing we'll do is cross-reference it with the stuff Okeke picked up. But we also can run it through the NDNAD and see if our man has left any trace of himself at a crime scene over the years.'

'If we get a match off that with any of the farmhouse profiles,' said Sutherland, 'then this really is Leon Martin.'

Boyd nodded. 'That would be the most likely conclusion.'

'In which case, guv,' said Okeke, 'should we talk to Kristy Clarke some more?' She reached across the table, pulled the tin of sweets away from Sutherland and dipped her hand in.

'If we bag Martin, boss... sounds like we're going to need Kristy Clarke's help, not just in visually ID-ing him, but maybe even his help before we interview him. He's the only person who really knows Martin,' added Minter.

Boyd nodded.

'And the message?' Sutherland reminded him.

'If we get our hands on a chargeable suspect, then, yes, graphology comparisons will help build a base for CPS,' Boyd said

'No, I mean the actual words. I know you want to keep that to your team... but look –' he held his hands out like Oliver Twist asking for more – 'I'm not going to run to the *Sun* with it. Plus, for Chrissake... I *am* your boss.'

There were a couple of sniggers at that, which came from the direction of Sully and Okeke.

Boyd glared at them, then shrugged. 'It looks like a song lyric, or a line from a poem.' He looked down at his notes. 'The lonely people slip aside, in the ground, their time to hide.'

34

'Ellessey Forensics. Good afternoon. How can I help you?' answered a male voice.

'It's DCI William Boyd, from Sussex CID,' said Boyd.

'Ah, yes. And how are you, Detective Chief Inspector?'

Boyd was almost certain, from the tone of his voice, that it was the same receptionist who had annoyed him on his first visit.

'Fine,' he said tersely. 'Can you put me through to someone in photographic forensics?'

'Of course,' came the silky reply. 'Would that be our *digital media* forensics department?'

'If that's what you lot call it, then yes... Please,' he added as an afterthought.

Boyd was treated to ten seconds of lift music, just long enough to have Lady Gaga lodged in his head like a splinter for the rest of the afternoon, then...

'Phil McNeil, digital media forensics team. How can I help?'

Boyd introduced himself again.

'Ah... you're the policeman that BBC Southeast had to bleep

out a few months ago – right?'

'Yes.' Boyd sighed. 'That's going to end up etched on my gravestone, I suspect.'

He heard McNeil chuckle. 'How can I help you, DCI Boyd?'

'Are you able to do some digital trickery on an old photograph?'

'I should think so. What sort of trickery are you after? Do you want it cleaning up?'

'No.' Boyd had no idea what the technical terminology was for it. 'I have a passport photograph of a man aged twenty-five and I'd like it aged up to look forty-six. Is that possible?'

'Ah, yes. You're talking about progressed skull morphology,' McNeil replied.

'Am I?' Boyd said. 'I'll have to take your word for that, I'm afraid.'

'Well, yes, unless you want to just download one of those phone apps that lets you take a selfie and then adds a few wrinkles and blemishes to your photo.'

'Nope. We're a bit more savvy than that over here,' Boyd lied – it had actually crossed his mind.

'Good to hear it. You see, the shape of a face changes dramatically from your mid-twenties into old age,' explained McNeil, even though Boyd hadn't invited him to. 'That's the bone tissue reshaping more than anything else, plus there's also the downward drift of fatty tissues and facial muscle atrophy.'

Boyd absently picked up his unused iPhone and gazed at his own reflection in the dark screen as McNeil continued.

'Gravity and age gradually pull everything downwards, like wax melting very slowly. Which, of course, is where plastic surgery can help out and move the soft tissues back upwards. But, really, the battle you're fighting is against the bone tissue. For example, the orbital sockets widen vertically, which makes the eyes look more sunken; it gives the brow ridge a raised sort of "permanently surprised" look to it.'

Boyd examined his brow ridge. It didn't seem like that to him – quite the opposite, in fact; it was lowered, grumpy-looking and not at all surprised by anything these days.

McNeil was still delivering an unsolicited TED talk. 'The lower jaw bone also begins to get narrower, making the teeth by contrast look larger and the chin point more pronounced. We call this the "witch" effect and –'

'Right,' Boyd said loudly. 'Phil, I'm sorry to interrupt. As I said, I have a passport photo, so it's small – can you work with just that?'

'Mmmm... probably,' McNeil replied. 'If it's not too blurred or degraded. We can use software to increase the image size and work at the age-rendering from there. Scan the picture and send it over to me via email. You'll get to me with P-McNeil-at-Ellessey-Forensics-dot-com. I can take a look and see if it's good enough to work with.'

'Okay, great. How long will it take?'

'A few hours – hopefully no longer.'

'To age it up or to let me know my photo's too shit to use,' asked Boyd.

McNeil took a moment to respond. 'The first one. I'll let you know immediately whether it's no good.'

Boyd checked the time; it was just after two. And it was Friday. 'If I send them over now, do you think you'll get something back to me before end of play today?'

'I'll give it my best shot.'

'Otherwise it's the weekend and you know... crime doesn't take weekends off.' Boyd realised he was pushing his luck. 'It would be great if you could.'

'I'll do what I can,' said McNeil. 'No promises, though.'

'Could you give me aged-up images with and without facial hair, too? Different types of hair, that sort of thing?'

'Indeed. I can give you a clown nose, if you like.'

Boyd decided he'd ignore that last comment.

McNeil continued smoothly. 'I presume this is going on Sussex Police's currently open contract? Contact... DSI Sutherland?'

'No. It's a gift for a young friend of mine,' Boyd said, unable to resist.

'What?' McNeil sounded confused and flustered. 'We don't do –'

'I'm joking!' cut in Boyd. 'Yes, please. Sutherland's the one you want to shake down for money.'

There was a pause. 'Send me the images, Boyd. I'll see what I can do,' McNeil said in a slightly clipped tone.

Boyd hung up. *Grumpy arse.*

BOYD SPENT the remainder of the day reviewing the investigation's action log from the very beginning – his review of the A21 grave alongside Sully, interviewing the two truckers who had found the first body, the post-mortem on the bones, interviewing DCI Gratton...

That made him stop for a moment.

It had been over a week since he'd visited Gratton. He wondered how the poor bastard was doing. He'd said he didn't have much longer to go – *weeks*, if he recalled correctly. Boyd wondered if he was still in a fit state to take a phone call. Not that Gratton needed anything from him, but he could call to update him out of courtesy.

Boyd took out his phone and thumbed the screen to access his recent calls list. He found the number for the hospice in Boston where Gratton was at. But then, thumb hovering over the number, he changed his mind.

The truth was, they had a new body, and more than a chance it was one of Leon Martin's. So far they'd managed to keep Martin out of the news, but he wouldn't put it past

Gratton to have joined up the dots. It was probably the last thing that Gratton would want confirming – that he'd let Martin slip away to carry on his work, years later and in another part of the country. That wasn't really news you wanted to go out on, was it? For something like that to be your legacy?

'Hello-o? Guv? Anyone in there?'

He stirred from his thoughts. Minter and Okeke were standing a few feet from his desk, pulling their coats on and getting ready to leave.

'Sorry, what was that? Were you talking to me?' he asked.

'Yes. I asked whether you're joining us for a pint down at the pier?' Okeke pointed at the wall clock. It was half five already.

'It's Friday, and it's finally thank-fuck-o'clock,' added Minter.

Boyd closed down the action log and signed himself out of his LEDS account. Monday would roll around all too quickly and by then, hopefully, Phil McNeil would have played around with whatever funky software he had and sent an aged-up image of Martin for them to look at.

A quick after-work pint sounded good. Anyway, Emma was going to be out again with Daniel tonight. At another gig.

'All right,' he said. 'Just the one, or I'll be walking home again.'

He got up and sent Emma a text to let her know he was having a drink with the troops, grabbed his jacket, then reached for the mouse to log himself out of his computer.

There was an email in his inbox.

From McNeil.

'You coming, sir?'

He looked up to see Warren and O'Neal passing by his desk. Both young men were heading out for a pint too. Okeke and Minter were just leaving the Incident Room, keen to start their weekend.

'Go on,' he called out. 'I'll catch you lot up.'

Boyd clicked on the email.

DCI Boyd

This is preliminary render based on the best of the image you sent of the passport-style photo. You say he was mid 20s in this image. So this is a rough render of how he'd look aged 45 to 46. I'll do another more thorough version next week.

Regards,

Phil McNeil

There, beneath the message, was a middle-aged Leon Martin. His face had been rounded slightly. The cheeks a little fuller, the jaw line heavier. The pale skin ever so slightly mottled with a suggestion of age-related blemishes and florid blood vessels. The neck had been made slightly thicker and the mop of wavy hair from the original photo had been trimmed back to a generic short haircut. McNeil had gone with no facial hair for this first draft render.

Boyd stared at the image for a solid minute. Leon Martin at forty-six looked entirely forgettable. That could be the face of an estate agent, a plumber, an accountant, a driving instructor... or a serial killer. A monster with an everyday face and a chirpy 'good morning' for his neighbours and work colleagues.

Boyd felt vaguely disappointed with the result. He wondered whether McNeil really had used his fancy-pants software – or just a cheap and cheerful Snapchat filter that he was passing off as something more technical and forensic. The rendered face looked so generic that Boyd honestly would have believed the latter.

'Sod it,' he said, closing the image file and logging off. He hoped that on Monday he'd get a better-quality rendering. And then... they could experiment with hairstyles and facial hair.

35

Boyd didn't race to catch up with them. He had a text from Emma, reminding him that she was off out with Dan, that there was a meal sitting in the fridge for him, and that Ozzie had been fed, walked and pooped and would be good for a couple of hours.

She ended her message with 'have fun with your mates' and a kiss.

Boyd finally met up with his team inside the Bier Garden. He saw Jay, Okeke's other half, was there at the bar, getting the drinks in. The rest – Okeke, Minter, Warren, O'Neal and a few other CID staff from the main floor – had commandeered a couple of tables and were chatting away. He just hoped that none of his team were going to spill the words of that poem or any other information from the case.

He wandered over to join them. 'Evenin' all.'

He was greeted by a chorus of 'guvs' and 'sirs' and over the noise he heard Okeke shouting that Jay was getting him a pint of lager.

Boyd nodded, then decided, since he was still standing, to give Jay a hand. He approached him from behind and slapped his hand on Jay's back between two muscular shoulder blades.

'Been a while, Jay.'

Jay turned round, beaming at the sight of Boyd. 'Boss!'

'I'm not your boss, remember?' he replied, though he couldn't help grinning. 'Just Boyd is good. How's things with you, big man?'

Since the Nix case (when Okeke's boyfriend had quite literally saved his life) Boyd hadn't actually seen him. He'd heard about Jay pretty much every day, however. Okeke talked about him as though he was a large, doting Saint Bernard. One who needed constant walkies and the odd bit of house-training.

'Good. Yeah. Still throwing drunk gits out of night clubs. Pays the bills more regularly than upcycling does.'

Jay had his own little business buying job lots of old furniture from house clearances, sanding them down and polishing them up for resale.

'Hey, Boyd,' he said. 'Sam tells me you're chasing down a serial killer.'

Boyd raised a finger to his lips. The pub was pretty noisy; with an old Kylie Minogue track and the noise coming from their group, it wasn't as if Jay had bellowed it out in a quiet library. But all the same...

'Yeah,' he replied softly. 'Although she *really* shouldn't have told you.'

He made a mental note to have a quiet word with Okeke about work talk at some point. Undoubtedly most of the force shared the worst parts of their working day with their partners, but they weren't supposed to. After their last big case when both Jay and Emma had been not just informed but involved, he supposed it was going to be a little trickier to enforce.

'Apparently he poses them like dolls? Is that true?'

'Sorry, Jay,' Boyd replied. 'Can't comment – and definitely *don't* repeat that, for God's sake!'

'Oh, right. Fair enough,' Jay said, unperturbed. The drinks started arriving on the bar. 'Oh, and some nuts, please, mate,' he said, fishing in his pocket for his wallet.

'I'll give you a hand,' said Boyd, carefully grabbing three pint glasses.

He plonked them into the middle of the table for his colleagues to figure out whose drinks they were and returned to the bar.

Jay was in the process of tapping his card.

'So, Boyd,' he said, finishing up and tucking his wallet away. 'Did you ever hear any more from those...' He raised his eyebrows and did a comedy left-and-right peek, before mouthing, *Russians*

At least he hadn't blurted the word out, Boyd thought. As far as he was concerned, it wasn't his job to whistle-blow on dirty money entering the country. To be honest, it seemed to be coming in from all directions now, and he wouldn't be surprised if the vast majority of career-focused MPs in Westminster weren't turning a blind eye and waving it in themselves.

Anyway, as that parcel had made abundantly clear, the Russians knew where he lived.

Boyd kept his face neutral. 'Nope,' he lied.

'They left you all alone, huh? That's good, mate. That's good.'

Boyd nodded. 'It's all in the past, Jay. Case closed, as we coppers like to say.'

Between them they managed to deliver the remaining drinks and nuts to the table and slot themselves into an ongoing, frank and noisy exchange of views about the latest *Love Island* goings on.

At the bottom of his pint, Boyd's resolve held firm and he politely excused himself from the increasingly noisy pub. The after-work drinkers were gradually being replaced by the younger and louder pre-club drinkers, and Boyd didn't fancy *walking* up the East Hill tonight.

He returned to the police station, picked up his car and drove home.

His headlights shone into the tall bay window of his lounge, picking out Ozzie on sentry duty. By the time Boyd had locked the car and come in through the front door, Ozzie was sitting tidily in the hallway, thwacking his tail noisily on the floorboards with a face that was almost certainly saying, *Standing on the back of the sofa? Nope! No, sir, not me.*

36

On Saturday morning Boyd woke up to the sight of a dark wet nose twitching inches away from his face. A nose dimpled, dark and shiny, like a quivering liquorice allsort.

Boyd focused on the rest of Ozzie's muzzle, then his face. Two determined eyes stared back at him, willing him impatiently to get out of bed.

'All right, Ozzie. I get the message.'

He got up and ran a hand through his hair. It was months since he'd last had a haircut and it was starting to look as though he was *trying* to grow it long. He vowed to get it sorted out this weekend.

Short back and sides, please. And don't spare the horses.

He wandered over to the bay window and looked out. Below he could see Daniel's blue transit van parked in front of his Renault. They must have come back after he'd gone to bed. Very quietly too.

Bless 'em.

Ozzie thumped down off the bed and onto the floor, his claws clacking on the floorboards. He nosed the door open and disappeared out into the hallway, intent on showing Boyd the way downstairs to the kitchen where his breakfast needed serving.

Boyd took the less-than-subtle hint and got dressed.

Downstairs he made a quick black coffee for himself and fed the dog, then put on Ozzie's car harness for a drive down to the seafront and a walk along the beach.

At nine on a Saturday morning, along Pelham Place, the car park was still half empty but filling up. By eleven it would be full. Boyd parked his car facing out to sea.

He unstrapped Ozzie, hooked him up to the extender lead and let him scramble out. 'All right, all right,' he muttered, hanging on to the lead, checking he had the car's key card and patting his back pocket for poo bags at the same time.

He made sure the car had locked, then took several steps across the tarmac, across the cycle path and onto the shingle – all the time, he realised, scanning up and down the beach looking for the woman previously known to him as Mia's mum. He glanced at the White Rock Theatre. He had a name for her now. Charlotte.

The sky was full of broken clouds today – a nice change from the relentless Tupperware grey that hadn't really changed since January. Top-heavy clouds raced overhead like tall ships. He savoured the flickering warmth on his face as the sun came and went to the slap and hiss of the lazy morning tide.

He let Ozzie lead him down towards the wet shingle, then onto the wet sand. The waves weren't threatening enough this morning to provoke a heroic defence of the beach. Instead, Ozzie snuffled around, looking for something interesting to either piss on or eat.

Boyd's mind inevitably found its way back to work. Specifically to the image he'd looked at just before packing up for the day and joining the others down at the pub.

The aged-up face had looked a tad artificial. But then, if

Sully was to be believed, there were algorithms behind the image, not just some berk with a copy of Photoshop and a tablet.

It may have seemed disappointingly generic to him at the time, but the more he'd thought about it, the more certain he'd become that it reminded him of someone. A little.

Dammit. Someone on TV? Someone he'd met? Someone at work?

It was too vague a resemblance to come to him, no matter how hard he racked his brains. Maybe on Monday, when he had McNeil's variations, a name would pop into his head.

Bollocks. It was frustrating.

37

It was Monday afternoon before Boyd finally received the additional images from McNeil. Despite his departing surliness on the phone, McNeil had gone the extra yard and given him a generous range of hair and facial-hair alternatives.

He stared at the images, ten in total. There were fatter and thinner variants, longer and shorter hair, different facial hair – from goatee to a full-on ZZ Top beard.

But the first image, the one with the standard short back and sides and a slightly more rounded face, kept calling him back for another look.

Dammit. I know that face.

'Didn't you interview him last week, sir?' came a voice from behind him.

He turned to see DC Warren peering at his monitor. He'd just come in from his post-lunch fag and still had his coat on. Boyd glanced back at the screen. Yes. *THAT* was who it bloody well was. Christ. The mental itch had been driving him insane all weekend.

'Mullen!' he nearly shouted. 'Dave Mullen. Shit. Yes!'

'Bloody hell, sir. Is he actually Leon Martin, then?' asked Warren.

Boyd looked again at the image. It wasn't Mullen's face exactly, but...

Shit... it was a strong likeness, yes.

'Maybe, Warren. He may well be.'

Apart from looking very similar to the computer-generated image, Dave Mullen also ticked some of the other boxes too: he was a delivery driver, he was the right age, he was the one who found the body. And... didn't the other Dave say something odd about him? About his reaction to seeing the body?

'Do you think we should call him in for questioning, sir?' Warren asked.

Boyd shook his head. 'Not yet.'

If Dave Mullen was Leon Martin, then he was good at disappearing, and at hiding his identity. 'Let's not give him a warning.'

Okeke drifted in and looked from Warren to Boyd. 'What's new?' she asked. 'You look like you're on to something.'

'We may have him,' said Warren.

'*What?*' She turned to Boyd. 'Really?'

'No,' he replied. 'Let's not pop the champagne corks just yet. We may have *something* here – that's all.'

Okeke walked round the end of the desk so that she too could see what was on his computer screen. 'That's the man you had in for a statement last week, isn't it?' she said.

'Mullen,' said Warren.

'It looks a *bit* like him, yes,' Boyd replied. 'A bit.'

He really wanted to keep a lid on the excitement. Bad decisions were made when you congratulated yourselves too quickly.

'Warren, I want you to see what you can find on him on our systems. Places of work, previous addresses, relatives. Medical records, criminal records, if any.'

Warren was already moving. 'On it.'

'Okeke?'

'Guv?'

'Social media. See if you can find a Facebook, Twitter or Instagram profile, then check his contacts, his posts, interests, interactions. See if there's any geolocation data on any posts he's made in the last week. We'll need to make a robust pitch to get access his private online footprint.'

'We'll need more than that computer render for the likes of Facebook to let us snoop around, guv.'

Boyd nodded. One piece of speculative evidence wasn't enough. They were going to need a lot more.

'Hold on,' he said suddenly. Okeke remained rooted to the spot beside his desk. 'Not you,' he said. 'You go and get... going.' His voice trailed off as he clicked through the action log to the index.

Okeke nodded, pulled off her coat and scarf, and made her way over to her desk.

Boyd's eyes remained on the screen. *Where is it? Where is it?*

He finally found what he was looking for – the link to Sully's image folder for the A27 layby. He opened it and scanned through the thumbnail images. There were hundreds of the buggers. He enlarged the thumbnails to a more helpful size and then, after a few minutes working his way down the list, he found what he was looking for and double-clicked the image.

It showed the message card that had been taped to the sign-post along with the flowers, and the blurred biro scrawl of those song lyrics.

Boyd felt a kick of adrenaline and wished to God he could turn it off until he had something concrete that he could get properly worked up about. He clicked back to the index and looked for the statement entries. He found Mullen's, clicked the link, and the screen flickered to show Mullen's signed, dated and printed statement.

Boyd compared that image with the photo of the card. The writing looked as though it *could* have been scrawled by the same person. There were variations, though, and any graphologist would tell you mood and fatigue affected the shape, size and lean of a person's writing. But there were tells, distinct ones that were always constant. The godsend was that he'd written the day alongside the date. Which gave them a 'y'. The tail of Mullen's 'y' was the same or a very, very similar vertical slash to those on the message card.

The lonely people...

'Okay, that'll do me,' he muttered under his breath. 'That's good enough.'

38

Boyd double-checked the address in his notebook. Thirty-seven Nightingale Avenue, Crawley. A quick call between Sutherland and the Chief Inspector for Mid Surrey had cleared the way for a knock-on and a warrant for entry.

He'd brought Minter and Okeke along with him. Okeke would question Mrs Mullen and Minter would make the arrest. That's if Mullen was even at home.

As they entered the cul-de-sac that was Nightingale Avenue, Boyd tried to keep a lid on things. They had just enough evidence to squeak over the warrant threshold, but not nearly enough to get them past the CPS's prosecution line. They could hold him for thirty-six hours. Hopefully, detailed questioning and a DNA sample would get them the rest of the way.

Mullen's house was semi-detached with a long, thin rear garden and a tall fence round its perimeter. According to Google's satellite images it backed directly onto a rail line.

They were fortunate. If Mullen was there and tried to make a run for it, there was pretty much nowhere to go. They pulled up outside his house, along with an accompanying patrol car from Surrey Police, which parked a bit further down the road.

Boyd had created a pretence for the visit, hoping to get inside the front door without too much drama; the employer details Mullen had given were out of date. It turned out that Mullen had ended his contract with the company over a year ago. So there it was – justification enough for them to turn up at his front door to clear up that little detail.

He checked his watch. It was gone five and the overcast sky had darkened enough to cause the sensor-triggered street lamps to flicker on.

'You ready, Okeke? Minter?'

They both nodded.

'I'm not going to piss around with him. As soon as we're in, it's a caution and cuffs for him and a house-search warrant for her. Okay?'

'And if she gives me reason to suspect she's involved... I'll book her too,' Okeke confirmed.

They'd discussed this possibility earlier. Karen Mullen appeared to have been his partner for seven years and his wife for two of those. There was every reason to wonder whether she might have an inkling about his dark past or a suspicion that he got up to something when he was out and about. If Okeke thought she might obstruct a house search or attempt to destroy evidence, then Karen Mullen was going to have to come in too.

'All right – let's get this done,' said Boyd. 'Okeke, you hang on here until we're in and come in behind us.'

He opened the door and climbed out. Minter followed suit and they walked up the garden path towards the front door. Boyd pressed the doorbell and turned to Minter. 'Smile – remember it's just a friendly detail-clarifying visit.' Minter flashed him a cheesy grin before dialling it back to something more professional.

Boyd heard the slap of approaching slippers on linoleum and through the frosted glass he could see someone emerging from the gloom within. A hall light snicked on and he could see it was a woman.

The door opened. 'Yes?'

'Mrs Mullen?' asked Boyd.

She was in her mid to late thirties, five or ten years younger than Dave Mullen. Her hair was scraped back into a blonde ponytail and her face looked blotchy and pink. She had the red-eyed look of someone who could do with a good night's sleep. Her eyes rounded the instant Boyd raised his warrant card.

'I'm DCI Boyd and this is DS Minter. Is Dave in? I'd just like a quick word with him, if that's okay?'

'Is he in trouble?' she asked.

'No, just... there are a few details in a statement he gave to us the other week that I wanted to follow up on.'

'You're the police?' she said rather loudly.

'Yes,' replied Boyd.

She leant to look past him at Minter, standing on her porch step, and the patrol car parked further along the cul-de-sac, already attracting twitching curtains from her neighbours.

'What's he done?' she said loudly again. He wondered if she was hard of hearing.

'Nothing,' he replied. 'I just need to have a quick chat with him and clarify a couple of things.'

'You want to come in, do you?' she said, again almost shouting. 'Could you not just have called?'

'Yes, we'd like to come in, if that's all right.' Boyd lifted a foot and put it on the lip of the door. 'We were in the area and thought it would make sense to drop by and get this sorted quickly.'

She shuffled forward slightly to block him. 'He's uh... he's in the bath. Upstairs.' She smiled. 'Let me just close this for a mo and I'll go and tell him you're here...'

Boyd held onto the edge of the door – strictly speaking a PACE infringement, but needs must, he reasoned. 'Why don't you just give him a shout, Mrs Mullen? I'll wait here!'

There was a strong whiff of amateur dramatics about this whole situation. Boyd glanced at Minter, a little confused. Mullen was obviously at home and well aware that they were there, thanks to Mrs Mullen's pantomime performance – but the only way out was through the front door or across the railway... He signalled, behind his back to Okeke.

Mrs Mullen backed up a step into the hallway, then cupped a hand by her mouth. 'Dave! You need to get out of the bath, love! You got some policemen here!'

She pressed out a tight-lipped smile for Boyd. 'Just give him a couple of minutes – he just needs to –'

Bang.

The noise of a door slamming came from the end of the hallway. 'Bollocks! He's doing a runner!' cried Boyd.

He pushed past the woman, down the hallway, barged the door open and almost fell into a small kitchen. He took the scene in in an instant. Dinner was on; there was something sizzling away in the pan. An iPad on the counter showed Alexander Armstrong and Richard Osman duelling with some pointless banter. It was a very normal teatime kitchen except the back door was still swinging on its hinges, having been thrown violently open.

In the pallid and fading daylight he could see Mullen running down the length of their garden towards the tall wooden fence at the end.

Boyd dutifully called out for Mullen to stop, but of course the stupid bastard didn't. He hurried out through the door and into the backyard.

'I mean, what's the fucking point?' he muttered to himself.

Okeke would have sent the uniforms around the back by now and there was quite literally nowhere for him to go.

39

Mullen reached the end of the garden and scrambled up and over the fence with an agility that belied his bulk. Boyd reached the fence just behind him and realised he wasn't going to scale it quite so effortlessly.

Seconds later Minter joined him, and Boyd wasted no time in saying, 'Come on – you're the body builder. Give me a leg-up!'

Minter ducked down and laced his fingers together so that his hands formed a cradle. 'Step in, guv.'

Boyd did so and with a grunt of exertion – more his than Minter's – he was lifted high enough to swing a leg over the fence. It wasn't a standard garden fence; it was something altogether more substantial, and – as he could see now – most probably built by British Rail to acoustically shield the rear gardens and houses that backed onto the line.

Boyd could see the fence was right up against a sooty brick wall that dropped down further to the weed-tufted gravel bed and sleepers.

'Watch out – it's a big drop this side!' he called down to

Minter, just as the big Welshman decided to leap, gazelle-like, up and over. He hit the ground awkwardly, mercifully missing the wall, yelped and clutched his leg.

Boyd swung his other leg over the fence and lowered himself down to the top of the brick wall. He could see Mullen running along the tracks, stepping from sleeper to sleeper.

'Mullen! STOP!' he called out after him. Where were the damn uniforms?

Of course Mullen took no notice and carried on.

'Call in some backup,' he shouted at Minter. 'Looks like it's *me* going after him, then.'

Boyd carefully dropped down onto the gravel and then sprinted after Mullen. He was only a hundred yards or so ahead, and either slowing down because he was running out of steam, or because maybe, like the big Welsh idiot behind him, he'd hurt himself dropping down.

Mullen veered suddenly towards the bank on the far side of the tracks, a steep incline covered with a carpet of nettles that led up to a line of stunted, soot-covered trees that looked as though they had long ago lost the will to live.

What the hell?

Mullen staggered uphill, waist deep in nettles.

Are you really doing this again, Bill?

'No choice, love,' he hissed as he crossed the railway line to the far side and ran along the bottom of the bank until he drew up to the partially flattened path made by Mullen through the mean-spirited, bastard nettles.

Boyd was no longer eyes-on. Shit. He began to climb uphill, realising halfway up that if he did manage to catch up with the man, he'd have precious little left in the tank to do anything with him.

As he scaled the top of the hill, he dipped under the skeletal low boughs of the trees and picked his way into a narrow apron of scrappy woodland. With the meagre daylight filtered out further by the branches and glimmers of sullen amber street lights blinking on beyond the trees, there was an eerie blood-orange tinge to this scrap of lifeless wilderness. It was the kind of hinterland that surrounded motorway service stations and out-of-town retail parks and ended up littered with needles, condoms and used nappies.

'Mullen!' he called out. 'Stop fucking around and give yourself up.'

His words rattled off the trunks and gnarled branches and startled a bird out of the leaves above him, making him jump.

'Mullen!'

Boyd felt a shove from behind and lost his balance. A moment later, as he tried to stop himself tumbling back out of the woodland and down the bank, he found himself pinned up against a tree trunk, one hairy forearm pressed against his throat and the glinting tip of a penknife blade uncomfortably close to his right eyeball.

Mullen leant forward and for one ghastly moment Boyd thought he was either going to nut him or kiss him.

'*You sad little people*,' he whispered hoarsely, as out of breath as Boyd. '*Can't you leave well alone?*'

'It's... it's over...' gasped Boyd. 'Do you... you really want to add killing a copper to your tariff?'

The dark form leaning over him paused for a moment. The tip of the blade trembling, so close to Boyd he couldn't even focus on it.

'DCI Boyd, you okay in there?' The shout didn't sound too far away.

'Best you take your KitKats and fuck off, then,' Mullen hissed, pulling Boyd forward and sticking out a leg, tripping him over. Boyd fell, tumbling down the steep incline, rolling through the bastard nettles and flattening them in a six-foot-wide path, before clattering heavily onto the bed of old gravel stones at the bottom.

He got to his feet slowly, not registering at first the myriad stings and scrapes on his skin, but instead thanking his lucky stars that the bloody waste of space uniforms had finally made it in the nick of time, and that Mullen had decided a police scalp *wasn't* on his Bucket List.

'Fuck,' he said to himself. He was still wheezing from the exertion and shaking with the adrenaline, both from his rapid descent and from wondering whether or not his right eyeball was about to be plucked out like a cherry tomato.

He heard the crunch of stones to his left and saw Minter hurrying towards him. 'Boss? You okay, boss?'

Boyd doubled over, resting his palms against his shins as he drew in a deep breath to stop himself from keeling over.

Minter was beside him a moment later. 'Boss?'

'He got away,' huffed Boyd. 'The bastard's got away. Again.'

40

'You were stalling us for him,' said Okeke. She leant forward, a gesture that landed halfway between accusatory and sisterly.

'Come on, Karen. You need to tell us where he's gone.'

Boyd was watching the interview on the CCTV screen in the neighbouring room. He'd let Minter and Okeke have this one, primarily because he wanted to be the fresh and friendly face for part two.

'I don't know,' Karen mumbled.

'I think you do,' pressed Okeke. 'You clearly knew enough to keep my colleagues on the doorstep long enough for him to get out the back door.'

Karen Mullen fidgeted with the cuffs of her shirt.

'You know, not helping us right now, when every second counts, is digging you deeper and deeper into trouble. Do you understand that?'

That's it, Okeke.

'Do I get a free solicitor?' Mrs Mullen asked.

'That's up to you, Karen,' said Minter. 'Do you need one? We're just asking a few basic questions here.'

'We're not after you, love,' added Okeke, more softly this time. 'But we do really need to find Dave.'

The camera in the interview room next door was high up on the wall, giving Boyd a less-than-useful view of the top of Mrs Mullen's head. But her body language was all tell.

She knows. This was an arranged escape plan.

'Not answering us, Mrs Mullen,' said Minter, 'will be seen in a courtroom as aiding and abetting. It will be seen as obstructing us. That's a criminal offence. Do you want to be charged with that?'

She shook her head mutely.

'Then you need to start being a bit more helpful.'

'Karen,' Okeke spoke softly again, 'how long have you two been together?'

'Seven years, eight years,' was the reply.

'And how long have you been married?'

'A couple of years.'

'And in that time Dave's always worked as – what? – a delivery driver?'

Mrs Mullen nodded.

'What does he deliver?'

The hapless woman shrugged. 'He's a man with a van. All sorts.'

'Does he deliver locally? Further away?' Okeke asked.

'Nationally,' Mrs Mullen replied. 'He's got his own website. MCS. Mullen Courier Service.'

Boyd pulled out his phone.

'He's got his own business website?' Okeke confirmed.

'Yes.'

Boyd tapped the company name into his phone and studied the screen for a moment. Minter had done the same. He showed the screen to Okeke, then got up and headed for the door. 'Be back in a second,' he said.

'For the recording, DS Minter has left the room,' said Okeke.

Minter entered the observation room next door and held the screen up for Boyd to see.

'He's got a business premises, boss. Did you get that?

Boyd held up his iPhone, showing an identical address and map that indicated a business unit in Crawley.

'The business park is just through those woods by the railway,' Minter informed him.

Boyd scrolled back up the page. There were photos of Mullen standing in front of two white vans: both Fords. A Ford Transit and a Ford Courier. Both vehicles had their rear doors wide open, revealing the space he had in the back, and, presumably for customer's peace of mind, rolls of bubble wrap and foam for protection in transit.

'He was heading for his van, then?' said Boyd. 'To drive it away? Or…'

'Or ditch something that was inside it?'

Boyd nodded. 'Get some uniforms over there right now.'

'Righto,' Minter said, heading for the door.

'And make sure you tell them he's carrying a knife,' Boyd called after him.

Minter hurried off to CID with his phone still clutched in one hand.

Boyd looked back at his own phone, at the photo of Mullen, standing proudly between his two vans, with a wide smile that resonated with the tagline below: *Any object, anywhere, anytime… safely, quickly and discreetly.*

Boyd tapped the screen and spread his fingers, zooming in on the picture.

'Gotcha,' he whispered. The number plates were legible.

Back in the interview room, Okeke broke the long, protracted silence. 'So come on, Karen. Where has he gone and why did he run? What's he been up to?'

No answer.

'If he's innocent, if he's got nothing to hide, then I'm sure we can clear this up really quickly. But we need your help, Karen.'

'He's a good man. He's been good to me,' she said.

Okeke nodded, offering the woman an understanding smile. 'But…'

'He's had trouble with you lot in the past,' replied Mrs Mullen. 'He told me what you lot are like, for picking on "likely sorts" all the time. He doesn't trust any of you.'

'Likely sorts?'

She shrugged. 'He's been done for some burglaries in the past. I'm not saying Dave's a hundred-and-ten-per-cent innocent, but he's done his time and he's clean now. But… every time something happens in the area…'

'He gets questioned?'

Mrs Mullen nodded. 'He said one day you lot were going to find something to stick on him and put him back inside.'

Okeke nodded sympathetically. 'If the face fits, huh?'

She nodded. 'They're just after him. They won't ever leave him alone.'

She'd said 'they', not 'you'. Boyd noted that Mrs Mullen no longer seemed to be including Okeke in her distrust of the police.

'My brother gets the same crap every day,' said Okeke softly. 'Black, male, living in London. I get what you're saying. I really do.'

Boyd watched the exchange on the monitor. *She's good at this.*

'Look, Karen. What I don't want to happen is for Dave to break any laws simply by panicking and running from us, okay? So tell me, where's he gone?'

Mrs Mullen shrugged. 'Honestly, I don't know. Somewhere in his van I expect, hopefully somewhere far away. And I don't blame him either.'

Okeke smiled at her, realising that she'd get little else out of her at this stage. 'Thanks Karen. That'll do us for now.'

~

DSI Sutherland looked up from the hastily completed form. He had his jacket on and had taken his dirty mug to the kitchenette – clear indicators that he didn't want anything else dropped in his lap right now, as he was finally ending what had been an unusually long shift for him and was getting ready to go home for a late supper.

'You want this ACT request to be submitted as a *high* priority?'

'Yes, sir.'

'But... we've already had Dave Mullen here in the station for questioning, haven't we?'

'Yes, sir, we have.'

Sutherland sighed. Submitting this high alert would, in effect, advertise the fact that Boyd had had the suspect on his radar much earlier. If Mullen really was Leon Martin and had killed and buried the A27 boy last week, well, it was just going to flag up that they'd let a killer slip through their fingers. Her Madge wouldn't be happy. And that was on Boyd.

'You really think it's him?' pressed Sutherland.

'As I said earlier, sir. There's enough to make him a Person of Interest. Plus... he did do a runner and threaten to stab me in the eye.'

Sutherland nodded. 'Well, he's guilty of something, then, isn't he?' He scribbled his name at the bottom of the form and handed it to Boyd. 'All right,' he said. 'Let's bring him in.'

Back at his desk, Boyd entered the ACT request onto the PNC and tagged it as 'High Priority'.

His options were 'Stop', 'Monitor' or 'Assess'. A 'Stop' would mean an instant pull-over, vehicle inspection and arrest. If there was nothing incriminating in the vehicle, if the van was swabbed for blood traces and DNA and turned up blank, then Boyd's team and their department would look like a bunch of trigger-happy, resource-hogging muppets. But the alternative was another dead boy and a record that showed he'd not given the all-forces request the right level of urgency.

Boyd was confident that Mullen's actions had shown he had something to hide. In his opinion, at best Mullen would be ditching stolen goods and, at worst, if he *was* Leon Martin... then right now he was most likely scrubbing his van clean, torching it somewhere in the middle of nowhere and heading off into hiding again. Speed was of the essence.

Do it, whispered Julia. *You want another child haunting you?*

Fuck it.

He hit enter.

41

PC Jake Smith was on his first unpartnered shift after six months of being stationed at Banbury. His mentor, Sergeant Adib, had signed him off on Thursday as being ready for a solo shift, and for his last three days off-shift Jake had been, well – basically – shitting himself.

The eight-hour shift, starting at 10 p.m., had thus far been a hectic five hours' worth of herding drunk idiots out of the pubs and clubs as they closed, followed by another hour spent dealing with a couple of elderly alcoholic sisters who'd had a proper hair-pulling, face-scratching, nail-breaking mud-pit tussle on the lounge floor of their shared home, during which one had ended up calling 999, claiming the other was attempting to murder her.

Both of them were out of their skulls and Jake had spent over an hour trying to unravel what had actually happened from a constant barrage of 'she said...', 'she said...'.

His ears were still ringing from their shrill, banshee-like screaming. That was sixty frickin' minutes of his life he'd never get back.

Drunks, especially old ones, were worse than bloody children.

He had an hour's patrol time left, followed by an hour back at the station to make good on his paperwork, and then – thank God – he could finally go home.

His first ever solo completed. Tick.

Jake was wrestling with the important decision of whether to stop for an end-of-shift Maccy D's or go full burn and have a KFC blowout, when the screen of his monitor flashed up an advisory.

He looked at the LCD screen and saw a low-resolution image of a white transit van. The point of view was low and close; it was from somebody's dash cam. He glanced up and saw the exact same white transit van cruising along just fifty yards ahead of him in the left-hand lane.

Fuck. It's MY dash cam. Shit. The advisory came with a red High Alert indicator and a one-sentence Alarm Note: *POI in murder case, approach with caution.*

He reached down below the monitor for the light/alarm keypad. His first official blues-and-twos. His finger hovered over the 999 button.

Shit. Just. Got. Real, Jake. Ready for this?

He wanted to say, 'No, not really.' But that wasn't an available option.

He hit the button and his patrol car lit up and squawked to life.

The transit van immediately dropped down to fifty miles an hour and Jake took the opportunity to move into the right-hand lane. He pulled up until he could see the dim silhouette of the driver to his left.

Jake jabbed a finger at him. 'Pull over! Pull over!' he shouted. Obviously the bloke at the wheel wasn't going to hear any of that, but hopefully he'd spot his frantically pointing finger.

Jake eased back behind the van in case the bastard decided to play wacky races and swerve *his* way, but, to his relief, he saw the van's indicator start blinking.

'Thank fuck,' he muttered, dimly aware that his chest cam was now undoubtedly activated by the siren and already recording.

Jake picked up the car radio's handset. 'Echo Mike Thirty-three to control.'

'Control to Echo Mike Thirty-three, go ahead,' the radio crackled.

'I'm pulling over a white Ford transit van, Papa Oscar Zero Nine Romeo Sierra Golf, following an ANPR ping for a murder POI. Location: A4260 heading into Twyford.'

There was no hard shoulder to work with, so the van just kept on going. Jake decided the first off-road they passed without turning into, he'd escalate this to a pursuit and call in for backup to intercede up ahead.

They passed a sign indicating an off-road a hundred yards ahead, then the three countdown signs. After the last, the van gently slowed down and veered to the left, onto the slip road.

Jake let out a breath. *Thank fuck.*

The slip road had two lanes and Jake flashed his headlights to indicate that the van driver should make use of the one on the left.

The van indicated again and ground to a halt.

Jake pulled up behind it, a cautious ten yards back in case the idiot attempted to reverse-ram him. That shit actually happened with forehead-slapping regularity.

'Here we go, then,' he said softly, aware once again, that the chest camera was picking up every little sound he made.

He opened the driver-side door and stepped out, in his head running through all those US cop dash-cam videos where a crazy-ass hillbilly decides to poke a gun out of the window. He could see the faint oval of the driver's face in the right-hand wing mirror. Which meant the driver could see him.

Jake raised his hand and beckoned the driver to step out. 'Out of the van, please!' he called. The driver remained perfectly still and for a moment Jake suspected the van was going to set off again with a scream of tyres on tarmac. But then the door opened slowly and a figure finally emerged.

42

Boyd was having a dream about Lego of all things. Specifically, the Star Wars Death Star Lego set that he'd always wanted to buy Noah one day, once he'd seen a few of the movies, of course.

It wasn't a cheap set, £400 or thereabouts last time he'd had a look. Not the sort of present you'd buy a little lad unless he was definitely going to become Star Wars fan number one, and you could justify the extravagance to the other half as a chance for a bit of father–son play-bonding.

In his dream, though, Julia had okayed it, and he and Noah had commandeered the dining table (for several days!) to build the bloody thing. There'd been nothing weird or wacky about the dream. It was just a blissful day spent with bricks, a hefty assembly guide and the son he was never going to get to know beyond the age of four.

The dream ended with his phone vibrating on the bedside table. Boyd reached out and grabbed his iPhone, grunting as he brought it within range of his bleary eyes.

That wasn't the culprit. It was his work phone. He cursed

and scrabbled around for that instead. 'DCI Boyd,' he answered, trying to sound vaguely awake.

'Morning. Are you the SIO who put out the ACT last night on a white transit van owned by one David Mullen?'

He was foggy minded and still half immersed in his Lego build. He blinked rapidly a few times and sat up. 'Yeah. You got him?'

'We've got him here,' the voice said.

'Where's *here*?'

'Banbury police station. Got him tucked up with a cup of tea in one of our interview rooms. What's the deal? You coming up to interview him or are we transporting him down to you?'

'What time is it?' Boyd asked.

'Same time as it is where you are, I expect.'

Oh, very funny. He leaned over and tapped the screen of his iPhone. It was just after six in the morning. 'Send him down to Hastings,' he said.

'His transit van's impounded up here. Do you want that transporting down too?'

Oh, for fuck's sake 'Right. Fine. I'll come to you. Who do I ask for?'

'DI Thomas. See you later, then, sir.' The line went dead.

Boyd sighed and he dropped the phone on the bedside table and looked out of the window. The sky had transitioned to its regular grey of dawn, making no promises about turning blue at any point later today. He got out of bed, leaving Ozzie snoring, his head on the pillow that in another life, another time, would have belonged to Julia.

He dressed quickly, grabbed his two phones and his car's key card, and shambled down the stairs, still trying to wriggle his feet completely into his work shoes without the hassle of having to fuck around with untying and retying his laces.

Boyd arrived at Banbury police station just before ten. He parked in the last remaining visitor's space and hurried inside the building. He flashed his warrant card at the desk sergeant and asked for DI Thomas. A few minutes later a slim man with comically Edwardian sideburns, wearing a tightly buttoned waistcoat that only a skinny arse could get away with, appeared beyond the electric barrier and waved.

'You DCI Boyd?'

'Yeah. DI Thomas?'

'Yup. Come on in.' He pressed a button on his side and the barrier clacked open.

Boyd followed Thomas through and down an echoing hallway.

'Thanks for coming all the way up, sir.'

'Got to be done,' Boyd said.

'I've been whiling away my shift, waiting for you to arrive, getting up to speed.' He looked at Boyd. 'Your boss –Sutherland, is it? – called my boss... Is this guy the actual Ken Doll Killer?'

Fucking great, Boyd thought. *So much for keeping that quiet.* 'Well, that remains to be seen, he said. 'He's looking like the hot favourite at the moment.'

Thomas seemed excited. 'Nice one.'

'Was he alone in his van?' asked Boyd.

Thomas nodded. 'The arresting officer said it was just him. No passengers.'

'Anything of note in the back?'

'Delivery items. He's one of those delivery freelancers – Pigeon Post Plonkers, as we like to call them.' Thomas sighed. 'Or White Van Mafia; they're a bloody nightmare these days.'

'How do you mean?'

'They're all over the shop, most of them. Driving too fast, working too many hours, falling asleep at their wheels. They're a damned hazard.'

'Good old zero-hour contracts. They should be bloody well

banned,' said Boyd, realising as he said it that he was sounding more and more like Emma these days.

Thomas pushed open two swing doors and then pointed down the corridor ahead. 'Mullen's in room two. I'll go and grab us a brew. Tea? Coffee?'

'Coffee, black. Thanks.'

'No problem. I'll be back in five.'

'Thomas?' Boyd called after him.

He stopped and turned. 'Yeah?'

'Can you grab me something to eat? I've not had any breakfast yet.'

43

Boyd entered the interview room.

Mullen was sitting at the table, hunched over so that his head was nestled on his folded arms. He was being watched by a uniformed officer. As the door swung shut behind Boyd, Mullen roused himself and looked up.

'Hello again,' said Boyd.

Mullen sat back slowly in his chair.

'I'm okay, thanks for asking,' said Boyd. 'Just a few scratches and nettle stings going down the embankment, but I've still got both eyes – which I'm taking as a win.'

'Don't know what you're on about, mate,' Mullen said, glaring at him from across the table.

'Oh, we're doing *that*, are we?' Boyd sat down. 'Fine.' He cracked his knuckles theatrically. 'Where do I start, Dave? We have you "discovering" that body, then apparently being reluctant to call it in.'

'What?'

'I'm just letting you know what the other Dave said.'

'He's lying.'

'Is he?'

'Yes.'

'We've also got you at the same age, same description, same build as a witness statement,' Boyd lied, hoping to unsettle him. A "speculative forensic likeness" wasn't going to have the same impact. He wanted to rattle Mullen before DI Thomas returned and the recording machine went on.

It seemed to be working. Mullen wasn't looking so cocksure of himself now.

'I know who you are,' said Boyd softly. 'Or, should I say, *were*.'

The colour drained from Mullen's face.

'Let's cut the crap, Leon.'

'Who, the fuck is Leon?'

The door clicked open and DI Thomas brought in a mug of coffee and a Mars bar for Boyd 'There you go,' he said, setting them down on the table.

'Cheers,' replied Boyd, not taking his eyes off Mullen.

DI Thomas looked at Mullen. 'Do you want a coffee?'

'No, he doesn't,' Boyd answered quickly.

Thomas sat down beside Boyd and reached across for the recording machine. 'Okay, you ready to start?'

Boyd nodded.

Thomas flipped the machine on and they waited for the beep to indicate that recording was now in progress.

'Present in the room are DI Thomas, DCI Boyd and David Mullen.' He sat back and nodded at Boyd to begin.

'I'm DCI Boyd, senior investigating officer on Operation Weatherman. We're investigating a recent and an old body, both of which are victims of the same murderer. I'm not going to disclose the evidence that links the two, but the person we're after is Leon David Martin, otherwise known as the Ken Doll Killer. Dave Mullen, we have reason to believe you're him.'

'What?!' Mullen blurted out.

'We had a chat with your wife,' continued Boyd.

'What? What the fuck? Are you harassing her now too?'

'We had a little chat about your past with her,' Boyd said. 'How she met you. What she knows, and more importantly what she doesn't know about you.'

'This is fucking ridiculous. I don't know who your Ken Boy is and I'm not a fucking murderer!'

'Your wife told us she met you in 2014. She says you've a history of petty crime that you served some time for before she knew you. She says you get picked on by the police all the time just because "they don't like you".'

'Fuck you!'

Boyd sighed. 'I can see why.' He picked up his tepid coffee. 'See the thing about you, Dave, is... there's no record of you having served time – either before or after 2014. You don't seem to have much of a backstory prior to 2014, in fact. No family. No friends. No social media footprint. It's like Dave Mullen winked into existence in 2014. Why don't we start from there? Why don't you explain to me why there's nothing of you before that?'

'I was lying low, wasn't I? Trying not to get fitted up again by you complete wankers.'

'Lying low? What name were you using before Dave, when you served time? Because it wasn't *Mullen*.'

Mullen's bluster and fidgeting simmered down. His expression was no longer outraged and fucked off with the inconvenience of it all – it went flat. Shut down. Like an ECG machine flatlining, Boyd thought.

He knows we know.

'No comment,' came the eventual reply.

Boyd picked up his coffee. 'Really?'

'No comment.'

Boyd took a sip. It was bloody awful vending machine coffee that tasted of coffee, chocolate, tea and soup at the same time.

'Dave, you're not in a great situation here. This is your

opportunity to show me I'm wrong. "No comment" really isn't going to help you do that.'

Mullen settled back in his seat slowly and crossed his arms. 'No comment.'

'Where were you living between 1987 and 2001?'

'No comment.'

'You have a trace of a Cheshire accent, Dave. I can just about hear it.' He turned to Thomas. 'Can you?'

DI Thomas nodded. 'A bit.'

'See, Dave, earlier, you said "fuck". Now, when I say it – and I do that quite often – it rhymes with "duck". But when you said it, it rhymed with "book". So, I'm pretty sure you didn't grow up down in Sussex. So how about we cut the "no comment? crap and you tell me who you are? Because one thing I'm certain of is this – you weren't born Dave Mullen.'

Mullen leant forward, arms still crossed. 'No, fucking, comment.'

~

BOYD AND DI THOMAS stepped outside the interview room some thirty minutes and several more *No comment*s later.

'I'm wondering whether to have him transferred down to Hastings. The van as well,' Boyd said. He had the case material down there, and he'd like Okeke to have a crack at him. She'd been talking to his wife and may well have better luck with Mullen too.

'He's been in custody since six a.m. It's now eleven,' Thomas pointed out.

'I know, time's ticking down.'

'You'll lose another few hours transporting him, then there's the mandatory travel rest before you can interview him again.'

Boyd sighed. 'I know.'

They had Mullen for twenty-four hours, then it was time to

either piss or get off the potty. Transferring him to Hastings was going to eat up too many of those precious hours.

'Have your CSI been through his van yet?' asked Boyd.

Thomas shook his head. 'Not yet.'

'But your arresting officer said there were parcels in the back, right?'

'Delivery items, he said. There are some small items of furniture, a large mirror, an antique clock. Fragile stuff.'

'Mullen bolted like a bat out of hell when we turned up at his house. And the first place he went to was his van. There's either something of interest in there now... or there *was*, not so long ago.'

'You want me to get some of our SOCOs in there?' offered Thomas.

Boyd nodded. 'It would be incredibly helpful if they found something I could waggle around in front of him. Try and nip this "no comment" crap in the bud.'

'You want to resume with Mullen?' asked Thomas.

'Nah, take him back to custody for now. I've got some calls to make,' Boyd said.

'Yes, sir.' With that, Thomas headed back into the interview room to collect Mullen.

Boyd pulled out his work phone and dialled Minter. He answered immediately. 'Boss?'

'All right.'

'How's it going?'

'No comment.'

'Ughh. I bloody hate those.'

'We're going to comb through his van for any forensic traces of Stephen Wooten,' Boyd said. 'If this is the van he used to transport the body, there's got to be something there. It's gonna be a few hours of waiting around, though.'

'Clock's ticking down, boss.'

'No shit. Look, he's giving me some crap about having a

history with the police as a result of petty crime, being a victim and all that. His wife said he did some time inside. See if you can dig anything up.'

'Righto.'

'And send Okeke up.'

'To Banbury?'

'Yes.'

Boyd thought he could hear a note of resentment in his voice. 'You're busy, Minter, and she's had a bit more luck with Mrs Mullen. Is she there?'

'Yes, she is, boss, I'll put her on.'

He heard the line rustle, then: 'Guv?'

'Okeke, I want you to come on up. We've got Mullen for eighteen more hours before we charge or release. I've called a stop to the interview while Banbury's forensics pick their way through the van, so nothing's happening for a while. You've got time to drive up. I need you in the room, talking with him about what his wife's been saying. You may have better luck than me.'

'No problem,' she said. 'I'm on my way.'

'And bring the case file on my desk. Save me printing out again up here.'

'Will do.'

'I'll have a brew waiting for you. Ask for DI Thomas at the desk.'

Boyd hung up, then dialled Dr Palmer at the Ellessey Forensic Services to check on their progress.

'Janet Bowler, speaking.'

'DCI Boyd, Hastings CID,' he said, momentarily thrown. 'Can I speak to Dr Palmer?'

'I'm afraid not; she's been taken poorly. Can I help?'

Fucking great, Boyd thought. *Of course she is.* 'Right. She did an autopsy for us five days ago,' he said.

'Ah, yes. Was that the no-ID one from the A27?'

'He *was* ID'd,' Boyd said. 'He's Stephen Wooten. Anyway,

she said she'd have DNA swabs from his hands and some other likely swab locations back by the end of last week. It's now Tuesday.'

'Oh, that's not very good, is it?' Janet said, sounding flustered.

'No, not really.'

'I'll have a look to see where we're up to with those.'

'Well, hopefully they're *done*, right?' asked Boyd. 'And I'm just waiting for the emailed report?'

'Yes, I'm sure they are,' Janet Bowler said, a note of panic creeping into her voice. 'Can I call you back when I've tracked this job down?'

'Please do.' He gave his number. 'As soon as you can. I'm interviewing a suspect and I'm a little pressed for time here.'

44

It was gone three o'clock in the afternoon by the time Okeke finally turned up at Banbury police station.

'Sorry, guv, the traffic around the M25 was bloody awf–'

Boyd rubbed the sleep from his eyes with the heel of his hand, jolted awake by her arrival.

'Napping, sir?'

'Thinking. With my eyes closed,' he answered. 'Helps me concentrate.'

'While lying flat out on their couch apparently,' she said, smiling.

DI Thomas had given Boyd use of the 'soft' interview room to spread out. Most stations had one of these now – they were designed to resemble a Premier Inn lounge as opposed to a Stazi interrogation room. They were there for sensitive conversations with more vulnerable types. This one had a sofa and two armchairs, a box of toys in the corner and a low coffee table with a vase full of plastic flowers and a box of tissues on it.

Boyd swung his legs over the edge of the sofa, sat up and

straightened his tie. 'I was running through the case,' he said sheepishly.

'Sure you were, guv.'

Okeke pulled the case file out of her shoulder bag. 'DI Thomas is getting Mullen up from the custody floor; we're going to be in interview room two.'

Boyd reached for the mug of coffee that Thomas had brought him a couple of hours ago. It was half empty and had formed a milk skin. 'I'm still waiting on Ellessey to send me a report on those Wooten swabs,' he said.

'It's been five days!'

'I know. Shit, right?'

She dropped the case file on the coffee table. 'What's Mullen been like so far?'

'One "no comment" after another,' he said, pushing the skin on his coffee to one side and taking a cautious sip.

'Great.' She rolled her eyes. 'One of those.'

'Not from the beginning; he was bolshy as hell then. He went quiet after I mentioned "Dave Mullen" didn't seem to exist before 2014.'

'Minter's been digging on that,' said Okeke.

'And?'

'No idea. I didn't hear from him on the drive up, so I'm guessing there's nothing yet. Have the SOCOs here found anything in his van?'

'Not yet. They're pulling it to pieces. Reducing it to kit form, hopefully.'

Okeke pulled out the page of aged-up Martin photos from a folder. 'Right – and this is all happening... based on one computer render?'

Boyd nodded. She looked at it silently for a moment. 'I mean, to be fair this one... this does look a lot like him, doesn't it?'

'Plus, he ran.'

'Well, you are a big bloke, guv. With a scary face.'

'He ran, and when I caught up with him he threatened me with a knife. You've got to be desperate to do that to a copper. He's got a van and he's changed his name. There's something going on.'

The door to the room opened and DI Thomas stuck his head in.

'Any news?' asked Boyd.

'Not great news, I'm afraid. Mullen's just asked for a duty solicitor.'

'Oh, for fuck's sake. How long will that take?'

'About an hour,' Thomas replied. 'To be honest, you might as well go and grab a coffee or something. There's a Greggs up the road.'

Boyd perked up. A Greggs sausage roll and a coffee were exactly what he needed right now.

'I can call you when the solicitor's clocked in and we're ready to resume the interview,' added Thomas

'Yeah, that actually sounds like a half-decent plan,' Boyd said, smiling for the first time that day.

'This is so bloody good,' muttered Boyd, spilling flakes of pastry from his mouth.

Okeke raised a brow. 'It's a baked-bean-and-sausage pasty.'

'Yeah, well, all I've had all day is a Mars bar and a stale vending-machine sandwich. After that, this gunk is bloody Michelin-star gorgeous.'

'They should have that as a franchise tagline... the last four words anyway.' She looked around the Greggs eat-in area. They were the only ones there.

Okeke bit into her salad wrap. 'If we don't get any forensics out of this van, we could always try the other smaller one back in Crawley?'

'No point,' he mumbled through a mouthful of pasty. 'Well... there is a point, to be thorough and all that, but he took this van, which I presume is because it had something in it that he didn't want us to find. If this is a no-show, I suspect the other van will be too.'

'There's his lock-up.'

'That's definitely of interest. I'd be surprised if Sutherland hasn't sent a team over already. But the vans are how he would have transported the body. And they're what I'm most interested in.' Boyd took another bite. 'The vans are our best bet. The other thing I'm counting on are those swabs from Wooten.'

'If that's a blank, guv?'

He shrugged. 'Worst case, I get to look like a right prat for jumping on the wrong suspect. But as I said – we'll get him for whatever he *is* up to. I'll give Minter a ring and see –'

Boyd's work phone vibrated in his pocket. He pulled it out, glanced at the screen and put the speakerphone on. 'Boyd?'

'It's Minter, boss.'

'I was just about to call you, to see how you're get–'

'Boss, gonna stop you there. Mullen's a dead end.'

'What?'

'Boss... Mullen changed his name by deed poll eight years ago. He was born David Pike. Pike's on the sex offenders' register for assaulting a minor back in 1999. He served a custodial sentence and was out on parole in 2002. So he can't be Leon Martin.'

Boyd felt the investigation clatter to the ground around him.

'He's been active on the dark web over the last couple of years peddling child pornography. From the exchanges – and it's all in anti-search term lingo – he takes his orders for the "coffee" online but delivers and receives payment in person.'

'Shit, bugger and bollocks,' muttered Boyd.

'He's delivering child porn like pizza,' added Minter. 'It's on plug-in hard drives.'

'That explains him being all twitchy at the A21 layby,' said Okeke.

'And making a run for it,' said Minter. 'Maybe he had some of those on him or in the van.'

Boyd nodded. 'Yeah.'

'I'm really sorry, boss,' said Minter. 'I thought we had a winner, too.'

45

They returned to the station, found DI Thomas and explained that the Dave in their cell wasn't the Ken Doll Killer after all.

Thomas looked almost as gutted as Boyd felt.

'His name is David Pike,' Boyd said. 'He's a registered sex offender. Your SOCOs might get lucky finding some computer hard drives and memory sticks, but they're not going to find any traces of our victim.'

'Arghh. That's annoying,' Thomas said.

And that's the understatement of the fucking year.

'Well, in positive news... you've got a kiddie-porn peddler in your cells. I'll get my DS to email over to you what he's pulled up on him.'

Boyd thanked Thomas for his help, then left the station, with Okeke, to head back to Hastings in their separate cars.

'See you in the morning, guv,' she called out as she ducked down in her car.

Boyd managed a half-hearted wave as he got into his. 'Yeah. See you tomorrow.'

He closed the door, pulled his seat belt round his waist and smacked the steering wheel with his fist.

~

BOYD GOT BACK HOME at just after ten to find Emma lounging on the sofa with Ozzie sprawled out next to her.

'Where's your young man?' he asked as he slung his jacket over the back of a chair.

'Bar shift,' she said.

There was a costume drama on TV and a half-finished bottle of J2O beside a subdued and glowing fire in the grate.

'How was work today?' she asked.

'You saw my note on the dining table?'

'Yeah. What time did you leave?'

'Silly o'clock,' he said, kicking his shoes off.

'Was it helpful? Did you get your man?'

Boyd loosened his tie and undid the collar button of his shirt. 'Got *a* man, just not *the* man. We picked up a sex offender who'd managed to go off radar, but he's not the man I want.'

'Oh.'

'Apart from that... what a waste of a bloody day, *that* was.' He nodded at her half-empty bottle. 'Not a bad idea.' He got up. 'Want anything from the kitchen?'

'There's an open tube of Pringles. Can you bring that?'

Boyd returned a couple of minutes later with the Pringles, a bottle of Malbec and two glasses in case Emma wanted to join him. He shook some Pringles from the tube and poured himself a generous glass of wine. 'Complete bloody waste of my time,' he repeated.

'Is this the layby body?' Emma asked, curious now.

He nodded. 'I can't really go into detail, Ems...'

'You did with Nix,' she pointed out.

'Yeah, well... you know I shouldn't have done that.'

'But you did,' she said. 'And I was helpful if I recall.'

He nodded. 'That you were.'

'So broad brushstrokes, then. Tell me.'

Boyd sighed. 'Unlikely though it still seems to be, we may just have a serial killer out there who's been preying on a victim pool that no one really seems to care about, unnoticed, for the last twenty years.'

'No way. Who's the victim pool?' she asked, sitting up.

'He selects his victims from among the homeless. Urban rough sleepers. They're anonymous, transient, virtually invisible so far as social care's concerned. Lads old enough that we class them as "adults" and completely wash our hands of them. They're off the radar; I suspect some of them aren't even officially listed as missing persons.'

'Oh God.'

'Right. As if life isn't shit enough, they've got this guy out there trawling for them.'

He really didn't want to think how many bodies might be out there, buried at the back of grubby roadside picnic areas, never to be found, missed or mourned.

'So this guy you went to interview today...' Emma got up, crossed the lounge and took the tube of Pringles away from him before he could finish the lot in one sitting. 'How does he fit into the case?'

'He was one of the men who found the body,' Boyd replied. 'Sometimes it helps to take a look at the unlikely. The ones who "innocently" discover the body.' He sighed. 'I thought we had one of those on our hands.'

'Men? As in plural?'

'Huh?'

'You said "men"?'

'Oh, right.' Boyd nodded. 'The other bloke was a truck driver. He was driving in Europe at the time of the death of our recent body. And he's too young for the old one. He'd have been in his early teens back in 2000.'

'Assuming that the old body and the recent body were killed by the same person?' she pointed out.

Boyd nodded.

'*Assuming*, Dad.' She repeated the word in case he'd missed it. '*Assuming*.'

He shook his head. 'There's sufficient evidence that it's the same person.'

'What's that? What's the evidence?'

'Can't say what, Ems. I'm sorry.'

She didn't press him, instead reaching for the wine. As she leant forward the tube of Pringles rolled from her lap to the floor. Quick as a flash, Ozzie, who had been fast asleep and snoring, was on his feet, straight on the floor and hoovering up.

Boyd laughed as Emma tried to wrestle Ozzie from the scene; she had to settle for saving the tube with the remaining crisps instead. Ozzie licked his lips, sniffed the floor and hopped back up onto the sofa as if nothing had happened.

'For God's sake, Ozzie – you're such a food cow,' Emma muttered.

'A *food cow*,' Boyd repeated, laughing again. 'And what the bloody hell is one of those?'

She grinned. 'You know. Cows are always chewing; he's always eating something or other. I don't know – it just fell out of my mouth. Anyway,' she said, 'don't change the subject. You were telling me about work.' She shot him a shrewd look. 'So this guy, the killer, where's he been? Why has he suddenly appeared again now?'

Boyd took a long glug of his wine and leant back. 'There was a previous investigation into him, back in the day, but he supposedly killed himself and the case was closed.'

'Supposedly? Surely they had his body.'

Boyd explained about Martin's van left at the cliff edge. The fact that he'd possibly allowed his last victim to escape, so that he could tell the police that Martin's intention was to kill himself.

'And they assumed he was dead?' said Emma. She repeated it again. '*Assumed?*'

'They didn't have much to work with back in 2001, Ems. Sometimes you just run out of leads and you have to pack everything up and move on.'

'Right.'

He took another mouthful of wine. 'I don't know.'

'What?'

'The previous SIO was pretty thorough. His CSM and forensics team were not so good.'

'CSM?'

'Crime scene manager. They charged in like a herd of elephants and completely screwed up all the scene evidence. They trashed everything and ended up with completely cross-contaminated unreliable DNA samples that belonged to dozens of different individuals.'

'Well, isn't that something you can just look up and match? Like a fingerprint database?'

'Now, in a lot of cases, yes. Back then, no,' he said. 'They had one dominant profile, which they labelled as the killer's –.'

'How did they know it was the killer's DNA?' she interrupted.

He looked at her. 'They matched it with some of his things from home.'

'Okay, but unless they actually like, what's the word, sampled...'

'Swabbed.'

'Yeah – swabbed the killer, there's no guarantee this dominant profile was definitively his, right? Or am I missing something stupid and obvious?'

Boyd finished his glass and reached for the bottle. 'No. You're spot on.'

'So, does he have family? Could a brother or sister be swabbed to verify that –'

'None.'

'None at all?'

She shook her head. 'So, like I said: how do you know it *is* his?'

He answered with a shake of his head. 'I'll admit, there's not much I can use with certainty from the 2001 evidence. Not gathered forensics anyway.'

'Could you gather some more, Dad? I mean... DNA samples last for quite a while, don't they?'

He looked at her. 'That's where my thinking's headed, Ems. We've got to go to the source and start over. His house was boarded up and never sold, so we may get lucky. It's worth a shot anyway.'

'Plus, forensic databases have changed a lot since then, haven't they?' she said. 'You might get a break that the other SIO didn't have.'

46

Boyd arrived at work early enough to catch the night-shifters clocking off. There were a couple of members of CID with whom he'd yet to exchange anything more than an 'All right?' since he'd started in January. They were the ones who actually *preferred* the night shifts – crazy bastards – and signed up for them routinely.

He dropped his coat and shoulder bag onto his desk and hurried to the canteen to grab a cappuccino and a pastry. Emma's breakfast fruit bowls with a spoonful of yoghurt just weren't keeping him going until eleven. He felt guilty that she was making them for him the night before, and he was scoffing them *followed* by a sticky cinnamon whirl.

The scales had shown a modest drop of only two pounds over the last month and Emma was scratching her head as to why the results weren't any better. He took the steps up to the canteen two at a time, in the hope of burning off a few extra calories. If he wasn't careful, there was going to come a point very soon when she would begin to question whether he was secret-eating at work.

He came back, set his contraband down on his desk and pulled open Gratton's case file.

This is going to be rendered redundant by Operation Weatherman, he thought. Mike Gratton's legacy was going to be a case that was never solved and, if Boyd had anything to do with it, superseded by an investigation that was going to make good on all their mistakes.

As Emma had said last night, they had the benefit of twenty years' worth of better science, better data technology and better practices and methods.

Boyd spent the morning picking through the details in the file. Looking at it with fresh eyes, and a post *Making of a Murderer* sensitivity to investigative blunders from the recent past, the daylight piercing through the worn threads of Gratton's work was blinding.

The farmhouse where Martin had been living had not been treated with the same forensic caution as a crime scene where the murderer was as yet unknown. As far as everyone had been concerned, they'd had Leon Martin's name from the first moment they entered the farm, and a certainty that this was the right place. Standard-issue boots and ungloved hands had completely compromised the scene and rendered any prosecution-ready evidence useless.

The van that Martin had driven to Wales, to supposedly take his life, had been searched then low-loaded back to the police station before a forensic specialist had had a chance to look it over in situ. The evidence pipeline was made more of a mess with two different exhibits officers from two different police forces handling the registration, tracking and storage of the evidence.

Gratton's investigation had been poorly resourced from the beginning because, as far as his senior officers were concerned, the case was already solved and Martin's final victim was alive and well. The other victim's identities were never followed up due to the workload that arrived after 9/11.

Boyd focused on the genetic evidence. The year 2001 wasn't exactly the early days when it came to handling DNA evidence, but it was early enough that thoughtless mistakes were still being made. DNA was, of course, all over the farmhouse: in the kitchen on crockery that hadn't been washed, on clothes waiting in festering piles to be laundered, in the semen stains of Martin's bed linen, in the grubby tidemark around his bath-tub. Martin was a young man living alone.

He hadn't exactly been house-proud.

The only deductions that had been extracted from the messy forensics were that two of the profiles were significantly dominant and had been attributed to Leon Martin and to his latest captive, Kristy Clarke.

The most dominant profile – the one that had been found on the steering wheel – had been pegged as Leon Martin's.

Emma's questioning came to mind. *If Martin wasn't swabbed, how did they know it was actually the killer's DNA profile?* The thought gave him a fleeting breeze of goosebumps up his arm.

Martin's suicide and Kristy's escape had seemed plausible to the police at the time. But what if *everything* had been staged?

The goosebumps continued up his arm.

47

Boyd flicked back through his notepad and found the number.

'St Barnaby's Hospice,' a voice answered cheerily.

'I'd like to speak to Mike Gratton. He's in room –'

'Nine, yes...' The woman on the other end of the line paused for a moment.

'Is he okay?' Boyd looked up at the ceiling. *Stupid bloody question.*

'Michael had a bad night last night, I'm afraid.' The voice was less cheery now.

'I'm sorry to hear that,' said Boyd. 'Is he asleep?'

'Yes, I should think so,' she replied.

'Are you sure?' Boyd nudged her. 'Can you check?'

'Mr Gratton needs to rest this morning, Mr...?'

'Detective Chief Inspector Boyd. It really is quite important. Could you check on him for me? If he's awake, let him know who's calling. Please.'

There was another moment of hesitation, then: 'One moment.'

The line clicked and he was left alone with a Take That song.

Okeke and Minter drifted into the Incident Room holding cartons of chips. Boyd glanced at his computer screen and realised the whole morning had passed him by and it was lunchtime. They exchanged nods. Okeke frowned and mouthed something at him. It looked like, *Got something new?*

He nodded again. 'Just checking up on something,' he said.

The music clicked off and the receptionist came back on the line, sounding annoyed. 'He'll take your call, Mr Boyd,' she said in a clipped tone and was gone, replaced with a ringing tone.

The phone rang several times. Boyd had a mental image of Gratton, lying in his hospice bed, his pillows being plumped up behind his back, and the phone being placed into one of his feeble hands.

Finally a weak male voice answered. 'Boyd? This is Mike.'

Boyd could hear the steady hiss of air from the respirator and the soft beeping of one of Gratton's monitoring machines.

'Gratton,' he began cheerily, 'how're you doing?'

'I've been better.'

'Right. The nurse at the front said you had a pretty bad night.'

'Most nights... are bad. Just want to... get this pain-in-the-arse over with... now.'

Boyd winced. *What do you say to something like that?*

'To *almost* quote Boris... "Get *exit* done", eh?' he quipped. The words were out of his mouth before he had time to think. He rolled his eyes at his own insensitivity.

Gratton – thank Christ – cackled. 'How's the... case going?'

'I don't know if you watch much news, but uh... there's been the discovery of a very recent body,' Boyd said. 'Stephen Wooten.'

'Oh?'

'Our two bodies – the old one and the recent one – had the same item buried with them.'

'What?' Gratton whispered.

'A carved figure. A soldier, a Coldstream guard.'

'The same as our body,' Gratton said. 'Shit.'

Boyd could hear the fatigue in his voice. 'Look, I thought you should know that you were right; it doesn't look as though Martin did go over that cliff and the case is active. I'm going to wrap this up and let you get some rest, Mike. We're expecting some fingernail swab results back from forensics –'

'You got...?'

'Scrapings? Yeah. From our lad Stephen Wooten. We're expecting a match against one of the DNA profiles from your investigation. I just wanted to double-check that Kristy's sample is clean – taken directly from him?'

There was a long pause.

'Mike? You okay?'

'We didn't take a sample from... Clarke.'

'What?' Boyd didn't want to force the poor sod to have to repeat himself, but this was confirmation of a suspicion he'd really hoped was wide off the mark. 'Why not?'

'We thought... we already... had our killer.'

Boyd held his breath to stop himself cursing. He heard the phone rustle; the hissing grew louder for a moment – Gratton catching up on the oxygen he desperately needed.

'Well,' said Boyd eventually. 'I need to get a swab from Clarke, then.'

'You should,' replied Gratton. 'To rule him out. He... deserves that.'

'You're convinced it wasn't him, aren't you?'

'I've seen trauma for... real and I've seen it *acted*.' Gratton wheezed in and out several times, then spoke again. 'You go test him, though. If it makes you feel better.'

'Results, as I'm sure you're aware, are much quicker these days,' said Boyd. 'We'll have a profile back pretty quickly.'

This time, I hope.

'Good,' Gratton rasped.

'Do you want me to call back when I know more?' Boyd asked.

'Yes... but best not... take too bloody long, eh?'

'I hear you.'

~

BOYD IMMEDIATELY DIALLED the charity group that Clarke worked for, Capital Reach, then remembered he had Clarke's direct home-office number. He hung up and dialled that instead, getting a voicemail message.

'Hi, you're through to donations. This is Kristy Clarke. I'm away from my desk right now, but if you leave a message and a number, I'll call you straight back.'

'Hello, Kristy. It's DCI Boyd. We spoke a few days ago. Could you give me a call back when you get this? My number is...' Boyd left his number and hung up.

They didn't swab Kristy Clarke? He couldn't believe that. The fucking halfwits had just presumed which profile was which.

'Jesus,' he muttered. That was shoddy. Really shoddy work.

48

Boyd summoned his team back round the Incident Room table after lunch.

'Right. So, yesterday's mad scramble to find and arrest Dave Mullen was a complete fuck-up. *My* screw-up.' He wanted to get that off his chest first. 'In the absence of any solid intel, I reacted to a bloody likeness in a computer-rendered photo of all things.'

'It really did look a lot like him, boss.'

'Thanks, Minter, but that was a very good example of how *not* to do things. And today, ladies and gents, I will demonstrate how to *actually* do things.'

There was a good-natured chuckle round the table.

'So, here's where we stand,' said Boyd. 'The Wooten forensics came back this morning.'

'Finally,' said Okeke.

'And the fingernail swabs are a match against the Leon Martin profile. It would appear Leon Martin, or a person calling themselves Leon Martin, is alive.'

'Okay, boss,' said Minter. 'It sounds as though you know something we don't know –'

'Right, well, this may sound like a bit of a reach... but I think we need to consider the possibility that our escaped victim, Kristy Clarke, might have been working with Leon Martin.'

Boyd paused to let this piece of information sink in. He looked at his team. All eyes were on him. The room was silent.

'I can see that,' said Okeke slowly. 'They only had Clarke's word for what happened to him.'

'They had DNA evidence,' Minter pointed out, 'on the restraints, in the back of the van...'

'I spoke to Mike Gratton earlier,' Boyd said. 'They didn't swab Clarke. They made an educated guess at the two prominent profiles they found.'

'*What?*' Okeke exclaimed, shaking her head. 'What was Gratton playing at?'

'Clarke had injuries,' Minter countered.

'Which could have been self-inflicted, or inflicted by Martin to suit their story,' Okeke replied.

'He went to the police for help when he escaped,' Minter said.

'He was picked up by the police,' Okeke said, 'and spun his backup story to explain his presence at the farmhouse. They could have planned it between them.'

'Look,' Boyd said. 'I'm not saying he *is* involved. He could be exactly who he says he is. Gratton believes one hundred per cent that he was a genuine traumatised victim. I'm just saying it's *possible*. Something's been nagging me about this case. Especially since Stephen Wooten's body turned up. Let's face it: Clarke had a bloody lucky escape, Martin's dead or missing, and now we have Stephen buried with another wooden soldier and the same message. I think he's involved somehow. Thankfully, there's a very easy way we can find out.' He mimed swabbing his cheek.

O'Neal laughed. 'Looks like... you're, uh... you know, giving someone a...'

Okeke nodded. 'You probably don't want to do that again, guv.'

'Jesus. I was miming a swabbing.' Boyd sighed. 'Come on – we're better than this, people.'

'Speaking of DNA, is there any possibility the Wooten scrapings could be old DNA?' asked Okeke. Sully pulled a face at her, but she continued. 'I'm just saying that it's possible our killer, if he's the person we *think* might be calling himself Leon Martin –' she looked meaningfully at Minter – 'had some of Martin's stuff with him and transferred it to the victim's body to throw us further off the scent.'

Sully shook his head. 'Dead cell DNA leaves different RNA transcripts. One of the things tested for routinely now is to verify whether the DNA sample was shed peri-or post-mortem.'

'The DNA on Wooten came from living skin cells,' said Boyd, 'and they match Martin's DNA profile according to the 2001 investigation. So our leading theory has to be that the person with that DNA profile is alive – and killing again.'

He nodded at Okeke. 'We need to tread very carefully with this one. Clarke is still a victim at this point. We'll get that swab so that we can rule him out quickly and, if he's innocent, let the poor sod get on with his life. We also need to chase up EFS on that bag of toiletries you recovered. Could you do that for me, please, before you set off?'

'Will do, guv,' Okeke said. 'Wait... *set off?*'

'Yes, set off. Minter?'

'Boss?'

'I want you and Okeke to go over to Clarke's place to get that swab done. We don't know how this is going to go, so I've arranged backup with the Kent lot and a warrant for Clarke's place. Liaise with them, please, and keep me in the picture. If he's who he says he is – and Gratton is convinced of that, by the way – then there shouldn't be any problems.'

'Right, boss,' Minter said, glancing at Okeke.

'O'Neal?'

'Guv?'

'I want you and PS Brown to continue home visits for the misper shortlist that Warren's already compiled. But collect DNA swabs from the parents where you can. They may not be able to ID any marks or tattoos in the photos, but let's get their DNA so we can check to see if there are familial links to any unidentified samples we have, either from 2001 or that we collect ourselves.'

'Yes, sir.'

'If we can start putting names to those victims,' said Boyd, 'we're building a nice prosecution platform for the CPS ready for when we catch this bastard. I'm going to arrange a recce of the Martin farm with Cheshire Constabulary. Warren, you've earned a field trip; you're coming with me.'

Warren grinned. 'Thanks, sir.'

'We'll be back late.' Boyd couldn't help himself. 'So, let your mum know.'

The others round the table made 'awww' noises and Warren, blushing, replied with two fingers.

'Sully, can you come along on this one with us?' Boyd asked.

'Ooh, I've earned a day trip too? Marvellous,' Sully replied.

'I want your opinion on whether the farm's still intact enough for us to squirrel out some valid forensics.' Boyd tapped his finger on Gratton's case file. 'The crime scenes were managed poorly.'

He then nodded at Minter. 'Minter managed to get a much better photograph of Martin just by going down to their evidence room and helping himself. It grieves me to say this, but I think we have to accept the Gratton case was a mess.'

Boyd looked at the faces sat round the table. 'This is going to be a long haul, folks – lots of bits to tie up. So let's get going.'

49

'Okay, this looks like us,' said Minter. He parked the car up on a grassy hump twenty yards down the leafy country lane.

Up ahead was the sign for Corner Cottage. Clarke's place.

Okeke looked up and down the lane. 'So where's our backup? They're meant to be here.'

'Late, obviously,' said Minter. 'Maybe they drove past a McDonald's and just had to pull in?'

She chuckled. 'You're not a big fan of Kent Police either?'

'I've had to co-operate with them several times. They've not been great.'

'I worked with them,' she pointed out.

Minter nodded. 'Oh, yeah – of course you did. Sorry I didn't mean to –'

'S'okay. I wasn't exactly happy there.'

'Why?' Minter asked. 'What happened?'

Okeke shrugged. 'Let's just say they have a pretty old-school culture over there.' She smiled. 'It's the kind of place where they still have old sweats who call female colleagues "love" or "sweet'eart".'

'That's a rubbish Kent accent,' said Minter. 'That was definitely Essex.'

'What the hell do you know? You're Welsh!'

'Well, you've got me there!' He laughed. 'I'm going to give their station a call; see where those muppets have got to.'

'Fine, I'm having a fag.' Okeke got out, closed the passenger-side door, pulled out her cigarettes and lit up.

She looked up and down the lane. It was overgrown, the tall trees on either side forming an almost continual tunnel of branches and budding spring leaves that cast the lane beneath in a fidgeting lattice of shadows.

'Not gonna lie,' she said quietly, puffing out a cloud of smoke. 'This is the perfect place for a serial killer to live.'

It was hushed, private, remote and best of all there was no CCTV or ANPR cameras. And no neighbours.

Minter opened his door and climbed out. 'Bloody rubbish lot.'

'What's up?'

'They got a shout, so they're off dealing with that.'

'They've got nobody else they can send?'

'Nope.'

Okeke looked over at the house. 'So what's the plan, Minty... Are we waiting until they can find a spare patrol?'

'I don't know, mate. Maybe give them another ten minutes?'

Boyd would have undoubtedly said, 'Sod it,' but Minter was more cautious. Minter's approach was right, of course. The professional thing to do, but...

'We could check and see if he's home,' said Okeke. 'While we're just fannying around out here?' She nodded ahead. 'I could go take a peek, see if his vehicle's there?'

Minter sighed. 'You really don't do patience, do you?'

'Nope.'

'Jesus. All right, but ditch the fag. That smell carries.'

'Okay.' She took one more defiant puff, then crushed the

cigarette beneath her heel. 'I mean it's only fifty pence I just wasted.'

He shrugged. 'If you have to smoke, why don't you vape instead?'

Okeke pulled a face. 'That's like asking a wine lover to drink grape juice. I'll just be a minute. You wait here.'

'Stay on the lane,' Minter said, getting back into the car.

'Yes, mummy.'

50

They stopped at a service station on the M6 because Sully desperately needed a piss break. Boyd couldn't resist ribbing him for not taking a leak before they set off, even though he fancied grabbing a coffee anyway.

As he and Warren queued beside the Costa counter, Boyd checked his work phone for any updates from Minter.

'Sir?'

He turned to look back at Warren. 'Yup?'

'I just want to say thanks again. You know, for bringing me along.'

'No need. This'll be good field experience for you. You need to walk a few crime scenes, get the hang of sniffing around them, before you can lead a murder investigation, you know.'

'Lead?' Warren asked, a shocked look on his face.

'Don't get your hopes up, sunshine!' Boyd laughed. 'Not yet. You're a couple of ranks shy of that just now.'

'Right. I know,' Warren said, colour rising in his cheeks.

'But you've done some good work.'

'Thanks, sir.'

'Crime-scene pacing's a knack. I don't know how Sully goes

about it – you'll have to ask him – but for me it's about getting a sense of the environment, the three-dimensional space in which a crime has happened. It makes it a lot easier to visualise crime sequences in your head.'

Warren nodded. 'Right.'

'Looking at a CSI report – the floor plans, the diagrams, the photos – is important,' continued Boyd, 'but you should always visit the place where it happened so you can *place everything*, if you know what I mean?'

'Yes, sir.'

Boyd shrugged. 'Some DCIs never step out of the office. That's not for me.'

'Think we'll find much today?' Warren asked.

'It's more of a quick recce today. If Lancs are wrong and there are signs the farm's been broken into and used, then it's probably not going to give us that much, if anything at all. Speaking of...'

Sully weaved his way, awkwardly stop-starting, across the service-station concourse and finally joined them. 'Busy here, isn't it?'

Boyd nodded. 'I s'pose.'

'I'm really not that keen on this many people in one place. It's unhygienic.'

Boyd raised his eyebrows at Warren. 'What are you having, Sully?'

'Since it's on the force, I'll have a mochachino, please. *With* the whipped cream and sprinkles. Don't forget that.'

'Christ, I said we're stopping for a drink, not pudding,' Boyd grumbled as he tapped his card to pay.

Sully looked over the rim of his glasses at Boyd's moderate pot belly. 'Some of us can allow ourselves those extra naughty calories.'

'Do you mind?' Boyd unconsciously sucked in his gut. 'That's a work-in-progress.'

51

'There's no vehicle parked there,' said Okeke. 'It doesn't look as though he's in. What do we do now?'

'Well, I guess we could have a little snoop around,' Minter replied. He got out of the car and gently closed the door. 'You're sure it's empty?'

'I'm sure.'

They walked up the lane and turned into the gravel driveway. Corner Cottage looked like the kind of home that some dear little old lady would share with a dozen or so cats. It was a bungalow, surrounded by a small lawn and bordered by flower beds and an almost impenetrable Maginot Line of leylandii hedges.

They stopped short of the front door.

'We should probably check he's definitely out before we have a look around the place.' Minter peered through a glass pane to the left of the frosted-glass front door and glimpsed a gloomy hallway.

He knocked on the door and waited.

'So much for "let's wait for backup",' Okeke said, sounding impressed.

Minter knocked again.

No response.

'Right, then,' he said. 'Let's glove up.'

'Thought you'd never ask,' she replied, pulling a pair of blue nitrile gloves out of her shoulder bag and snapping them on. Next, she took out a DNA swab kit. 'We're looking for things outside that Clarke would routinely touch and no one else.'

Minter nodded. 'You look for that and I'll do a quick lap round the house to check what I can see inside.'

He turned round, treading carefully past a flower bed and peering into another window further along.

'I've already done that!' said Okeke.

Minter waved a hand over his shoulder. 'It doesn't hurt to check, Okeke,' he said as he disappeared round the corner.

She turned to inspect the door in front of her. The handle would be a good place to start. There might be other profiles present... but certainly Clarke's was most likely. She unscrewed the vial of the forensic tub and gently lifted out the swab attached to the cap, making sure it didn't touch the sides as she did so. Between uncapping and capping, the only thing the tip should touch, or even brush against, was the subject surface.

She moistened the tip with a drop of distilled water, then, carefully, she leant towards the door handle and made a motion to grab the handle as a person would normally do, getting as close as she dared, to identify which part of the handle would make the fullest contact. Then she gently stroked the tip of the swab along it several times. She capped the sample and filled in the location 'front door handle' on the container's label.

Okeke took one last look at the handle and was about to move on when she caught a glimpse of a dark fingertip ridge pattern on the brass plate just to the right of the keyhole.

She leant in closer.

'Hello,' she said softly. 'You look like blood.'

She pulled out a photographic ruler and some tape and gently fixed it to the door beside the brass plate, then took a couple of pictures as close as she could get without losing focus.

'Good. Very good,' she muttered as she checked the images she'd taken. The fingerprint ridges were as clear and defined as black ink. She pulled out another swab vial, moistened the tip and stroked one side of the tiny bloody print several times until the moisture hydrated the print and caused it to blur.

Against the white tip of the swab, the moistened black had turned dark red. 'Bingo.'

Okeke capped the swab, filled in the label and dialled Minter.

'What is it?' he answered.

'We've got blood on the handle. Which means we've got reasonable cause.'

'Well, that's good, because I'm actually already inside,' he replied.

Through the frosted glass, she could see movement in the hallway. There was a click as the lock was turned and the door swung inwards. She saw Minter putting his phone back into his hip pocket. ''Ello again.'

'How did you –'

'There was a cat flap in the back door.'

'Don't tell me you squeezed –' she began, momentarily confused.

'Yes, Okeke, I managed to squeeze myself through the cat flap,' Minter said seriously.

She pulled a face. 'Sorry.'

'I did, in fact, manage to reach through the cat flap and turn the back-door key.' He grinned guiltily. 'Which is all fine now you've found some suspicious blood.'

Okeke raised a brow.

'Of course, you found the blood *first*, and *then* I found my way in,' he said, moving aside to let her in. 'Right?'

Minter checked his watch. It was three in the afternoon. 'Do you think we should call Kristy's work? To make sure he *is* there and doesn't surprise us?'

While he looked up the number, Okeke took a few more steps into Corner Cottage and peered into the kitchen. It looked pitifully old-fashioned; the units seemed as though they'd been installed in the seventies, all cream MDF, with the veneers chipped at the corners and some of their doors hanging at an angle. The floor was worn lino, a black-and-white chessboard pattern with the black squares almost worn to white.

She could hear Minter talking to someone as she picked her way carefully around the kitchen. It was tidy. That much she'd noticed instantly. Unusual for a man living on his own, she mused, thinking of Jay and the permanent piles of unwashed dishes at his place.

Minter hung up. 'Okeke? Where are you?'

'In the kitchen!'

He poked his head in. 'He's not at work. They said he's on annual leave.'

'On holiday?'

'Apparently he takes a week off at the same time every year and drives up to the Lake District to take pictures of the birds and wildlife there.'

'Which means he could be there or –'

'Shit,' Minter said. 'He could be back any minute.'

'Well, we'd better get on with it quickly, then,' said Okeke.

52

Warren checked the maps app on his phone. They had a postcode to get them close, then a description, from the local police station, of how to get to the Martin farm. Being a rural postcode, it was annoyingly vague, and to add salt to the wound it had started raining heavily with big viscous spatters of rain drumming on the windscreen.

Boyd had taken a shift at the wheel after their second pit-stop, courtesy of Sully's pea-sized bladder.

'Is it left up ahead or not?' he asked, trying to keep the irritation out of his voice.

'I don't know... It's doing that pausing thing again,' Warren said.

Boyd upped the rate on the windscreen wipers. The front one was a noisy bastard, whip-guuurrrrn, whip-guuurrrn, whip-guuurrrning as it struggled to clear the rain.

'Warren? I need an answer. Preferably today.'

Boyd had slowed down to an almost stop at a turning, indicator blinking right to show his intention. Behind them a truck rolled to a begrudging halt.

'It's still paused. I think it's the signal,' said Warren.

'Or lack thereof,' Sully offered, helpfully, from the rear seat.

The truck honked loudly.

Sully jumped and turned round to look out at the monster hovering intimidatingly close behind them. He flipped a birdie at the driver.

'Sully! For Christ's sake,' said Boyd.

'He's bullying us,' Sully said. 'I won't tolerate that.'

The deafening honk reverberated around the inside of the car once again.

'Let's just be professionals here,' Boyd snipped, glaring at Sully through the rear-view mirror.

'Maybe it isn't this turning,' said Warren. His pale cheeks blotching. 'I'm sorry. I really don't know, sir.'

'Give me the bloody phone!' Boyd grunted. He looked at the frozen screen. The blue direction arrow had given up the ghost and vanished completely.

They were on a single-lane A road with a number of rural roads splitting off to the right, each one snaking in radically different directions for no apparent reason. It could have been this road, or the one before, or the one just a little further along.

'Oh, for fuck's sake,' he muttered.

The truck honked again. Boyd had had enough. He wrenched open his door, stepped out into the rain and slammed the door behind him. He pulled out his warrant card and waved it around, pointing at it with his other hand in case the truck driver wasn't getting the message.

'WE'RE THE FUCKING POLICE!!!' he shouted, although most of that was lost in the noise of the drumming rain. He got back in the car, soaked.

'Better?' asked Sully.

Boyd twisted in his seat, his road rage not entirely spent.

Sully, not in the least bit intimidated, spread his hands and smiled. 'Let's just be professionals, eh?'

IT WAS gloomy inside Corner Cottage. Minter snapped the hallway light on, which bathed everything in a sickly vanilla glow that gradually grew in intensity. The hallway was lined with dark and faded floral wallpaper, and by the front door was a coat rack that held a single anorak and several bunches of keys.

'Okay, so the kitchen's tidy,' said Okeke. 'Not just tidy, but tidy-tidy. There's no milk in the fridge, the bin's empty – it looks like he might well have gone on his trip.'

'Right,' said Minter. 'That means we don't have to rush this, then. Let's see what there is to see.'

He advanced cautiously towards the door ahead of them, gently eased it open and found himself looking into the lounge.

The décor was exactly what he'd expected – old lady chic. The only thing missing was a flight of porcelain ducks on the wall over the mantelpiece and a row of Toby jugs.

'The lounge,' he announced over his shoulder as he stepped in.

Okeke followed. 'God, this is like stepping into a time capsule,' she said.

Two brown armchairs and a beige sofa, quite possibly fashionable fifty years ago, almost filled the room and a TV that was so ancient it had a wood veneer on the sides, stood in the corner.

'Hello, nineteen-eighties,' said Minter.

'Nineteen-sixties more like,' said Okeke. 'Eighties was MFI. All chrome, black ash and futons.'

'Great. Thank you for that, Lucy Worsley. So how old is Kristy Clarke?'

'About forty, I think.'

'Right, so he's not old. Not *this* old, I mean.'

'I think Boyd said he rents this place. So maybe it's not his furniture,' said Okeke.

Minter carried on studying the room in a slow rotation. There was an old oval mahogany dining table in the corner. He could see paperwork scattered across it and the house phone – an old one with a rotary dial.

'So there's his work-from-home space,' he said.

Okeke dug into her forensics kit. 'I'll get some swabs.'

Minter nodded. 'And I'll go and check out his bedroom and bathroom.'

He left her to it and disappeared into the hallway.

She approached the dining table. As well as the paperwork and the phone, there were some files and folders, a half-full mug of tea with a skin on it and a plate with crumbs. She noted the mug as a good place to get a swab and turned to look at a notepad, which was covered in writing.

There was nothing that screamed serial killer at her, to be fair – just a list of names and telephone numbers, some crossed off, some yet to be called by the look of it.

Clarke's day job – cold-calling for charity donations. She snapped a photo of it on her phone.

Pushed aside, further along the dining table, was more paperwork. She could see a well-used AA road map of the UK spread out on the table with felt-tip scribbles and lines drawn on it. There was a small stack of notebooks with dark burgundy covers and red elastic cover bands. And a crafting mat, Stanley knife and off-cuts of glossy white photographic printer paper.

Carefully, she eased the elastic band off one of the notebooks and opened the cover. The first page was covered with a meticulously tidy handwriting that had an old-fashioned care taken over the curls and loops.

It was a diary entry.

. . .

12TH SEPTEMBER, 2011.

Life is no more precious than any chemical reaction. Go deep enough, that's all it is. Chemistry. Go deeper than that and it's just electrons in motion. When we pull back and look at things in large-scale, we like to think we see patterns in the white noise and we call those patterns names like 'intelligence' or 'God' or 'consciousness'.

It's just noise. Electrons bumping around like ants in a nest, commuters in a train station, all of them lost.

OKEKE FLICKED through the book to see more of the same and put it to one side.

She picked up another and flicked through that. She was about to put it down when she caught sight of something on the inside of the back cover. She opened it and saw that something had been written in what looked like biro, bang in the middle.

The lonely people slip aside, in the ground, their time to hide.

'Minter!' she called out, heart thumping. 'You should come and see this!'

She expected to hear his approaching footsteps down the hall, but there was silence.

'Minter?'

Still nothing.

Okeke crossed the lounge and stood in the doorway. The doors leading from the hall had been opened, Minter's way of indicting that a room had been visited.

'Yo, Minty! You there!' she called.

She took a step down the hallway and noticed that the front door was open. She'd been last one through it and was certain she'd closed it behind her.

53

'Whoa, okay, so here it is. *This* turning has to be ours?' said Warren, who, in a bid to prevent Boyd from having a heart attack, was now behind the wheel.

'Well, we've been down every other bloody one,' Boyd grumbled.

He looked up from his phone. He couldn't see anything that looked like a proper turning. But Warren's eagle eyes had.

Warren diligently indicated right, even though the road was deserted, and pulled into a completely missable gap between two overgrown trees.

They drove up a deeply rutted track that might once have been tarmac but was definitely now honest-to-God dirt. The trees on either side had grown brazen, their limbs reaching across to each other overhead, while nettles and brambles had staked a claim along the ridge of mud between the wheel ruts.

'Probably should have thought ahead and grabbed a Land Rover from the pool,' offered Sully as the car bucked and rolled along the soil trenches, and undergrowth scraped the underside of the car noisily beneath them.

'A tractor might have been better,' replied Boyd.

Their pick from the pool, a Ford Galaxy, was struggling, and Boyd was beginning to think they should have parked on the roadside and walked down, when the car dipped into a deep rut and they came to an abrupt halt, the front bumper wedged in the mud.

'Reverse!' he said.

Warren eased the car backwards a few yards and tried to steer to the left to go around the rut, but the tyres refused to scale the sheer walls of the deep muddy trench.

'Bollocks,' said Boyd.

'Well, we now know it's not easily accessible,' said Sully. 'We may still have our untarnished crime scene.'

The track ahead curved to the left and Boyd could see sky. Presumably, where the woodland ended, the farmhouse was. 'It looks like we're walking from here,' he announced.

Sully chuckled. 'Does England have its own version of Louisiana swamp-inhabiting, banjo-playing weirdos?'

'Yeah. That's Norfolk. Come on,' Boyd said, trying to open the passenger-side door. The bottom bumped against a dirt ridge. 'Arse! What about your side?'

Warren's door scraped open. Barely.

'We're out your side, then,' said Boyd.

Warren was just about able to get out, but Boyd's tall body wasn't built for manoeuvring in tight spaces. Somehow, though, he managed to get himself over the hand brake and gear stick and emerge from the car.

'It's up ahead, sir. Not too far,' said Warren, pointing.

Sully emerged from the car, pulling faces at the mess the mud was making of his smart work shoes. 'Jesus. These'll be ruined. I'll be putting a claim in for new ones.'

'Probably should have thought ahead and grabbed wellies, then,' said Boyd with a smirk on his face.

Sully dead-eyed him.

The Martin farmhouse was every bit the forlorn-looking carcass Boyd had been expecting to find. It had been left empty for twenty years but sealed tight: most of the downstairs windows were boarded up with plywood, police tape still stuck across them. Minter had been quite right about that.

The building looked intact, structurally sound but weathered to a palette of dull olives and browns. What had once been whitewashed stipple walls were stained mint green with moss and algae. The paint on the exposed windowsills was flaking and several roof tiles had slipped or been pushed aside by blisters of moss.

The farmhouse and outbuildings formed a three-sided arena round an overgrown courtyard of gravel. To the right of the house was a rusty corrugated barn – more a large shack than barn, to be truthful. Boyd could see a variety of retired farm equipment and tractor attachments lurking in the gloom.

To their left was a long ground-floor annexe that looked as if it had served as a garage or a garden shed at some point. Halfway along was a shutter door that was almost completely pulled down. He could see cobwebs, some plant pots, jerry cans and canisters in the narrow gap at the bottom.

Boyd looked up at the thick, grey overcast sky. It had, thankfully, stopped raining, but it was certainly threatening to start again, and soon. The light was beginning to fade from the sky. If they hadn't spent so much time getting lost, they'd have caught more of the daylight hours. Not that it mattered, he supposed. He suspected it was going to be pitch-black inside the farmhouse anyway. He pulled a penlight out of his pocket, one of the LED aluminium ones you could pick up at the till in any twenty-four-hour petrol station. He checked the battery was still good.

'What's the plan, sir?' asked Warren, also taking in the heavy sky.

'We'll do a once-around the outside, then I want to see if we can prise one of those plywood boards loose.'

'We're going in, guv?' he said.

Boyd nodded. He could see consternation on the lad's face. 'It'll be fun. Like an episode of *Scooby-Doo*.'

'MINTER?'

The first open doorway on the left was the bathroom. There'd be rich forensics pickings in there, but that was for later. Right now Okeke was feeling decidedly on edge.

'Will you please bloody answer me!' she snapped angrily.

The door to her right opened onto a cellar. She could see steps leading down and the faint glow of a light.

See, now this is how the token black character in a slasher movie usually dies.

Only it wasn't the middle of the night, and she wasn't wearing a nighty. *Don't be stupid, Sam.* She was allowing her imagination a little too much freedom. She took a deep breath and stepped onto the top step. 'Hey, cloth ears... Are you down here?' she called into the gloom.

'Yes,' Minter replied. 'Okeke, I've found something. You should come down here and take a look.'

Extremely relieved to hear his voice, she clattered quickly down the wooden steps to find herself in a small stone-walled rectangular space with a low ceiling. There was a single mattress on the dirty floor. A pillow and a quilt. Beside that was an electric heater plugged into an orange extension cable that was coiled up at the bottom of the stairs.

'Shit,' Okeke said.

'I don't think Clarke's making money on the side with Airbnb,' said Minter grimly, pointing to a rusty metal ring, cemented into the wall beside the mattress. The rust was worn away around the middle, exposing a glint of iron. 'There's rust flakes on the floor,' he said. 'It looks as though someone's tried to pull this ring out.'

Okeke swore again. 'He's been keeping someone down here.'

'There's also what looks like blood stains on the mattress and the quilt. Not a fatal amount, I don't think, but...'

She squatted next to the mattress to inspect the spatter of dark droplets for herself.

'I think we've found the Ken Doll Killer,' she said.

Minter nodded. 'Or at least one half of him.' He stood up. 'Let's get out of the house. We don't want to contaminate things any more.'

Back outside the cottage, mercifully in the daylight once more, Minter reached into his jacket for his phone, just as the Kent uniforms finally arrived at the bottom of the driveway. He thumbed Boyd's number on the screen, waited for three rings, then heard Boyd's answer message.

'Boss, it's Minter here. We're at Kristy Clarke's place. I forced entry. There's blood in a basement room. He's been holding someone prisoner down there. He's not here. Work says he takes a week's holiday up in the Lakes this time of year. So –'

'And there's a pad on his desk,' said Okeke. 'That song... the lyric's written down in there.'

Minter nodded. 'Don't know if you got that, but bottom line: Clarke's the killer. At least the recent one. Call me back as soon as you get this, boss.'

54

'You two go left,' said Boyd 'I'll go right and meet you at the back.'

Warren and Sully set off and Boyd made his way across the courtyard to the corner where the barn and the house almost met. There was a walkway in between. He looked back to see Warren squatting down and peering into the long shed, panning a more substantial, long-handled flashlight up into its dark interior.

Boyd made his way along the side of the house, past a ply-boarded window towards the rear, feeling an unnerving sense of déjà vu.

The last time he'd done something like this, he'd been jumped and nearly lost an ear. He looked up at the drab grey sky, complete with the inevitable crows circling overhead, then across at the nearby trees, their skeletons still visible from winter.

Yup, the setting was virtually identical.

The rear of the farmhouse looked even more scabby than the front. All the downstairs windows had been boarded up here too, though the tiny upper windows had been left alone.

They were murky, almost opaque, with two decades' worth of algae. That was encouraging. If kids had chanced across the place, then almost certainly at least a few of those boards would have been smashed.

In the middle of the stone rear wall was the back door. Plywood had been screwed firmly across it, leaving the upper and lower panes of glass just visible at the top and bottom. There was even a strip of police tape still stuck to the ply, the detached end flapping and rustling, stoically hanging on to the wet wood to inform all that this was, indeed, a crime scene and – Gandalf-like – *None shall pass!*

A rusty padlock dangled from an equally rusty hoop secured to the door frame.

It was unlocked.

Warily Boyd stepped back. An unlocked door had been his undoing last time. The criminally minded and the utterly insane tended to have the same lax attitude to household security.

He looked to his right, expecting to see Warren and Sully, but there was no sign of them . They were probably still checking the outbuildings.

His gaze returned to the unlocked door. *This place has been or is being used.*

'Okay,' he whispered. 'Don't be an idiot again.'

Boyd firmly believed that you either learned from those little life lessons or deserved what you got. He pulled his phone out to see check the signal situation.

Still shit. Nothing, in fact.

He looked again to see if the others were approaching yet. Hopefully one of them would have a signal. Between their police phones and their own, one of them should have at least a bar.

He heard footsteps. It was Warren.

'Where's Sully?' Boyd whispered.

'There's a transit van in one of the sheds,' he replied. 'He's swabbing it right now, sir.'

Boyd quickly raised a finger to shush him. He pointed at the unlocked padlock.

'You think someone's in there?' Warren whispered.

Boyd nodded.

'Shit. What do we do?'

'We learn from my mistakes. It could be Martin or Clarke. You got a phone signal?'

Warren pulled his phone out and checked it, then shook his head.

'Go back and ask Sully if he's got one. If he has, call in for backup. Now!'

Warren nodded and was about to hurry back the way he'd come when they both heard a whimper coming from inside the farmhouse.

They looked at each other.

'Was that –' Warren began.

'Go!' said Boyd urgently. Then quickly added: 'And come straight back.'

There was another whimper.

Boyd flapped a hand at Warren. 'Give me your flashlight.'

Warren handed it over. 'You going in?'

Boyd sighed. 'Yes. And, Warren? Hurry the fuck up, would you?'

55

Boyd gently pushed the back door inwards. Mercifully this one didn't creak like some theme-park haunted house. He switched on the torch and found himself in an old rustic kitchen. In the middle of the room was a large wooden table, corners knocked off with age – 'characterful' an estate agent would call it. To his right stood an old range with a hob on top, and beside it a cracked porcelain sink. Pots and pans dangled on hooks from the low ceiling beams. If it wasn't for the multiple spiderwebs in the corners and the accumulation of years of dust, plus, of course, the fact that it had once been home to a serial killer, it would have a certain rustic charm.

He panned his torch around the room. It reminded him of photos he'd seen of Captain Scott's abandoned base camp. Or a diorama in a museum – *Farmhouse kitchen, circa 1955.*

He heard the whimpering sound again, more clearly, and another voice, male, softly spoken.

Go in loud with a called-out warning? Or go in quiet?

If Boyd had had an armed response unit with him, he'd have happily opted for the former. Instead he crept across the kitchen floor to an open door that very clearly led down to a basement.

Closer now, he could see that the worn stone steps descended, not into darkness, but into the faint, flickering light of what must be a candle's flame. It was casting shifting, dancing shadows against the old brick wall.

Basements – why the fuck do psychos always seem to have fucking basements?

He took a cautious first step down, relieved that the steps were stone and not wood that would more than likely creak treacherously beneath his weight. He took another step. A couple more and his shoes would be level with the gently shifting shadows. Potentially in view. He heard a man's voice, singing softly.

Boyd heard the clank of metal on metal – a tool, or tools, being gathered.

'*So, sunshine, let's get this done, shall we?*'

The whimpering intensified in both volume and pitch.

Boyd had heard enough.

'POLICE!!!!' he yelled, scrambling down the last steps and aiming the beam of his torch directly at the back of a man who was leaning over something.

The scene in front of him seemed to freeze in time. An image that Boyd forensically examined in the space of a heartbeat. There was the flickering candle. Beside it a threadbare burgundy sofa that he instantly recognised from the photos in Gratton's case file. A young man was lying on it, hands and feet tied. Mouth gagged.

The man on his feet – a narrow-shouldered and unassuming figure wearing a roll-neck sweater, long hair pulled into a grey-brown ponytail – was leaning over him. He slowly turned round to face the beam of light.

'Kristy Clarke?' Although Boyd had been half expecting it, it was still a shock to see him.

Clarke blinked in the stark light, raising a hand to shade his glasses. Boyd could see various expressions flickering across his face as he wondered what to do next.

'Don't do anything stupid,' Boyd said. 'I'm aiming a gun at you.'

Clarke's face creased with the hint of a smile. 'Oh, DCI Boyd.' His smile widened. 'Now, we both know that's not true.'

'Put your hands up where I can bloody well see them!' Boyd tried again.

Clarke shook his head slowly. 'No, it's okay. I'm good as I am.' In his right hand was a long thin-bladed knife, mercifully not covered in blood. Yet.

Boyd glanced at the boy on the sofa. He was deathly still, his eyes pleading with Boyd to do something.

'Drop the knife!'

'Again, no. I think I'll keep hold of it, thanks.' He smiled. 'You look shocked. A little startled. I'm guessing you weren't expecting to find me down here?'

'Wrong,' Boyd said. 'We know you were helping Leon. You helped Leon fake his suicide and then...'

'Poor, poor, traumatised, sobbing Kristy. Weak, dirty, barefoot, terrified. Poor boy,' Clarke said, his voice sliding into a mocking approximation of Gratton's northern accent. '*Need to go gently with him; he's barely an adult and he's been through so much.*' He tilted his head. 'Interesting theory, Boyd. Though I wasn't helping Leon,' he paused. 'You could say Leon helped me. *I'm* the Ken Doll Killer. Stupid wretched name. But it's a name, right?'

'It's over, Kristy,' said Boyd firmly.

'Sir?' Warren's voice came from the kitchen above.

'DOWN HERE!' Boyd shouted back. 'BASEMENT!'

Within seconds Warren came bounding down the steps, loud, clumsy and heavy-footed. He paused at the bottom, trying to process what he was seeing.

'Come on, Kristy,' said Boyd. 'Drop the knife.'

Clarke met Boyd's stare; his eyes looked menacing behind the lenses of his rimless glasses. He smiled but kept his hands by his side.

'We've got FTOs outside,' said Warren shakily. 'It's over, mate.'

'Didn't know school was out,' Clarke said, looking Warren up and down. 'You could be one of my boys. You're not too old, you know.'

'DROP THE FUCKING KNIFE!' barked Boyd.

Clarke sighed and began to bend down as if he was going to place it on the floor. Then suddenly he twisted and plunged the long-thin blade into the screaming boy's chest.

'FUCK!' shouted Warren.

Boyd lunged forward and swung the torch down at Clarke's knife hand, hoping to knock it out of his grasp, but Clarke ducked and sidestepped.

Boyd flung his torch in a roundhouse sweep with the aim of catching Clarke on the backswing to knock him off balance, but again met nothing but the swoosh of a wasted effort. In the confusion of the flickering candlelight and lurching shadows, Boyd had lost his bearings.

He was vaguely aware that Warren was beside the sofa, behind him. 'Jesus! Sir! He's bleeding out. He's bleeding out!'

Boyd glimpsed movement in the corner of the room. He aimed his torch in the direction of the movement and found he was looking at the steps leading up to the kitchen. In the confusion he'd swung around 180 degrees. He caught a glimpse of Clarke's feet scrambling up the steps and out of view.

'See to the lad!' said Boyd. 'I'll get backup to radio for an ambulance.'

'They're not here,' Warren said, stricken. 'I left Sully trying to get a signal –'

'Oh, for fuck's sake!' said Boyd.

He climbed the steps in pursuit of Clarke, taking them two at a time.

At the top he heard feet on old rattling floorboards to his left and turned to follow the noise deeper into the farmhouse, once again scolding himself for being a stupid, reckless arsehole.

56

Boyd followed the receding noise into a dark, windowless hallway. Up ahead pallid daylight spilled across the floor from an open door to the right. Boyd slowed his pursuit as the sound of fleeing ceased.

He's still inside.

Boyd eased himself up to the door and peered in. He could see two small Hobbit-sized windows punched through thick stone walls, the glass lead-lined with uneven diamond shapes and weeping with condensation. They spilled pale shades of the fading afternoon into a room that had once been used as a lounge.

'Kristy,' he called out. 'This ends worse for you if you stab a police officer. It's not worth it.'

There was no answer. Boyd found an old TV dinner tray on a bureau to his right, just by the door. He grabbed it as a makeshift shield. If Russell Crowe could manage with a shield this small against other gladiators, a TV tray had to be a fair match for a kitchen knife.

'Kristy,' he said again. 'There are more police are on the way, and they *will* have guns.'

Again, no answer. Boyd took a step further into the lounge.

He was in a crowded room of silhouetted shapes: a grandfather clock, a tall bureau, a winged chesterfield chair and a standing lamp. To his left he noticed a dusty glass display cabinet. Inside it were several shelves full of porcelain knick-knacks: hedgehogs in bowler hats, cats in bonnets, rabbits with waistcoats. Leon's mother's, Boyd guessed.

On one of the shelves were half a dozen soldiers in red tunics and bearskins. He quickly panned his torch across them. They were the carved wooden figures. The same as the one they'd found clasped in Wooten's hand.

'Why the wooden figures? Why did you bury those with the lads?' he called into the gloom.

Faintly he could hear the boy in the basement crying and moaning and Warren's voice trying to soothe and reassure him.

Then Sully's voice, louder, closer. 'Boyd?' It came from the courtyard. 'Everything okay in there?'

'STAY OUTSIDE!' Boyd shouted back. 'He's in here!'

'Backup's coming!' replied Sully.

'Good. We've found a boy. We need an ambulance. Now fuck off back to the car and stay there!'

He heard the crunch of footsteps on the gravel and saw Sully's shadow crossing one of the tiny windows, momentarily darkening the room even further, like a passing cloud.

Something tumbled over and shattered on the wooden floor. Boyd heard a door latch snick and suddenly blue-grey daylight speared into the gloomy room at the other end of the lounge.

Clarke was outside.

'Fuck!' Boyd stumbled through an unseen obstacle course of shin-high obstructions: a coffee table, a coal scuttle and finally a magazine holder.

He made his way to the open door only to see Clarke

sprinting through long grass for the treeline that surrounded the farm.

Boyd gathered a couple of deep breaths and sprinted after him.

Clarke disappeared into the shadows beneath the low bough of an evergreen. As Boyd approached, he slowed to let his eyes adjust to the daylight and then to the darkness of the wood beyond.

'Kristy!' he called out again.

Of course there was no answer. Boyd stepped forward, ducked slightly under the bough and readied his tray-shield to block any sudden attack.

He emerged into woodland. A wood that hadn't been managed by anyone for decades: there were no beaten paths, no recent felled trees, no branches waiting in scruffy piles to be cut up into logs. If those windows had been Hobbit windows, then this was Mirkwood – creaking with old trees and every now and then the short jackhammer taps from a woodpecker nearby.

Fifty yards further in he could see a large wooden storage barn.

He picked his way cautiously towards it, through knee-high clusters of nettles and brambles that tugged at his trousers.

Closer, he could see the shack was a dilapidated framework of wooden beams and green-stained slats. A structure held together, more likely, by the ivy that had engulfed it than rusty old nails and screws.

He stepped slowly up to the barn-like entrance. As he entered, he heard a creak above him and looked up to see horizontal slits and squares of daylight shining through where shingles had shifted, slipped or warped. Moving among them, a dark formless shadow, stepping from one support beam to the next.

'I'm going to say this again. This only makes matters worse for you if you attack me,' Boyd warned him.

The shifting form froze. 'I can't think how, Boyd. But I'm happy to talk for a bit.'

'It's over, Kristy. Why don't you come down?'

Boyd took another step forward and aimed his torch up into the loft. It briefly caught a hand grasping a beam, then the hand disappeared back into darkness. He panned the torch around, but the more he moved the beam, the more moving shadows he created.

'All right, then. Let's talk,' Boyd said, fumbling in his pocket for his phone. 'You can start by telling me where Leon is. Did he fake his suicide after killing those young men?' he paused. 'Or was it all you?'

'Leon... that poor idiotl he was harmless.' Clarke was silent for a few moments, then: 'I've read about people like me. I've self-diagnosed. I know what I am.'

'And what's that?'

'I'm a predator, Boyd.'

'I don't think you're remorseless, though,' Boyd said. 'Why the flowers, that message? Why the toy soldiers?'

Clarke laughed. 'Oh, that was just part of the false trail. Part of poor Leon's legacy. The boy who grew up lonely, parented by a broken man and a suffocating mother. His father's face was ruined; you know he was a soldier in the Falklands?'

'Yes, I knew that.'

'They both rather selfishly died and left him all alone.'

Boyd heard Clarke moving around above him, the old wooden beams creaking.

'Leon was so desperate for companionship; he'd have befriended anyone.'

'And that's why he brought you back here?'

'Of course.'

'How long before you killed him?' Boyd asked.

'I let him live long enough to understand him. To know his background, how pitiful a life he'd led. Long enough to realise he would tick all your profile boxes.'

Boyd heard the board above him creak again. He panned his torch around, but this time picked out nothing. There were stacks of logs in the eaves and areas where floorboards had been laid down. But no sign of Clarke.

He's up to something.

'So that's Leon. What about you, Kristy?'

Clarke laughed. 'Oh no, you don't get to hear my story, Boyd. That's for the history books.'

'History books?'

'Oh yeah. People love a mystery, don't they? You think six dead women in Whitechapel would still make the news today if Jack the Ripper had been named? Of course not. Not knowing something is what drives people crazy. Don't you think?'

'You should come down,' Boyd tried again.

'And you'll take me into custody and there'll be interview after interview with another dumb copper who thinks he's worked me out.' He laughed. 'Poor Mike Gratton. He felt so sorry for me. He was so gentle with me.'

'There'll be an armed response unit in here any moment now. If you bugger about with a knife in your hand, they'll be going for head shots. You do understand that, right? So, the smart move,' he continued, 'would be to drop your bloody knife, come down here, and I'll arrest you. No need for me to fill in any unnecessary firearms paperwork that way.'

Clarke laughed. 'I like you, Boyd.'

'I wish I could say the same, Kristy. So how about it?'

'No. I don't think so. I don't plan to become some sad old lifer trading titbits about myself for jail privileges. Where's this body? Where's that body? Were you abused when you were young? Did you have mummy-attachment issues?' Boyd could hear a rustling sound from above. 'You'll just have to work out who I was for yourselves.'

The wooden beam just above him creaked loudly as something suddenly leapt down at him out of the darkened loft space above. He managed to swing the torch up just in time to see Kristy Clarke's face – eyes perfectly round, mouth parted wide with a *whoop* of exhilaration, descending towards him in a blur of movement.

Then the movement lurched to a sudden, jarring halt and dust, dirt and shards of rotten wood cascaded down in a shower.

Boyd heard a visceral crack and an *'ooof'* of expelled breath as Clarke's body spasmed and jerked involuntarily for a moment before coming to a rest: a sack of lifeless ballast that swung lazily like a builder's plumb line.

57

Boyd finished the briefing, then cleared his throat. 'Okay, I'll take one or two questions now.'

The press room was rammed. And suddenly very noisy with dozens of voices shouting out at once. Boyd pointed at a guy in the front row.

'Stephen Hall, the *Sun*.'

Bad choice. 'Okay,' Boyd said, nodding. The room fell silent.

'Do you think Leon Martin played *any* part in the killings back in the nineties?'

'On the balance of evidence, probably not. In fact, we suspect that Leon Martin might have been Kristy Clarke's *first* victim. Next question.'

'Could Leon have been coerced by him?'

'No. To be clear, we think Leon was a victim. I'll take another.'

The room filled with voices once again. Boyd tried to pick a journalist who didn't look like a tabloid hack. But then... *What does a hack look like?*

'Georgina Bart, *Daily Mail*.'

Oh, for fuck's sake.

'You used Clarke's name, but then you said earlier in your opening statement that his identity hasn't actually been confirmed yet.'

Boyd nodded. 'That's true. We're hoping to get lucky with familial DNA at some point, or maybe someone who knew him when he was younger will call in.'

'Why do you think he killed himself?' She quickly barked the second question.

The room was pin-drop silent once more.

Stupid bloody question.

Boyd took a breath and said, 'Perhaps the thought of spending the rest of his life in prison was too grisly a prospect to contemplate.'

However, the most likely answer, certainly in Boyd's mind, was the narcissistic one. Fame. Or, more precisely, notoriety. The sick bastard didn't want to give anything away. *People love a mystery, don't they?* he'd said.

Boyd picked another eager raised hand.

'Alex Francois, *GB News*. There are unconfirmed reports that he left flowers where he buried the bodies, along with a message: a song lyric. Is that true?'

Boyd wasn't going to let Clarke even have that – that line of crappy prose that meant absolutely nothing. If he quoted it here, it would end up becoming some bloody meme; sick-in-the-head fuckers would probably treat it like a piece of Shakespeare, like it had some kind of obscure wisdom baked into it. 'The message was meaningless, random and unclear and had no real bearing on the investigation. I can't even remember it, sorry.'

He looked for another question and this time hoped he'd picked a grown-up.

'Kelly Lambert, *Independent*.'

He nodded for her to continue.

'Do we have an update on the boy found at the farmhouse? How's he doing?'

'He's in a stable condition. He'll be okay. Thanks for asking that one.'

She went on. 'Do you think you'll be able to name and locate Clarke's other victims?'

'We believe so. He kept a diary with his victim's names in and an old AA road map marking the graves. We've recovered nine bodies so far. Some of these bodies are quarter of a century old, so we are dealing with just bones, which makes them more difficult to track down. We will find them all, though – that much I promise. They deserve a proper burial.'

'Have the victim's families been informed?'

'Yes. And, as far as we're concerned, their identities will remain confidential.' He looked briefly to the side to see Sutherland and Her Madge beaming like unlikely proud parents.

'It's clear that he used a position of trust as a charity worker to canvas for potential victims. There'll be some more work to do to determine if he was guilty of any more abductions and murders. For that reason, *mainly* actually, we won't be releasing victim names to the press.'

There were more hands going up, but he decided the expected form of picking three or four questions to answer was enough. 'Right, that'll do for now, folks.' He backed away from the lectern and the nest of microphones and followed Sutherland and Hatcher out of the press-briefing room.

'You handled that well,' said Hatcher, outside.

'Thanks, ma'am.'

Sutherland closed the door on the noisy room, and the corridor outside was quiet again. 'Well done for not swearing. See you Monday morning, Boyd.'

Boyd nodded and watched as his two senior officers headed

up the corridor. He could hear Sutherland bending Her Madge's ear about keeping hold of some of the unspent magic money tree she'd offered him last week.

'No, Iain...' The start of her answer was just discernible. 'If it's not been spent, it comes back into my discretionary pot...'

58

It was late afternoon before Boyd was able to emerge from the police station. After the press conference, there had been the remainder of the case paperwork that needed completing before the very short-lived Operation Weatherman could be wound down.

He got home, and to his relief there were no press waiting outside his house. Emma, though, was in for once.

'Where's Daniel?' he asked.

'He's got a gig over in Somerset. A small music festival. It was a last-minute thing.'

'Really? Well, what the hell are you doing here, then? I'd have thought that was right up your street.'

She smiled. 'I thought it would be nice to have some Dad-'n'-Dog time, if that's all right with you?'

Boyd gave her a long hug. Grateful that she was home for him, grateful to have something in his life that didn't feel tragically twisted, broken... or just plain sad.

'You can let go now, Dad,' she said, laughing.

THE NEXT MORNING, after a lazy slow start, he took Ozzie down to the beach for a walk. Or, more accurately, Ozzie took him.

As he wandered along the shingle towards Hastings Pier, he wrestled with the question that had been sitting in his head all weekend: whether or not to give Mike Gratton a call.

Presuming he hadn't seen the news, would he want to know he'd had the killer right in front of him all those years ago, feeding him tea, biscuits and sympathy? Clarke's diaries had revealed that four more victims had been taken since Leon Martin's supposed suicide.

Probably not. But maybe he could try to edit the truth for him. Let the poor sod know that the killer was dead and the case was now closed. He decided on balance, if he was in the same situation, he'd want to know.

Boyd pulled his phone out and found the number for the hospice. He dialled it and got an answer after half a dozen rings.

'Can I speak to Mike Gratton,' he asked. 'He's in room nine.'

'May I ask who's calling?' she replied. 'Are you family?'

'No, just a... just a work colleague,' Boyd said.

'I'm afraid he passed away last night,' said the receptionist. 'He'd been unconscious for a couple of days and he just slipped away.'

She was halfway through a scripted response about the contact number for the funeral company when Boyd made his excuses and hung up.

It was an odd feeling. Relief tinged with regret.

Relief that he didn't have to tell Gratton that he'd been duped by Kristy Clarke. Relief that he hadn't seen the press conference and realised how many other young men had died as a result of his blind spot.

Regret that Mike Gratton had been fooled because he was a good man.

59

He was getting wet in the rain and was almost certain he was wasting his time standing by the slip road from the service station that led to the motorway.

There were so many video nasties made about hitch-hikers these days that thumbing a lift had become something of an old-fashioned and dying art.

He was about ready to give up and head back to the service station to try his luck at striking up a conversation in a queue. He could be charming. He could easily come across as wretched and harmless, enough for someone to offer him a lift.

Just then, a vehicle indicated and pulled over.

A white van.

A young man stuck his head out. 'Would you like a lift somewhere?' he asked.

He nodded. 'Yeah, that'd be great. Thank you. It's wet out here.'

'My name's Leon,' said the van driver. 'I'm driving up towards Manchester. Is that where you want to go?'

He nodded. The driver – Leon – sounded much younger than he looked.

He smiled at him. 'Manchester's perfect, Leon. Absolutely perfect.'

'Climb aboard, then,' said Leon.

He walked around the front of the van, opened the passenger door and climbed up and into the cabin.

'So, what's your name?' asked Leon. 'Mine's –'

'Leon, you said already.'

'Oh, right. Yes.' Leon shucked out a nervous laugh.

My name? He looked out of the windscreen. A lorry was pulling out of the petrol station to the side of them. He made out the name 'KRISTY CLARKE HAULAGE' in dirty black letters on its side as it trundled down the slip road to the motorway.

'Kristy. Kristy Clarke,' he said, smiling across at Leon.

'Cool,' said Leon shyly. 'Now I've got some company for the ride.'

Kristy nodded. 'That you do.'

Leon signalled to pull out and, as he waited for a big enough gap in the traffic, he looked down at his passenger's feet. 'Hey, are those actual Nikes? Like the Fresh Prince wears?'

'Uh-huh, got them last week. Cool, aren't they?'

Leon nodded. 'They're very expensive, I think.'

'They are.' He looked at Leon and offered him a warm and winning smile. 'I need somewhere to stay tonight. I won't be any trouble. I don't suppose... '

Leon immediately looked uncomfortable. 'I... don't bring friends back to the farm. It's –'

'It's just for tonight. Please?' Kristy said, smiling at him again. 'You can have my trainers if you want? As, like, a trade? A thank you? How does that sound?'

Leon eyed them again. They did look so good. And new. And pristine. 'Okay,' he said. And smiled back at his new friend.

THE END

DCI BOYD RETURNS IN

A BURNING TRUTH available to pre-order

here

ACKNOWLEDGMENTS

The second book in a series is usually the hardest to write. You're looking to take what worked in book one and translate those ingredients into a whole new story. The risks are that you don't take too much forward, because you're trying not limit the new story, or you take too much and write something that feels like a repeat. As with all 'second things' (book, album, act, child... only joking) it's difficult to get it right, but, if you do, you'll have an easier time with the rest.

So, yup, *Old Bones...* was a bugger to write and get right. For that reason, my acknowledgements are even more heartfelt. Firstly, a huge thank you to my wife, Debbie, who took a badly wounded book and made it better. She really is the other half of a process for which I get all the credit. Thanks to Wendy Shakespeare for her forensic work as our copy-editor and continuity guru. I must also extend my gratitude to some people who have proven to be invaluable with their comments, their feedback and their support: Maureen Webb, Lesley Lloyd, Lynda Checkley, Donna Morfett, Paula Shaw, Mary Ryan, Pippa Cahill-Watson and everyone in the amazing Team Boyd - I appreciate all that you do! Not forgetting, of course the larger body of people in the Facebook group UK Crime Book Club. Thank you for your support.

And, finally, my heartfelt thanks go to Spaniel Aid UK, for allowing us to adopt our adorable boy Ozzie in 2017. He's as much our dog as he is DCI Boyd's. If you would like to know more about Spaniel Aid UK and the work they do, please visit their website: www.spanielaid.co.uk

ALSO BY ALEX SCARROW

DCI Boyd

SILENT TIDE

OLD BONES NEW BONES

BURNING TRUTH

THE LAST TRAIN

Thrillers

LAST LIGHT

AFTERLIGHT

OCTOBER SKIES

THE CANDLEMAN

A THOUSAND SUNS

The TimeRiders series (in reading order)

TIMERIDERS

TIMERIDERS: DAY OF THE PREDATOR

TIMERIDERS: THE DOOMSDAY CODE

TIMERIDERS: THE ETERNAL WAR

TIMERIDERS: THE CITY OF SHADOWS

TIMERIDERS: THE PIRATE KINGS

TIMERIDERS: THE MAYAN PROPHECY

TIMERIDERS: THE INFINITY CAGE

The Plague Land series

PLAGUE LAND

PLAGUE NATION

PLAGUE WORLD

The Ellie Quin series

THE LEGEND OF ELLIE QUIN

THE WORLD ACCORDING TO ELLIE QUIN

ELLIE QUIN BENEATH A NEON SKY

ELLIE QUIN THROUGH THE GATEWAY

ELLIE QUIN: A GIRL REBORN

ABOUT THE AUTHOR

Over the last sixteen years, award-winning author Alex Scarrow has published seventeen novels with Penguin Random House, Orion and Pan Macmillan. A number of these have been optioned for film/TV development, including his best-selling *Last Light*.

When he is not busy writing and painting, Alex spends most of his time trying to keep Ozzie away from the food bin. He lives in the wilds of East Anglia with his wife Deborah and four, permanently muddy, dogs.

Ozzie came to live with him in January 2017. He was adopted from Spaniel Aid UK and was believed to be seven at the time. Ozzie loves food, his mum, food, his ball, food, walks and more food...

He dreams of unrestricted access to the food bin.

For up-to-date information on the DCI BOYD series, visit: www.alexscarrow.com